FALLEN KING

RESTLESS KINGS

BELLA MATTHEWS

Editor: Jessica Snyder, Jessica Snyder Edits

Copy Editor: Dena Mastrogiovanni, Red Pen Editing

Cover Designer: Jena Brignla

Photographer: Michelle Lancaster, Lane Photography

Interior Formatting: Savannah Richey, Peachy Keen Author Services

Savannah ~ There are no words big enough to thank you for everything. You were the first person to join my team, and I never would have made it to book seven without you by my side.

I love you not because of who you are, but because of who I am when I am with you.

— *ROY CROF*

PLAYLIST

- Shape of You – NOTD Remix, Ed Sheeran, NOTD
- The Call, Regina Spektor
- Kiss Me, Ed Sheeran
- Use Somebody, Kings of Leon
- You (with Marshmello & Vance Joy), benny blanco, Marshmello, Vancy Joy
- Dancing On My Own, Calum Scott
- Satellite, Rise Against
- Heart Attack, Demi Lovato
- New York, Snow Patrol
- Way down We Go, KALEO
- Cool for the Summer, Demi Lovato
- Sign of the Times, Harry Styles
- Always, Gavin James
- Lost Without You, Freya Ridings
- Stubborn Love, The Lumineers

https://spoti.fi/38mo1hu

DAPHNE

"HAVE YOU TOLD YOUR MOM YOU'RE NOT GOING BACK TO California yet?" My best friend, Carys, just came home after having spent the past two years going to college in San Diego. Her mom thinks she's home for the summer. But I know she's home for good.

"Nope. Not even thinking about it yet." I'm not used to being able to talk to her on my way to work. Usually, she'd be three hours behind and still sleeping. But today, the skinny bitch is finally starting to sound winded as she jogs around Boathouse Row in Fairmount Park. She tried to convince me to go with her this morning, but that wasn't happening.

I don't do the whole get up early to exercise thing. I'd rather sleep in and not sweat. But that's just me. I stop at the light at the corner of Broad Street between the Philadelphia Kings football stadium and the Philadelphia Revolution hockey arena and wait for it to change from red to green. I swear it's the longest light in the city.

A fifty-foot-tall LED screen with Carys's stepbrother Declan Sinclair splashed across it greets me from the wall of the state-of-the-art Kings complex, where he quarterbacks the championship-winning team. It stands in stark contrast to the hockey arena my family owns. I've been bugging my dad to do some renovations for a while now. But he typically just nods his head and blows me off.

As I turn into the parking lot of the arena, the drastic difference between the two buildings glares back at me. I'm not sure the Revolution has ever been state-of-the-art. But these days, it looks really rundown in comparison.

Maybe I'll mention it to Dad again.

The late-July heat engulfs me the second I take an unsteady step out of the car, teetering when the new heels I found yesterday at my favorite vintage shop get caught in a crack in the old parking lot. Okay, so maybe purple satin 1950's peep toes aren't the most practical for work. But in my defense, they look perfect with my black lace sundress, especially since I cinched my waist in with a cute belt.

Once I'm stable again, I push my earbud back in before it falls out and continue to listen as Carys tells me all about her crazy weekend at her stepsister's wedding.

I take two steps toward the Revolution offices before turning back around.

Shit.

Almost left the coffees in the car.

I swear, I am *that* person. Ask me which Revolution player had the most shots on goal last season—no problem. Van Buren. Three hundred and one shots last year, and two hundred and fifty-eight the year before that. Ask me where I put my keys this morning and it'll take me for-*freaking*-ever to remember.

With my laptop bag in one hand and my purse dangerously close to slipping from my shoulder, I reach back into the car to grab both coffees, then hip-check the door shut, barely managing to avoid getting any lace caught in the process.

Okay. Deep breath. I think that's everything.

My first few weeks spent as my dad's executive assistant have been intense and not at all what I thought I'd be doing a month out of college. We'd talked non-stop over the past year about me reestablishing the charitable division of the Philadelphia Revolution, the professional hockey team my family has owned for decades. I thought I'd be slipping right into the position when I graduated.

Apparently, my father had other plans. Now I need to get through one year working as his assistant and learning the ins and outs of the team before I can start my charitable foundation.

Still totally worth it.

I figured out early on that Mondays are better for both of us after a quick stop for coffee, and it's now become part of my regular routine.

"D . . . Are you even listening to me?"

Oops. "Sorry. I'm scrambling this morning." Carys and I have been best friends since we first met in our local summer theater program. She was eight, and I was ten, and we both wanted to be Dorothy. Instead, we ended up being the Scarecrow and the Tin Man, and we've never looked back.

She knows me better than anyone ever has.

It's not like she's surprised when I'm not paying attention.

"Whatever. It's fine. When am I going to see you?" Carys flew home a week ago, and as far as her family knows, she's only spending the summer in Kroydon Hills before going back to San Diego. I'm pretty sure only her business partner, Chloe, and I know the truth.

For two years now, she and Chloe have secretly been working on a high-end lingerie line and boutique, and they've finally decided now's the time to make it happen. But family dynamics can be messy, and Chloe's brother just married Carys's stepsister in the wedding she flew home for. So they know everyone will have an opinion when they make their big announcement.

I think them having an opinion is going to be the least of her problems when they all lose their minds over her decision to drop out of school. But she refuses to change her mind, so my job will be to hold her hand and pick up the pieces when it's done.

I push through the front doors of the offices and training facilities for the Philadelphia Revolution, and the cool air chills the bare skin of my arms as I hurry along. "I thought you were coming to the house tonight for Margarita Monday."

"Sounds good. I'll drag Chloe with me. Seven work?"

"Yup. That's perfect. See you then." I huff as I make my way to the elevator, carrying all my crap. Maybe if I ran like my bestie or took one of the yoga or dance classes taught by my roommate, Maddie, I'd be in better shape. But I've never been a fan of breaking a sweat and have no desire to start now. I mean, my ass could be a little smaller or my stomach a little more toned, but if I have to wake up early and go to the gym to do it, it's not happening.

Curves are sexier anyway.

When I finally make it to my desk outside Dad's office, the area is eerily quiet, which is kind of strange for a Monday morning. Coach O'Doul's lights are off, and Dad's door is closed. Once my computer boots up, I check his schedule for the day and find a meeting with the entry locked, which is odd. I know I didn't put it there, and Dad isn't typically organized enough to put anything into his calendar. I grab his coffee, knock on his closed door, and wait.

"Come in," is bellowed loudly enough to make me jump. I guess he's here.

I push through the door and force a smile on my face because it's a Monday morning, and nobody, not even me, is happy to be at work on a Monday morning. But it's a smile nonetheless.

My father is dressed to the nines in a three-piece suit instead of the polo and khakis he's been rocking lately.

Well . . . *trying to rock*. It hasn't been a great look for him, but today, his hair is styled, and his face is freshly shaven.

I'm hoping this is a good sign. Maybe he's finally getting himself out of the funk he's been in the past few months. I'm not sure what's caused it, but he hasn't been himself since the beginning of the year, and he's absolutely refused to talk about it whenever I've brought it up. Hopefully, he just needed time to work through it. "Mornin', Dad. Here's your coffee. I checked your schedule, and it looks like the only meeting you have today is at nine. You've got about thirty minutes before it starts. The event was locked on your calendar, so I couldn't actually see what it was. Do you need me to get you anything for it?"

Dad raises his bloodshot brown eyes to meet mine and frowns." Sit down, Daph. We need to talk."

Oh, this can't be good.

I've only been here a few weeks. I haven't even had to make travel arrangements for the team yet, so I can't imagine what I could possibly have done for him to look so disappointed in me.

I guess I'm about to find out.

My palms start to sweat as I gingerly take the seat across from my father.

He's lowered his eyes to the whiskey in the heavy crystal glass fisted in one of his hands. I hadn't noticed that when I walked in, but now that I've seen it at eight-thirty in the morning, it's hard to not stare as panic begins to edge in. "Dad . . ."

His broad shoulders rise and fall with his deep inhale and exhale before he closes his eyes and raises his face to the ceiling. "I've been trying to figure out how to tell you this, Daphne, but we're out of time. I'm selling the Revolution," he glances down at his wrist out of habit, but his Rolex isn't there, "in about thirty minutes. That's my nine o'clock. The

Kingstons are buying the organization. I didn't want you to know until I was sure the deal was going to go through."

"What are you talking about?" My world tilts on its axis as my head spins. "You can't do that." The words are bitter as they cross my lips. "This was Grandpa's team. *Mom's* team. How could you do this?" A sob catches in my throat that I refuse to set free.

The Kingstons are Philadelphia royalty. They own this city and the professional football team whose stadium is across the street from the hockey arena. They'll come in and change everything.

It won't be the team Grandpa loved.

This team was his pride and joy. My mom was supposed to run it after he died, but I guess you never really plan for what happens if you outlive your child. Mom died when I was eight. I barely remember her. But when this office was Grandpa's, the shelves were covered in pictures of her growing up here.

Dad changed very little once he took over two years ago.

It's almost like a shrine to happier times.

Now that I take a moment to look around the room, I see nothing but boxes.

Holy shit. He's really doing this. The office is empty. Ready for its next occupant.

The pictures that lined the shelves are gone, leaving nothing but dust in their place.

The trophies have all been packed up.

Any traces that this is his office have been removed.

Dad started working with Grandpa after Mom's death. It made sense. He might not have loved the team the same way as Grandpa, but I never would have expected this. Nothing about this makes any sense, and I fight back the hot tears burning behind my eyes.

He's selling our family's history.

My future.

"Why? Why do this? Is it because I don't want to run the Revolution? I'll do it if I have to. I'll do it if it means you don't give up the team."

"No, Daph. I got myself into some trouble, and selling the Revolution is the only answer." He runs a shaky hand through his salt-and-pepper hair, and my anger mixes with hurt, creating a toxic combination. He's really doing this, and he didn't even talk to me about it first.

I play his words over in my head and get stuck on one word. *Trouble*. "What kind of trouble did you get in, Dad?"

He raises his glass to his lips and finishes the contents with a flourish before slamming his glass against the ornately carved desk. "The kind where this was the only answer. Now listen to me. I've negotiated for your job. You and most of the management are guaranteed your positions for the next twelve months. Use the time to get the experience you need so you can get whatever job you want when you're done here."

When I sit there, staring out the window instead of at my father, he slams his open palm against the desk. "Do you understand what I'm saying?"

My head snaps back to him as a trickle of fear skates down my spine. "I don't understand any of this."

"You don't need to understand. You just need to do as you're told. Now, go set up the conference room. The Kingstons will be here soon."

I stumble out of his office, my mind racing and my pulse pounding.

I love my father as only a daughter can.

He may not have been the greatest dad, but he did his best, and that was enough.

I never knew he'd be the man who breaks my heart.

MAX

I'VE BEEN WAITING FOR MY SISTER FOR TEN MINUTES BY THE time she slides next to me into the back of my SUV. You can always count on Scarlet to be what she'd consider fashionably late, and it's only gotten worse since she found out she's pregnant. Like she needs extra time to make sure the baby bump approves of her wardrobe choices too.

We were supposed to have left ten minutes ago. "You're late." I look up from the contract I'm reviewing one last time before our meeting. Scarlet and I have been working on this deal for three months, and today, we'll finally put it to bed.

Scarlet rolls her eyes and offers a good morning to my driver, Luka, before she takes the iPad out of my hand and closes it, then sets it down on the briefcase by my feet. "You ready for this, Maximus?"

Why are siblings such assholes?

I've hated my name since the damn *Gladiator* movie came out years ago, and all eight of my siblings know it. Doesn't stop them from using it though. Especially when I'm in a shit fucking mood.

Scarlet sits next to me on the leather seat, rubbing her bump absentmindedly while she smiles like this is the greatest day of her life.

I guess for her it is.

"Ready to get this over with . . . ? Yes. Ready for the pain in the ass I think this is going to be . . . ? No."

Yesterday, I was the General Manager and President of

Operations for the Philadelphia Kings football team in addition to being the CEO of King Corp. A position I inherited when our dad died unexpectedly six years ago, making me the youngest to ever hold those titles. My first move was to bring on my former college coach, Joe Sinclair, as the team's new head coach, and together, we've built an even better Kings team than Dad left behind.

Now, in less than five years, our team has won two championships, and the entire organization is running at peak performance. Scarlet and I have worked tirelessly alongside Becket and our little sister Lenny to maintain our family's legacy.

Adding the Philadelphia Revolution to our holdings is the next step in expanding our sports empire. Everything has been decided by lawyers and looked over by my brothers and sisters, who are all equal shareholders.

Equal to each other, but thanks to Dad, not to me.

He was a bit of a patriarchal dick and wanted me to have controlling interest since I was the oldest of his kids. He knew by making me his number two, when and if the time came, I'd be the person promoted to CEO of King Corp.

To be the man in charge, like I'd been groomed to be my entire life.

Our great-grandfather had it written into the company bylaws that there always had to be a Kingston as the acting president, and that position not only gave me final say in the company business but also controlling interest in King Corp.

It also placed me at the top of our family empire. But at the end of this meeting, Scarlet will be stepping into what is now my old position with the Kings, and I'll be the new President of Operations for the Revolution.

When we started looking into this acquisition for King Corp., it was with Scarlet in mind as the new president of the Revolution. I never imagined I'd leave the Kings. But once we found out she was pregnant, we agreed it wasn't the right move for her. It wasn't fair to ask her to step into this position, knowing that she would only have a few months before my niece was due. Scarlet would never have felt comfortable taking the maternity leave she deserves that soon after starting with the new team.

The answer was obvious.

Scarlet can run the Kings with her eyes closed and hands tied.

We grew up with that team. It's been in our family for over sixty years.

Nobody will ever know it the way the Kingston family does, and Scarlet has been the driving force of the organization for years.

She was born to run the Kings.

It also gives me the chance to grow our family's legacy.

To do something my father never did.

To prove myself.

It was easy to take the Kings to the next level of football. They were already a great organization when I took over. The Revolution is struggling. Bringing them up to the level of the other great hockey teams out there won't be easy. But I've never been scared of hard work.

I want King Corp. to be synonymous with Philly Sports.

Scarlet reaches over and places her hand on my arm to get my attention. "Are you having regrets, Max?"

"No. This is the right move." Excitement wars with concern as I lay my hand over hers and squeeze to reassure her. "Just wondering what kind of shit show we're walking into."

The two stadiums that house the football and hockey teams are across the street from each other in the Center City district, but that's where the similarities end. We pull up to the front doors of the large brick complex, and I take note of the worn-down building and parking lot that's in disarray. Definitely time for an update.

My bodyguard and driver, Luka, holds the door for Scarlet, and I follow her out of the SUV.

"Does he wipe your ass for you too, Max?" She smirks and walks ahead of me, straight through the unlocked doors into the building.

A woman sitting at the front desk asks who we're here to see, then tells us to take the elevator up to the top floor. I scan the lobby while we wait for the doors to open and find one security guard, who's scrolling and watching something on his phone.

That's going to have to change.

"Jesus, you're a pain in my ass. You know that, right? You need a bodyguard too, Scarlet. You're about to experience a whole new level of exposure after this deal is announced." I've tried to have this conversation with her before. We all have. But she's stubborn and not listening.

You can't have the level of success our family has had and not expect to deal with crazy. I've tried to shield her as much as I could, but this move is going to take it to a whole new level for her.

After the elevator doors open, we head inside before moving slowly up to the third floor. The phone in my pocket buzzes with an incoming message from Becket.

Becks: How's it going?
Max: It hasn't started yet, moron. Scarlet was late. I'll call you after.
Becks: Is she okay?
Max: She's fine. The baby's fine. Our sister likes to make an entrance.
Becks: Don't forget. Drinks at Kingdom tonight to celebrate.

I turn my phone to Do Not Disturb and slide it back into my pocket.

When the doors open, Scarlet and I step off and almost flatten the woman waiting on the other side. And that would've been a damn shame because she's mouth-watering. Standing in front of us, her white-blonde hair is a stark contrast to a black-lace dress accentuating sinful curves. The kind a man aches to get his hands on. And when she looks up, it's with the palest blue eyes I've ever seen.

They're such a light blue, they almost appear to be silver.

And they don't look happy to see us. "Welcome to the Revolution. Please follow me." When she speaks, her tone is clipped but raspy as hell.

Like a woman who spent hours calling out her lover's name while she got fucked hard on her knees, begging for more last night. And my cock takes notice.

Scarlet leans in and lowers her voice. "I guess not everyone's happy to have us here."

"Yeah. Looks like." I nod, shaking myself out of whatever the hell I was just thinking, and discreetly adjust myself before following the women down the hall.

That was unexpected.

I don't dip into the workplace pool. I'm not a fourteen-year-old kid whose dick gets hard every time he sees a beautiful woman. But there was something about the stubborn glint in her eye. She may look small and meek, but my gut tells me there's a hellcat buried under all that lace.

She escorts us into a conference room with windows overlooking the empty ice below, and I take a minute to stand there and take it in, like a king surveying his kingdom. The navy-blue and red Revolution logo sits at center ice as the Zamboni makes its way slowly around the rink. Multiple red banners hang from the ceiling above with navy-blue lettering. They list numbers that have been retired, MVPs and championship titles. The last title win was seventeen years ago, and my first goal as the new president is to get a new year listed on that damn banner.

My thoughts are interrupted by the feisty blonde giving me a death stare. "Mr. Brenner will be in momentarily. Can I get either of you anything?"

This woman can only be five foot two at most, putting her at an entire foot shorter than me, but she straightens her spine and stares me down like she's six feet tall.

I hold my hand out to shake. "No thank you, Ms. . . ." I leave the statement open-ended, urging this woman to introduce herself.

"Ms. Brenner." She places her palm in mine, and electricity skips between us like a live wire. "Daphne Brenner."

Fuck. She's Will Brenner's daughter and my new administrative assistant.

I pull my palm back. "Nice to meet you, Ms. Brenner."

Eyes the color of moonlight glare back at me. "I wish I could say the same, Mr. Kingston."

DAPHNE

ONCE MY FATHER AND THE LEGAL TEAM HAVE JOINED THE meeting, I'm left sitting at my desk like a voyeur, as the pit in my stomach grows impossibly larger. All I can do is wonder what signs I could have overlooked and curse myself for missing them. Dad and I have never been overly close, but how could he be in this kind of financial trouble . . . the kind that would force him to sell the team without me seeing it?

Have I been that wrapped up in myself that I missed it?

Or has he been that good at hiding it?

Five days a week, I sat just a few steps from his office, and he didn't say a word.

Now I'm stuck waiting for answers I might not get for hours, and waiting has never been my strong suit. Instant gratification is more my speed. But my father asked me to wait outside instead of sitting in on this meeting, so I put my internet stalking skills to work in the meantime.

In less than a minute, Google tells me everything I need to know about every Kingston sibling from their list of romantic partners and net worth to shoe size.

But I narrow down my focus on the two in my office: Max and Scarlet.

There are endless articles and websites about them both, but there's no mention anywhere of today's sale or their interest in expanding their kingdom.

I'm surprised a sale that's bound to be as newsworthy as

this one, in a city this big, where the elite keep their circles so small, could be kept hush-hush.

Before I can think better of it, I pick up the phone and call Kelly, the VP of Human Resources and my godmother. She was my mother's best friend in the world before she died, and she tried to fill that role for me as much as she could through the years. She picks up on the second ring, and I don't waste any time. "Did you know?" I'm surprised by the catch in my voice and the angry tears threatening to fall.

I might as well have asked her if she was in on the betrayal too.

"Well, hello to you too, Daphne. How was your weekend?" A chastising tone is evident in her answer. "Mine was fine. Thank you so much for asking."

I wish I was calling just to check in or schedule a lunch date, but neither of those is happening today. "Kelly . . . Did you know?"

"D, it's Monday morning. My inbox is full. I have two files sitting on my desk, waiting for my attention, and I've just sat down with my second cup of coffee. You're going to have to be a little more specific. Did I know *what?*"

I glance around the empty office before trying to get a clear view of the suits sitting in the conference room. I can see them through the glass walls covered in life-size images of our hockey players. I lower my voice. "Did you know Dad's selling the team?"

"What?" Kelly's voice jumps five octaves before she yelps. "Shit. I just spilled my coffee." There's movement on her end of the call before she blows out a long breath. "Okay. Now, tell me what the hell you're talking about."

I tear my eyes away from what Google informed me earlier was the oldest and hottest Kingston sibling. Not that I needed Google to tell me that, but seriously . . . Last year, he was declared Philly's most eligible bachelor, and the pictures online don't even do him justice. According to my stalking, I now know that he's the youngest GM in the football league's history and is as opposite of the other stuffed suits as he could possibly be.

He wears his dirty-blonde hair a little too long. Thanks to a few candid photos, I can see his designer suit covers drool-worthy muscles wrapped in colorful ink. And his eyes . . . His eyes are the color of a dark ocean wave you drown in miles from shore. "Dad's selling the Revolution to the Kingston family. He told me when I got in this morning, then Max and Scarlet Kingston walked through the doors a few minutes later. They're all in the conference room now. But from what Dad said earlier, I think today is just to finalize everything. It's already a done deal."

"What the hell is he thinking? He didn't say a word to me." I know Kelly well enough to know the exact look of annoyance accompanying those words.

"Me either. Not until this morning. And our conversation left me with more questions than answers." The door to the conference room opens, and my skin prickles with awareness as the Kingstons walk through, followed by my father. "Shit, I've got to go. I'll call you back."

I hang up the phone just as the three of them approach my desk.

Dad seems small and lost, sandwiched between these two powerhouses.

And while I might be mad as hell at my father, I'm heart-broken to see him like this.

I want to reach out and wrap my arms around him protectively, hoping he'll tell me he has a plan. That everything's been handled and not to worry about anything. That the team is still ours.

But that's not going to happen.

Scarlet stands on my father's right, looking flawless and

smiling from ear to ear as she reads something on her phone while her hand rests on her pregnant belly.

She was born into this world the same way I was, but looking between us, we couldn't be more different. Scarlet is dressed from head to toe in designer labels, and I get excited about vintage thrift store finds. She exudes confidence, and right now, I feel like I'm balancing in my heels across quicksand.

It's like she's on top of the world.

Why wouldn't she be though?

Her father didn't just sell her family's business right out from under her.

Nope. Her kingdom just grew while mine vanished.

Max Kingston stands to my father's left. At thirty-two, the oldest Kingston sibling is already a titan in the sports world, and I don't need an article to tell me that acquiring my family's team just massively increased his portfolio. I suddenly feel like the clock is ticking for me to make my mark on the world.

There's something about the way he's standing at my desk . . . as if he's the master of the universe and expects the planets to revolve around him. And I get the impression I'm supposed to be one of those planets.

Like I don't already have my own orbit.

My father shoves his hands in his pockets and looks over at the man next to him, who's currently sucking all the oxygen from the room. "Daphne, I'd like to introduce you to Max and Scarlet Kingston. Max is stepping into the President of Operations position for the Revolution. After today, you'll be reporting directly to him."

And just like that, my orbit changes.

The rest of the day moved so excruciatingly slow that I wondered if it was ever going to end. A company meeting was held, followed by a Q&A session and a catered lunch. As if lunch from Bagliani's was going to make everything better. Later that afternoon, I followed my father to the King Corp. home offices in Center City, Philly, for the official news conference regarding the acquisition before finally being told to go home.

Geez, a whole hour early.

Thanks for that.

After a quick trip to the liquor store—because was there seriously any other way to handle this day that didn't involve alcohol?—I drop my bag onto the kitchen counter and wrap my fingers deftly around the bottle of tequila. I know tonight is supposed to be Margarita Monday, but hey, it's five o'clock somewhere . . . right?

By the time my roommate, Maddie, walks into the kitchen, I'm already enjoying the burn of the tequila as it slides down my throat, promising to dull the ache in my chest.

The two of us have been staying with her brother, Brandon, since the lease on our campus housing expired after graduation last month. Mads is the only one who calls him by his first name. The rest of us were given strict instructions to call him "Dixon."

I can appreciate that. I'm not fond of being called by my name either. Daphne, the ditz from *Scooby Doo*, ruined that for me at a young age.

We're supposed to be looking for our own place, but Dix isn't in any rush for Maddie to move out, so we've been taking our time. He isn't hurting for space in his house that looks like it's just waiting for a family, complete with a wife, two point five kids, and a golden retriever. Dixon's the starting center for the Philadelphia Kings football team, and this house was his first big purchase when he got his signing bonus. Guess he isn't the bachelor-pad kinda guy.

He and Maddie grew up in foster care, getting bounced from home to home. She doesn't like to talk about it, but one night, she told me Dix likes the stability this house represents. It's something neither of them had growing up.

I think he'd keep her here with him forever if she'd let him.

She snatches the bottle of tequila from my hand and holds it above my head.

"What the heck, D?" Mads never curses. "Heck" is about as strong as it gets for her.

When I reach for it, she holds it higher. "Not until you tell me what's got you doing shots straight from the bottle."

She tilts her head to the side, watching and waiting for me to answer.

Maddie and I were placed in the same dorm room our first semester in college. I'd been so worried about living with a stranger that I begged my dad to let me commute instead of living on campus, but it turned out to be unwarranted. Mads is amazing, and other than both of us being blondes, we're polar opposites. She's tall to my short. Graceful and athletic compared to my uncoordinated self who hates to sweat. I'm book smart, and she's the street-smart friend you want by your side when you're walking through the city.

But most importantly, her heart is huge, and she wears it proudly on her sleeve. Not that I don't have a big heart, but mine might be a tad bit more closed off than hers.

Four years later, she's one of my closest friends.

She's a dance teacher by day at Hart & Soul Academy of Dance in Kroydon Hills, teaching dance and the occasional yoga classes for the owner, Annabelle Sinclair. Belle's husband, Declan, happens to be Carys's oldest stepbrother and the starting quarterback for the Philadelphia Kings. In case we needed our lives to be even more Six Degrees Of Kevin Bacon, Mads also runs her brother's social media accounts by night, and Belles has asked her to consider taking on her husband's as well.

I swear, you need a string board to keep track of how everyone in this town is connected.

Guess not much has changed since high school.

I pull myself up to sit on the kitchen counter behind me and drop my head back against the cabinet. "You're never going to believe the day I had."

She puts the tequila down on the table and empties the rest of the contents from my shopping bag as I tell her about my morning and the staff meeting that followed before we were all given the rest of the day off.

Maddie's blue eyes blink back at me. "Holy cow, D. You had no idea?"

"Nope." I pop my "p," reach into the cabinet next to me, and grab the margarita pitcher and glasses before jumping off the counter. "Now, am I allowed to start drinking?"

Maddie grabs the cutting board and limes, then hands me the knife before thinking better of it. "Let's keep the sharp objects away from you tonight, okay?"

I glare at her as I throw my hair up in a bun. I'm a bit of a klutz. Knives and I may have a bit of history. "That was one time, Mads. Come on."

She waves the paring knife in front of my face. "One time and twelve stitches. I'm not in the mood to go to the hospital tonight, D. Now, sit down and tell me what it was like meeting Max Kingston."

My cheeks flame when I remember the current of electricity that jolted between us outside the elevator. "He was an arrogant jerk. A hot one, but definitely a jerk who expected everyone to bow to him. He was just . . ." I trail off, searching for the right words, annoyed with myself that my mind chooses to focus on that instead of his family stealing the team out from under mine.

"Oh, he really is. I've met him once or twice at Brandon's games. Max Kingston wears his power like a second skin I'd like to run my fingers all over." She runs a lime over the edge of our margarita glasses before rimming them with salt and pouring the sweet nectar of the gods in.

Once she hands me one, we clink glasses.

"He's going to be my new boss, Mads. I will *not* be touching his skin." Not if he was the last man on Earth. The lie filters through my head so easily, I almost believe it.

"Whose skin?" comes from a familiar voice in the doorway.

Followed by Dixon's baritone, "New boss?"

I turn my head and squeal when I see Carys and Chloe standing next to Dix. Jumping from my chair, I wrap my arms around Carys. "Oh my God, you're never allowed to be gone this long again." I haven't seen my best friend since Christmas. I think I cried when she told me she was going to college in California. "Seven months is too long. And no, phone calls don't count."

She squeezes me back, then pats my arm. "I missed you too, but I can't breathe, D."

Dix grabs a bottle of vitamin water from the fridge and smiles. "Hey now . . . I found them out front. Why don't I get greeted like that?"

Chloe rolls her eyes from across the room. She's known Dixon for a few years. Her brother, Brady, and Carys's brother, Murphy, both played football with him in college. "Whatever, Dix." She sits down at the table and pushes out the chair next to her for him. "Now, where are we ordering from? I'm starving."

"Okay . . . Let me get this straight." Carys dips the crust of her pizza in the ranch dressing on her plate, then points it at me. "You told your father you'd stop by tonight, and he told you not to come. Did he tell you why?"

"Did he seem okay?" Maddie adds.

I sip my second margarita and lick the salt from my lips as I shake my head. "He said he needed some time. I wanted to scream at the top of my lungs, *'Thanks for saving my job, Dad. But maybe a heads-up would have been nice.'* It just didn't seem like the right time or place to do it." I look between the three of them. "Don't get me wrong. I'm grateful he guaranteed my job for the next year, but I'm just so . . . I don't know. I'm angry, and I'm sad. And I think I'm hurt too." I run my finger along the salt falling down the side of my heavy, green stemmed glass. "I might not have ever wanted to take over the team, but I wanted to run the charitable department. I wanted to be a piece of the organization my grandfather built. That my mother was supposed to run." I wipe at my face before the tears can fall. "I love that team. I guess I just thought it would always be a part of my family."

Cinder, our gray-and-white long-haired cat, jumps up on my lap and nudges her head under my hand, directing me to run it over her back the way she likes before she swishes her tail in my face and moves on to Maddie. Mads and I found her as a kitten who'd been left out in a box during our sophomore year of college, and we took her in. She's a prickly little girl, but even she feels bad for me.

Fuck. I hate pity. Even coming from a cat.

"I'm going to stop by the house tomorrow after work. My mistake today was giving him a heads-up. Tomorrow, I'm just going to show up. What's he going to do? Turn me away from the house I grew up in?" It wouldn't be the first time. Dad shut down for months after Mom's death. It was awful. I was only a little girl, and I still remember how alone I felt.

I hope to God he doesn't do it again.

Maddie pushes her salad away and stands from the couch. She's a diabetic, and pizza is not something she tends to indulge in. It can wreak havoc on her sugars. "Maybe you should give him some time, D. If you push him before he's ready to talk, you might not like what he has to say."

"I guess. But I have a feeling, after my first day working for Max Kingston tomorrow, I'm going to *need* the answers from Dad. Not just want them."

"Max isn't that bad, D." Carys's stepbrother isn't her only family member working for the Kings. Her stepfather is their head coach.

I bristle at her words. I don't want to hear that he's not the bad guy right now. Not yet. Because if the Kingstons aren't the bad guys in all this, then I think my dad is.

"Give him a chance." She says it more like an order than an idea.

"Easier said than done." I watch Carys play with the bracelet on her wrist. "Speaking of chances. Are we going to discuss why you decided to end things?"

"Good luck," Chloe snorts. "She hasn't told me shit."

Maddie walks back into the living room with a full pitcher of margaritas in hand. "Ohh, wait. I want to hear this too. Has there been a status change with . . . wait . . . what are we calling him?"

Chloe and I both answer, "He who shall not be named," much to Maddie's amusement.

"First." Carys points her finger around the room. "You guys are assholes. And second . . . Yeah. It's over." She reaches over and takes the pitcher out of Maddie's hands. "But let's focus on a much more fun topic of conversation. If we're going to talk love lives, I want to know if we've found someone worthy of popping Mad's cherry yet."

We hear a distinctly male groan coming from the kitchen, where Dixon's eating his dinner, before the rest of us burst into laughter, and poor Maddie just shakes her head.

And with that change in subject, my pity party is officially over.

Well, at least for tonight.

MAX

"How's it feel to finally be out of Dad's shadow?" My brother Sawyer stands on the opposite side of the reclaimed wooden bar, pouring shots of Macallan for Becket, Hudson, and me, while our youngest brother, Jace, leans back on his chair with a petulant look firmly planted on his face. He's still a few years away from seeing twenty-one, and the fact that Sawyer owns Kingdom doesn't mean he gets a pass just yet.

I ignore the back-handed compliment on today's acquisition.

At least I try to.

When I don't answer him, Sawyer raises his glass high in the air. "To you, Maximus. May this be the first step in allowing yourself to stop living Dad's life and start living your own."

Sawyer swallows the amber liquid in one swig while he watches me carefully.

Knowing he hit a nerve with that toast.

But that's what he does.

Sawyer is smack-dab in the middle of five brothers.

He pushes boundaries.

He observes reactions.

He calculates his next moves.

He refuses to bend to the wants and expectations of other people.

That's why he owns one of the most successful bars in the

city. None of us thought this was what he was going to do with his life. Dad pushed him to work for King Corp., the same way he pushed the rest of his sons. I even tried when we decided to buy the Revolution. Sawyer's got an innate ability to understand exactly what a business needs to turn a profit, and it would have been nice to have another Kingston representing the company. But Sawyer never wavered. He'd built and sold three successful businesses by the time he was twenty-five when he went all in with Kingdom, his baby, which he offered up for the celebration tonight.

The bar is crowded for a Monday night, but Kingdom always is, weeknight or not.

The former warehouse may have a new life, but the old, industrial feel is carried throughout with a high open ceiling, showcasing matte black pipes, a large dancefloor off to the right, and a big old, refurbished bar to the left. Tonight, we're at the top of the long metal staircase, enjoying the VIP area overlooking the dance floor below. When we all get together, it's easier if we're up here.

A round of cheers bounces between the five of us, and I savor the velvety smooth whiskey before flipping my glass over and slamming it down on the bar next to my bottle of beer. "Thanks, asshole."

They can't really be this oblivious, can they?

My family loves to make snide remarks about me following in Dad's footsteps. But what fucking choice did I have? Poor little rich boy, groomed to take over a family and an empire. I've got zero fucks to complain about in life. I've got everything I need, more money than God, and a family who loves me. I may have been raised to protect them, but I think I'd want to do that either way. "Tell me you realize I live Dad's life so none of you have to."

Becks shrugs and flips his glass over next to mine. "Don't

look at me, man. I work in the office one floor down from yours. I'm part of the Kingston machine too."

Sawyer grabs the rag tucked into his jeans and wipes down the bar. "You work for the family, Becks, but it's different. Max lives in Dad's house. He works in Dad's office, doing Dad's job. He runs Dad's company—"

Jace snaps a bottle cap between his thumb and forefinger, then turns his attention back to me. "Let's not forget you also stepped up as my legal guardian after Dad died."

There are nine of us siblings. Dad had four wives and a mistress.

His final wife, Ashlyn, was pregnant with our youngest sister, Madeline, when Dad died.

My little brother Jace was the only one of us who wasn't eighteen when it happened. His and Lenny's mom had passed away a few years before Dad married Ashlyn. Somebody had to step up and take care of him.

"I'm the oldest. It's my job to make sure you're all good. Christ, Lenny was starting her degree." I turn toward Hudson. "You were busy fucking your way through Philly." I point my bottle at Becks. "And you were still finishing your damn law degree. We barely even saw you that year."

Sawyer flips our glasses back over and pours another round. "Nobody is saying you did anything wrong, brother. We're saying you did it all for all the right reasons. Now it's your turn to do it however you want, for whatever reasons you want. And we're gonna give you the kick in the ass you need to start doing it on your own damn terms. We know what you've sacrificed for us." Sawyer looks behind me, his eyes locking on something. When I turn, I see Scarlet and her boyfriend, Cade, wrapped up in each other on the dance floor. She's glowing, and he has his hand wrapped possessively around her. "We know what you gave up for her.

You're the best of us, Max. Now, stop taking care of Dad's shit and start taking care of your own."

Those words play hell with my thoughts for the rest of the night.

I take care of my own shit.

They act like I'm Mother friggin' Theresa.

It's not the first time one of my brothers has pointed out that I stepped into Dad's shoes after he died. When you're the oldest of nine, it's what you do. Somebody had to, and because I did it, none of them would ever have to be crushed by the burden.

They'd get to pick their own path and chase their own dreams without the weight of King Corp, the family, and all our futures coloring the way. I made sure we stayed close and present in each other's lives and didn't drift apart after we lost Dad.

But have I used it as a crutch?

Have I gotten too comfortable living this life?

When Dad died, I asked Jace if he wanted to stay at the house or if he wanted to live with me at my place in the city. Jace chose Dad's house because he didn't want to switch schools and didn't want the hour-long commute that living in the city would have equated to with traffic each morning. So I made it work. But Jace has grown up and moved on. He lives in the hockey house at Kroydon University now. While I still live at Dad's.

Maybe it is time to start making some changes.

I make a note on my phone to have my new assistant get me set up with a realtor tomorrow. Knowing part of the deal with Will Brenner was guaranteeing his daughter's job, I asked Taylor, my assistant with the Kings, to stay and work with Scarlet. Her assistant didn't want to transition out of marketing, so he'll be working with the new head of that department, and Taylor will run Scarlet's world.

If I can't get rid of Daphne Brenner, I might as well use her.

Which leads to me recalling the haughty way she told me she wasn't happy about us buying the team this morning. The level of nerve that took surprised me. She stood in front of me, looking every bit the image of a 1950's pin-up model with her sinful curves, shiny blonde hair, and her chin tilted up. Refusing to back down. Intriguing me more.

Little does she know, strong women are my kryptonite.

In the boardroom *and* the bedroom.

Not that Daphne Brenner can ever be in my bedroom.

That fantasy has to be packed away.

I've crossed quite a few lines, all in the name of King Corp, but sexual harassment has never been, and never will be, one of them. Imagining my mouth on her skin is as far as that can go. Maybe tomorrow she won't make my mouth water and my cock jump.

The next morning, I'm in the office before anyone else, ready to get started like any other day. Movers came in last night and cleared out Will's office, then set mine up so I didn't have to miss a beat. The only problem is the woman sitting right outside my door, who hasn't stopped humming since she walked in unless it was to give me a death stare.

Pretty sure she's tried to kill me with her eyes a few times so far.

As the office comes to life, Daphne has a conversation with each employee who walks by her desk. Every single one. She smiles and talks with everyone. Which is more than she did with me yesterday, or today for that matter, and it's beginning to grate on my nerves.

It's not my fault her father was an asshole who decided

not to tell his staff until after the deal was signed. His CFO was the only officer he looped into the deal, and as the finance guy, I don't think there was much choice.

I obviously would have handled things differently, but this is the shit show I'm going to be dealing with.

She's shown no initiative yet.

Really the only thing she's shown me is that she's capable of slamming drawers and socializing. That doesn't bode well for her. It should be interesting to see who's left standing at the end of the day.

Taylor anticipated all my needs. If I had a meeting on my schedule for that day, the agenda and any necessary information were in a folder on my desk when I sat down that morning. She had a system in place for everything and didn't like anyone to interfere. It worked for me.

My sister . . . I'm thinking not so much.

And with that thought, I realize I've given enough attention to my sister and her assistant instead of dealing with my own angry little spitfire of an assistant. Pushing up from my desk, I walk out into the hub of this wing of the building. There are two executive admins, including Daphne, and two offices other than my own. One is the General Manager/Head Coach's office. The other is empty right now.

"Daphne." I wait patiently until she looks up from her computer.

When her pale blue eyes meet mine, they appear frostier than yesterday. "Yes, Mr. Kingston?" falls from her lips like an insolent schoolgirl, and my palms itch to spank her perfectly heart-shaped ass while she's panting my name, bent over my desk.

"I'd like to speak with you in my office." My words come out with smooth practice, not betraying my body's reaction to this woman, and I wait until she's standing, then follow her into my office. Today, she's wearing a sleeveless white blouse, with a little ruffle at the neckline, tucked into a bright pink pencil skirt that would look amazing rucked up around her waist, and a pair of sexy black heels, adding at least three more inches to her legs.

I close the door behind me and wait until we're both seated to begin. "I think we got off on the wrong foot yesterday, Ms. Brenner." A beautiful red flush covers her cheeks, and I swallow. "I'm sorry the sale was kept from you, but that decision was not mine."

"D." She sits straighter in her chair. "Please call me 'D.'"

It doesn't fit her in the least, but I give it a try. This job will be a lot easier if my assistant doesn't fucking hate me for the next twelve months. "Okay, D. Call me Max." She relaxes slightly. "How about you tell me what exactly you did for your father? Then we can discuss my expectations."

"I basically did whatever he needed." She crosses her legs and relaxes her body, and I follow the movement before quickly averting my eyes. "I haven't worked here very long. I graduated from Kroydon University last spring with a master's in non-profit management and started here in June." She runs her teeth over her bottom lip, then sighs. "To be honest, Max, this position isn't my long-term goal. I had a deal with my father before he sold the team."

I lean forward, intrigued. "What kind of deal?"

"Are you aware that the Revolution's charitable foundation was closed a few years ago?" This grabs my attention because I never saw that mentioned in any of my research.

"No. I wasn't aware. Do you know why?" I make a note to find out more and wait for her to continue.

"No." She clasps her hands together tightly in her lap and holds her head higher. "Unfortunately, I don't. I just know what I planned to do with it. If I worked for him for twelve months, my father was going to let me reopen the Revolution foundation and run it." She tucks a lock of blonde hair nervously behind her ear, then smiles. "Any chance you'd be interested in a charitable division? I want to call it the 'Start A Revolution Foundation.' I'd like to focus on kids. Hungry kids. Kids with no homes. No families. Kids who can't read. There are so many ways the kids in our own city need help, and I want to fill that void."

The hopeful smile that graces her face could light up the entire arena.

"I'm not sure how much you know about me, Daphne, but the Kings and King Corp. both have charitable divisions."

Her shoulders drop. "So you don't need another one."

"What I'm saying is I believe in giving back. My family always has. I'd like to get the foundation back up and running. But for now, I've got to focus on the team, and I'd like your help."

"My help?" Gray eyes look up, seemingly shocked.

I stand and walk around my desk, closing the space between us, then lean back on it and cross my arms over my chest. "Yes, *your* help. Judging from the parade of people who've stopped by your desk this morning, it seems like a safe bet to assume you know most of the employees. At the very least, you know the team sitting on this floor. I need you to be my right hand through this transition. Help me make it as smooth as possible."

"And in return . . . ?" She scoots forward on her chair as if she's trying to physically touch the answer she's waiting for.

"In return, I'd like you to take any down time you have during the day to put together your proposal on how you'd like to start the foundation. I want a mission statement that's in line with the history of the organization. I want to know what your focus will be and how you intend to raise the funds, as well as what type of startup capital will be required." That smile reappears, spreading across her face and hits me square in the chest, frustrating the hell out of me.

I'm not this guy who fantasizes about his assistant. His very young, very beautiful, very mercurial assistant. "There's no timetable on this. I'm not sure if or when I'll give you the go-ahead. But these are the first steps. Walk me through how you'll do it."

She jumps to her feet and throws her arms around me.

Soft curves press against the hard lines of my body, and I hold my arms out to the side like an asshole who doesn't know what to do. Because seriously, what the fuck are you supposed to do when your hot-as-sin assistant, who's at least ten years younger than you, presses her full tits against your chest?

Lifting her up to fuck up against the wall sounds like fun in theory, but in actuality, it would probably get me sued.

"I'm so sorry, Max." Daphne backs away, her cheeks red with embarrassment. "I . . . It's just . . ." She looks down at the floor, pursing her lips. "Thank you. This means so much to me . . . I . . . I really appreciate it."

That makes two of us.

I sit back down behind my desk, hiding the effect a happy Daphne has on me, and we go over my schedule for the remainder of the week.

When she's standing and ready to leave the office, I stop her for one last thing. "Daphne. Could you please find me a realtor? I need to purchase a new home and would like to work with someone reputable and discreet. I don't need it plastered on social media."

She laughs. Actually laughs. "Max, I'm pretty sure I can do whatever you want if it gets me my foundation." She practically skips out of my office, completely unaware of what she just said and the filthy fucking images she left in her wake.

DAPHNE

WHEN MAX ASKED ME TO FIND HIM A REALTOR LAST WEEK, I had no idea that would mean I'd be going with him to view properties this week. But I've quickly learned Max Kingston doesn't believe in wasting time. The busy streets of Philadelphia have flown past us as we make our way around Center City for Max's first appointment. And here I am, sitting on the buttery soft leather seat of his Range Rover, being driven by a man who looks like he could crush a walnut with his bicep, as Max and I discuss the results of the meetings he's been holding with the heads of the departments over the last few days.

This man never stops.

He's in the office earlier than all of us each day.

I keep trying to get in before him, but I'm sorry, it's not happening. I'm starting to think he's sleeping on the couch in his office. It's a big couch. He'd fit. All six-feet-plus of his way too pretty for a man's body. Today, he's dressed in a dark-gray suit with a navy-blue tie that nearly matches his eyes. And if it weren't for the tiny little pale-blue pin-dots covering the tie, I might not have noticed he's got matching pale flecks hiding in the depths of those eyes.

And . . . now, I sound like a creeper.

"Daphne?"

I lean forward, knowing I'm a busted creeper. Judging by the raise of his brow, he caught me staring. I've been doing that a lot lately too. Max has an open-door policy and leaves his door wide open whenever he's in his office. And I've got a million-dollar view of this company-stealing hottie from behind my computer.

Max Kingston looks like Jax from *Sons Of Anarchy* and Christian Grey made a baby.

Hot as the nine circles of hell hot.

He repeats my name.

Only . . . growlier.

Why does he always have to speak and ruin the fantasy?

"D." The correction leaves my mouth before I think better of it, and I remind myself he's my boss, and I need this job. He's my new gatekeeper to the Revolution Foundation. Gotta play nice and stop ogling the boss.

Besides, he might hold the keys to my future with the foundation, but he's still the ass who owns my family legacy.

A muscle ticks in his jaw before a smug smile replaces his look of annoyance.

I wrap my fingers tightly around the edges of my iPad to keep from flicking his ear the way I would Dixon's. *No touching the boss.* Jesus, I've got to get laid. Who knew sexual frustration could manifest itself like this? Not me. That's for sure. I mean, so it's been six months . . . wait, or is it seven? And that wasn't even good sex. Damn it.

"Did you confirm my meeting with O'Doul?" Max has his own tablet sitting in his lap and a damn smartphone in his hand. He can see I confirmed his meeting if he'd open up his schedule on either one.

I adjust my shoulders and cross my ankles like the lady I was raised to be. "Yes, Max. You're meeting with the GM this afternoon at four. He needs to be out by five. His daughter has a soccer game tonight." He nods his head, and I point at the screen. "If you'd checked your schedule, you would've seen that I took care of that this morning."

He opens the device and hands it to me. "I did check. There's no note."

"Double-tap, Max." I don't even take the device from his hands. "You have to double-tap for the additional information."

"Fucking double-tap," he grumbles, more to himself than to me. "Swear to God, we need better systems. Everything used to be there before. I didn't have to go searching." He places the offending piece of equipment in his briefcase. "When am I meeting with the head of IT?"

"Friday," I answer without needing to look at the calendar to know. Donya, the head of our IT department, was pissed about Dad selling the company and even more furious it was the Kingstons who bought it. She's holding a big old grudge about something she wouldn't share.

Max checks his watch as we sit, stopped at a red light. "Can you add software to the agenda for IT?"

"No." His head jolts up at an unhealthy angle, and I smother a laugh. "You already asked me to put it on the agenda. I don't need to be asked twice to do something, Max. I like to do it right the first time."

The Rover turns into an underground parking garage for One Riverside. This building is one of the priciest in the city with a breathtaking view of the Schuylkill River. Once we're parked, Luka gets out and opens Max's door first, then rounds the car and opens mine.

"Oh, no. Thank you, but I'll just wait here." I pull my purse from the floor and reach for my phone to keep myself busy.

Max stands next to Luka, waiting for me. "No, you won't. Come on, Daphne." His long legs stride to the door where the bellman's waiting, and I can't help but wonder if this man is ever told "no."

It's like house-hunting with a very wealthy but very picky Goldilocks. We've seen three beautiful penthouses, and he hasn't liked a single one. Too much natural light. Not enough windows. Too sterile. Too cluttered.

And my favorite so far, *"The dining room isn't big enough."*

Holly, the realtor who missed her calling on the catwalk, has been eyeing him like a carb she absolutely refuses to eat but really wants to lick. She makes yet another note before she leans into him, boobs first. "No problem, Mr. Kingston. I can have another set scheduled for later this week." I wonder if she sees dollar signs or husband potential when she looks at him because she's definitely seeing something, and considering he's barely spoken to her, it can't possibly be his winning personality.

He takes a step back. "Great. Thank you. Just call Daphne to schedule." *Selling Sunset*: East Coast Edition looks like she just sucked a lemon at the mention of my name. She glances over as if just realizing I was in the room and quickly assesses me, apparently deciding with a single flick of her eyes that I'm not competition, before giving me her back.

Oh, honey. Don't worry your pretty little highlighted head about it. I will not get in the way of you trying to bed Mr. Kingston. But even as that thought trickles in, I take a step back to avoid the impending lightning strike for the tiny little lie I just told myself.

Because seriously, who wouldn't want to bed Max Kingston?

I don't bother trying to convince myself I don't want to know what he looks like under the thousand-dollar suits he seems to live in. I mean, the man is smoking hot, but I also think that there's more to him than Gucci suits and a Colgate-worthy smile.

And that's what scares me. I don't want to like him.

Once Max and I are alone in the elevator, his body relaxes, and he leans back against the wall. "I used to have a penthouse like this."

My interest piqued, I ask, "Why'd you give it up?"

His eyes close briefly before his shoulders tense. "Family obligations."

"Have you considered going back?"

"You can't rewind time. There's no use trying." It's the first personal exchange we've had since that initial meeting in his office.

And when Max turns his attention to his phone, it seems to be over.

That's until my stomach takes that exact moment to make a very unladylike growl, and I cringe and bite down on my bottom lip.

The elevator doors open, and Max surprises me by placing his hand at the small of my back, singeing my skin through my sleeveless red shirtdress and ushering me to the waiting car. Once we're buckled in, Luka asks, "Where to?"

"Ms. Brenner and I need to grab some lunch before we head back to the office." He turns to me. "Any place in particular you'd like to stop, Daphne?"

I take a deep breath in through my nose before releasing it out again. He's never going to call me D, but I appreciate him asking where I'd like to eat. Hmm . . . So many good places to pick from. "I bet your favorite place to eat is somewhere formal and stuffy, isn't it?" I can just imagine the black-suit-clad maître d' greeting Max by name in a posh downtown restaurant where the tip alone is a car payment.

Luka laughs knowingly from the front seat.

"I'm right, aren't I? You're kind of easy to read." I sit up a little straighter and maybe a little too proud of myself until Luka cuts off my premature celebration.

"You couldn't be further from–"

Max clears his throat. "Dim Sum & Noodle."

"What?" I am so confused.

"That's my favorite place. It's not far, if you want to try it. But it's far from fancy, if that's what you're in the mood for." I can tell from his waiting expression I'm about to be judged by my answer, but now it's my turn to surprise him.

"That sounds great. I don't like fancy." I consider myself quite the foodie. It doesn't need to be expensive to be good.

"Oh yeah?" When I nod my head, Max smiles. "Where's your favorite place to eat?"

I don't even have to think about it. It's been my favorite place to eat forever. "Fat Jack's."

Judging by the set of his eyes and the crooked smile I'm rewarded with, he approves of my choice of food truck. "My brothers and I have never agreed on which fat sandwich is the best."

Seriously? He likes my favorite food truck?

I really didn't want to like my new boss, but he's making it hard for me. "It's definitely the Fat Jack. You can't go wrong with his signature dish. It's a classic for a reason."

Max laughs like I'm absolutely dense as he loosens his tie. "Luka, can you swing by Fat Jack's for lunch? I've got to school Ms. Brenner."

"You can try to school me all you like, Mr. Kingston, so long as you feed me first."

Max's eyes hold mine for a moment, his dark pupils dilate before he looks away and goes back to scrolling through his phone. And just like that, the moment's gone.

When we grab our order, Jack, the owner of Fat Jack's, greets Max by name, and he asks about Becket and Scarlet.

Yet another reason not to hate my new boss.

If I'm being honest with myself, I kinda like him.

Maybe a little too much.

MAX

The Revolution's head coach, Bobby O'Doul, is well respected. He's also a pompous ass with an ego the size of the Liberty Bell. As one of the few men in this league who hold dual GM and head coach titles, he's earned it . . . to an extent. It's more common in professional football than hockey. After fifteen years spent as one of the league's top defensemen on the ice in California, he retired and switched coasts to work with this organization as one of the assistant coaches. Two decades later, he's sitting at the top of the food chain.

At least, he thinks he is.

But owner trumps GM.

And while I haven't spent my life learning hockey the way I've learned football, I will not be disrespected in a building I fucking own. "I don't think you're hearing me. I wanted to be included in the discussions. I will be included in the decisions. If it's happening in this organization, I'm the first to know."

His face reddens like a plump tomato, ready to burst, while I sit back in my chair, waiting for the inevitable explosion.

O'Doul shoves back from his chair and plants his hands on the edge of my desk. "Brenner never needed that."

"Do I look like Will Brenner to you?" I wait until he straightens, then rise from the chair. Bobby O'Doul doesn't intimidate me, and respect is earned in my world. So far, he hasn't earned mine. "I've never been a micromanager before, and I don't intend to become one now, but I've always known my organization, inside and out. Every employee hired, every cent spent. If this team fails, it ultimately comes back on me. So for now, you're stuck with me in your meetings and on certain calls. We're barely a month away from training camp, and we both know that any changes that need to happen behind the scenes need to be finished by then."

O'Doul stands there, stoically staring at me. I offer him my hand, hoping he'll take the olive branch for what it is. "This would be a hell of a lot easier if we were on the same side."

"Yeah well, we'll see how it goes. Won't we?" He begrudgingly shakes my hand, then hurriedly leaves my office, closing the door behind him.

I cross the room to reopen the door only to see he's stopped to speak with my ever-perky assistant, who has a smile stretching across her face for everyone but me. She always seems to be looking at me with a mix of suspicion and surprise splashed across her beautiful face. She's asking about his daughter's game, and O'Doul happily shows her what I'm assuming is a photo on his phone before heading to the elevator. Apparently, pleasantries are given out freely in this office to everyone else.

I've never had such a hard time winning over staff.

But the culture of this office is different from the Kings.

And that needs to change. Starting from the top down.

Daphne turns back to her computer and jumps when she sees me standing in the doorframe. She runs her teeth over her plump bottom lip the way I've noticed she often does.

The urge to free that lip with my thumb before I suck it into my mouth immediately follows like it's been doing all week. I'm going to fucking hell.

She's worked for me for one week, and thoughts I shouldn't be having invade my brain daily. She's nothing like the women I've been with. All soft curves and smiles, covered in feminine dresses and delicate pearls. Not a power suit or designer handbag in sight.

Daphne Brenner would never date a guy just to be seen.

She'd rather eat at the local food truck than The Four Seasons.

She exudes happiness and laughter for everyone but me. I'm the villain in her fairytale, and for some reason, that bothers me. I didn't steal this company away from her father. He came to me for a fucking rescue boat.

When she starts packing up for the day, I stop her. "Have you had any thoughts about what we discussed last week?"

Her phone buzzes on her desk before she has a chance to answer me, and she quickly picks it up and glances over the screen before her face falls and her skin pales. "I'm sorry, Max . . . I've got to go." She logs off her computer and hurries out of the building without a backward glance.

What the fuck was that?

And why am I left with a feeling of loss when she leaves?

KINGSTON FAMILY GROUP TEXT:

Scarlet: Does anyone need an extra ticket for Crucible's fundraiser this weekend?
Lenny: Like I would pass up a chance to watch your boyfriend flex his MMA muscles?
Lenny: I'll take two.
Hudson: Are you sure you're happily engaged, little sister?
Lenny: Look, but no touch, Huddy. There's nothing wrong with it. Besides Bash has his own muscles that I touch as much as I want.

Hudson: Oh God! TMI!

Sawyer: Is there a woman left in Philly you haven't touched, Hud?

Becks: Ooh. Burn.

Jace: No one says burn anymore, old man.

Becks: Who you callin' old, tweenager? Have your balls dropped yet?

Jace: I'm nineteen.

Max: Aww. He's nineteen. In two more years, he can buy his own drinks.

Jace: Whatever Maxi-pad.

Max: Great comeback, jack-off.

Scarlet: Focus people. The benefit. The tickets. Who needs extra?

Amelia: I'll be home with the baby. But Sam is going and bringing Dean.

Lenny: Are they driving the Impala?

Amelia: Ooh, now that's a sexy picture.

Hudson: Don't forget who the MC for the night is, people.

Sawyer: WTF, Scarlet. You're giving him a microphone? Did Karaoke night teach you nothing?

Scarlet: I'm not the one organizing this. Just being a supportive girlfriend.

Scarlet: Cade's giving him a microphone. Actually, Cade's sister made the decision.

Becks: Bad move.

Jace: The worst.

Hudson: Fuck off, assholes.

Scarlet: I give up. Call me if you need an extra ticket.

My father's been gone for six years, and I've never changed a thing in his home office. Never made it mine in the years since I've moved back into his house. I haven't wanted to. A few years ago, my brothers and sisters and I came in here and went through his things. It was the first step in the healing process that never went further. It provided some closure. But not enough. It was also a day that would be burned into my brain as the day half my siblings admitted to having sex in here.

A silent laugh shakes my body as I remember Scarlet announcing she lost her virginity on this desk.

Leave it to her to go for shock and awe.

I raise my crystal rocks glass and run my finger over the condensation dripping down the side as I scan the room in a silent toast to my father. I stare at the portrait of us kids hanging on the wall. I was in my early twenties, and I think Jace was ten, so everyone else was scattered between the two of us.

We had no idea Amelia existed back then, and Madeline wasn't born yet.

It was the seven of us.

The world was in front of us for the taking.

For the living.

I think I forgot to live it though.

A knock on the open doorframe alerts me to Ashlyn, my father's final wife. He died when she was just a few months pregnant with my youngest sister, Madeline. The two of them still live here with Hudson and me. "Hey, Ash."

"What's up, Max?" Ashlyn was shy when Dad brought her home. None of us really understood what was between the two of them. He'd lost Jace and Lenny's mom a few years before that, and she was the love of his life. Not my mom or Sawyer and Hudson's mom. No one compared to Kristen. But then, one day, he brought home this Olympic figure skater, who was younger than everyone, except Jace and Lenny, and they told us they were married.

We were shocked. But not as shocked as we were a few months later when he had a heart attack in bed with a model, while Ashlyn was home, pregnant with Madeline.

"I wanted to talk to you about the house."

Ashlyn sits delicately down in the chair across from the desk and eyes my drink. "You've been drinking more lately, Maximus." Even Ashlyn likes to bust my balls now.

"You're not my mother, Ashlyn."

She reaches forward, takes the tumbler from me and takes a sip, then hands it back. "And thank fucking God for that, Max. Just a friend noticing something. I'm a good listener if you need one was all I meant."

I suddenly feel bad for my response.

I suppose Ashlyn has opened up more over the past year or two. I still don't understand the relationship she had with my dad, but it doesn't matter now. I never considered her a stepmom the way I did the others, but I'd call her a friend.

"Listen, I wanted to let you know that I'm moving out. I looked at places today. I haven't found anything yet, but I'm hoping to soon." I swallow the last of the whiskey and listen to the clink of the ice cubes before meeting her gaze. "We're not selling this house though. This is your home as much as it's anyone's. You and Madeline belong here."

With an almost imperceptible nod of her head, Ashlyn studies me for a long, uncomfortable moment. My siblings and I have always been loud and outgoing. Some might say *too* loud. But in a family as big as ours, you had to fight to be heard.

Ashlyn has always been at the opposite end of the spectrum.

Quiet.

Introspective.

She gracefully stands and purses her lips before speaking.

"If you're feeling crowded or antsy in this house, Madeline and I can move out."

"No. This is your home. It's her home. It's where she should grow up. I'm not crowded, Ashlyn. I'm tired of living in the shadow of a ghost. I had my own life before Dad died, and it's about time I get that back. I got comfortable, filling in for him. It's time to be more than John Kingston's son." Long past time.

"Don't make change for the sake of change, Max. Do it because you want to. Because it's the right move. Don't do it because it's what you think you're supposed to do."

It's my turn to return her stoic nod as she leaves the room.

Why does everyone in this family think they have the right to tell me what to do with my life? And why does what she just said completely unnerve me?

DAPHNE

"OKAY, WALK ME THROUGH IT AGAIN." MY HANDS SHAKE uncontrollably as I sit on the couch with my roommate and practically beg her to tell me she made a mistake. That what she's already told me twice was wrong.

Because she can't be right.

My dad can't just be . . . gone.

I flew out of the team offices and raced through the streets of Kroydon Hills after I got her text, hoping that I could catch up with my dad before he did something stupid.

He'd already left Dixon's house, so I practically broke the land speed record, hoping to catch him at his house before he made good on whatever his plan was. It didn't matter how quickly I got there though. There were no cars in the drive-way, and my key wouldn't open the front door. But there was a black metal box hanging from the doorknob.

The kind of metal box realtors place on houses that are for sale to hold the keys.

I walked around the front of the house, peering through the windows to find the house empty from what I could see. The perfectly manicured green grass and brightly colored, cheerful flower beds hide the gloom.

I called his cell phone, but the line had been disconnected.

What did you do, Dad?

I tried the cemetery next, thinking maybe he'd gone to talk to Mom. He used to go once a week and lay fresh flowers on her grave. He used to always ask me to go with him, but I never needed a cemetery to talk to my mother. Her body may be resting beneath that ground, but she's been with me whenever I needed her, no matter where I've been.

She's not answering me now though.

And I have no idea where else to look.

By the time I made it back to Dixon's house, I'd searched everywhere I could think, trying to find my father. I'd called everyone I thought might possibly know anything. But I was no closer to getting any answers to my questions.

Maddie nudges the brown box closer to me. Cinder struts around it as if she's going to inspect its contents before deciding it's far too boring for her, and then struts out of the room. "When I answered the door, your dad was standing on the other side. I told him you weren't home from work yet. And he said he knew, but he wasn't here to see you. He was here to see me." She laces her fingers through mine and squeezes. "He asked me to give you this box. He wanted me to tell you he loves you and he's sorry. I texted you as soon as the door closed, D. He scared me. He sounded . . . broken. Like he'd given up."

With the fingers of my free hand, I trace the top of the box, not sure what to do next.

"Are you going to open it?" She wraps her other hand around our joined ones, giving me her strength.

"I'm scared." My words are whispered.

A quiet plea that the contents of the box don't destroy me. The fear is real.

He sold the family business.

He changed the locks on the door.

He's not answering his phone.

"I'm scared when I open that box, there'll be a suicide note in there, Mads."

"I know, D. And that's why we're going to do this together."

48

Dixon, who's been sitting quietly across the room in a recliner, gets up and leans against the arm of the couch next to me. "We've gotcha, D. Whatever you need." His hand squeezes my shoulder in silent support.

I slide my finger under the unsealed flap of the old box. The four top flaps are tucked into each other. They aren't even taped, so it opens easily enough. Sitting on top of everything is a handwritten note scrawled on a piece of Dad's monogrammed stationery.

Dearest Daphne,

You deserve answers I can't give you, but I hope this helps. Saying I made a mistake doesn't seem strong enough. I thought selling the team would fix it, but it didn't. It only provided a band-aid that wasn't as strong as I'd hoped.
I'm sorry to have to tell you this, but I've sold the house and closed the accounts. I have to go away for a bit while I figure out what my next steps are. I can't tell you where I'm going. I know I've let you down. Believe it or not, I'm doing this all for you. You're safer this way. It's the only way to make sure my mistake doesn't touch you. I'm sorry, honey.

I love you.
Dad

I read the letter two more times before handing it to Maddie and grabbing my phone from my purse to pull up my banking app and log in. My father is the executor of the trust fund my grandfather left for me. He's the cosigner on my account until I turn twenty-five, two years from now. Until then, I have a limit on how much I'm allowed to access each month.

On my twenty-fifth birthday, the entire account belongs to me with no strings attached. In my grandfather's will, he said this was so I wouldn't decide to give away all his hard-earned money to the homeless dogs of Philadelphia before I was old enough to realize what other good it could do for me and the world.

He told me to think bigger.

He knew me too well.

I guess there really won't be a need for big thoughts after all, because I'm looking at an account with a big fat zero balance in it where there used to be seven figures.

Maddie reaches up and wipes the tear from my cheek before I even realize that I'm crying.

"I don't have a home. He sold the house I grew up in. And he didn't even tell me. Didn't warn me. He didn't let me clean out my room." My voice grows progressively quieter with each word. "He sold the team without warning me, so why should I be surprised he's selling the house without saying a word?"

Dixon wraps a big arm around me and holds me against his chest. "You'll always have a home, D. This is your home for as long as you want." His big, callused hand rubs circles on my back like only a big brother could. But instead of a calming effect, a hysterical laugh bubbles up in my throat.

When I can't contain it anymore, I step back and hold up my phone. "He emptied out my trust fund. He *stole* the money. What kind of trouble could he have gotten into that would make it okay to steal from his daughter? It's all gone. Every last penny." Dixon wipes a tear from my cheek. "I would have given it to him, if he'd just asked."

"Do you want to file a police report?" Dix asks as gently as he can.

I stare at him in horror. "No. No police. No one needs to know any of this."

"Do you want to go through the box?" Maddie's in fix-it mode. She's good at not getting overly emotional. "Maybe you'll get some answers." She holds the top open, and I glance inside. It's a bunch of frames.

My fingers slide over pictures of my family that once sat on beautiful white shelves in my childhood bedroom.

That's it.

That's what he's reduced my childhood memories to.

A few pictures.

I had a closet full of old hatboxes brimming with memories.

Photographs.

Keepsakes.

Journals.

Things that meant too much to bring them with me to college when I knew they were safer at home. Things I'll never be able to replace because they were invaluable to me.

And now they're gone.

And so is my dad.

DAPHNE

"DAPH . . ." A LIGHT KNOCK ON MY DOOR PULLS ME FROM THE warmth of my dream. I was building a sandcastle on the beach while my mother laughed at something I said. It wasn't so much a dream as a vivid memory from my childhood. And whoever insists on knocking again isn't allowing me to slip back into my happy place.

Dammit.

I ignore my intruder and pull my pillow over my head when the door creaks open, listening as someone walks gently into my room. It's not Maddie. She's already over my pity party. She told me yesterday that pity was a self-indulgent luxury, and since I no longer had that option, it was time to get up and go to work.

Mads isn't a sugarcoater.

According to her, that's another luxury she's never had.

It seems calling off work the day after my dad dropped his bomb was acceptable, even though I was a coward who sent an email instead of picking up the phone. But apparently, you only get one day of mourning when your father upends your entire life. The fact that I've now taken two and still don't want to face my life is unacceptable. When the bed shifts under the weight of my intruder, I peek out from under my pillow.

Carys has pulled her legs up in front of her chest and is tugging at my duvet.

"Go away," I moan.

She ignores me and turns from gentle to bulldozer in about two point two seconds, yanking my duvet from me and tossing it to the floor. "Don't think I can do that, D. Time to get up."

"No." I swing a pillow back at my best friend, and the bitch laughs and snatches that away too.

"You're going to get up, get in the shower, and go to work. You've had two days to wallow. And I get that may not be enough to unpack everything you're dealing with, but life goes on, Daph. You've got to get the hell out of bed." She sniffs the air, then covers her face. "Definitely take a damn shower. You stink. Come on."

"You're not going away, are you?"

She grins and shakes her head.

"Fine." I swing my legs over the side of the bed. "What time is it?"

Carys scooches her butt further down the bed until she's sitting next to me. "Too fucking early for me to be here convincing you to go to work. Yet, here I am. Don't make me get Dixon in here because I bet I could convince him to throw you in the shower if I need to." She wraps her pale arm around my shoulder and leans her head against mine. "Maybe you could convince him to shower with you. He's gorgeous, after all. Shame to let all that go to waste." With one more gentle squeeze, she hops off the bed and offers me her hands. "Now. Get. Up."

"Carys . . ."

"Nope. No whining. Get. *Up.*" She takes my hands in hers and pulls me up, then walks into my adjoining bathroom. The shower turns on, and steam quickly starts to billow from the open door before she returns and throws a towel at me. "You've got one minute before I open your bedroom door and ask Dixon for help. And just saying . . . I think he'd be really happy to help you, D."

I reach forward and smack her with the towel. "That's the last thing I'm thinking about right now, C."

"Men suck, but they're a lot of fun." She tugs my arm until I follow her into the bathroom. "Life goes on. It has to. Now, shower and brush your damn teeth, please. Then get dressed. You're going to work today if I have to drive you there myself."

"Fine." I stomp my foot like a toddler. "But I'm going to remember this the next time you and *he who shall not be named* break up." I take off my night shirt and throw it at her face. Nothing she hasn't seen before. "No sympathy from me."

Carys laughs, but the sound is forced and laced with regret. "We'd have to get back together for us to break up again, D. And we're not getting back together. I fucked it up this time, and I'm not even sure why. I'm so fucking stubborn." And I'm an ass for bringing him up. "You're going to work today, and tomorrow night, we're going out. I think we need drinks to deal with the dumpster fires our lives have become."

"Fine. But you're buying. I'm poor."

Carys picks my nightshirt up from the floor and tosses it in the hamper before agreeing.

The door clicks shut behind her, and I thank God for my tribe.

As I kick off my panties and step under the hot spray, I consider crawling back under the covers and hiding for one more day, but I know the girls are right. I've got to get up and get functioning.

I need my job now, more than ever before.

The team my mom and grandpa loved. That *he* sold.

And here, in the privacy of my shower, I slide down the wall and let the hot spray wash away my tears for everything I've lost one last time. I won't give *him* any more of my tears.

Not today.

Not ever.

I haven't spoken to Max Kingston since I got Maddie's text the other afternoon. I emailed him the past two mornings to let him know I wasn't coming in to work and needed to take some personal days. I had no idea the reception I'd get when I walked into the office today, but it certainly wasn't what I got.

A beautiful woman, who looks like she belongs on Themyscira with Wonder Woman and the other Amazonians, is sitting at my desk, arguing with someone on the phone.

Max couldn't have replaced me after two days . . . could he?

That thought rocks my world like everything seems to be doing lately.

I stand, stuck in place for a moment before deciding to bypass her and walk right into Max's office. Unfortunately for everyone within a five-mile radius, my give-a-fuck meter is running really low. If he replaced me already, I need to know. *Now*.

Max is on a call, so I drop my vintage green leather messenger bag on the floor next to his desk and wait for him to look up with my hands on my hips.

When he finally does, I cross my arms over my chest and cock my brow, then wait him out.

The look on Max's face is a cross between annoyance and amusement. "Let me call you back, Becks." Once he hangs up the phone, he leans back in his executive chair and crosses his arms, mirroring me. It's barely eight o'clock in the morning, but he's already got the sleeves of his black dress shirt rolled up his forearms. Colorful ink dancing along corded muscles makes my mouth water until he speaks . . . "Welcome back, Daphne. Are you feeling better?"

"I'm fine, thank you." Why does this man insist on using my full fucking name? I chose not to waste what little patience I still have on that question and go for the gold instead. "Who's sitting at my desk?"

I'm not even attempting to temper the attitude I'm throwing.

Stupid? Yes. But I'm past the point of caring.

I'm done allowing myself to be moved like a pawn on a chess board.

I knew I shouldn't have left my damn bed.

Max doesn't seem phased at all by my outburst. Calm. Cool. And collected, as always. "My assistant."

"*I'm* your assistant." I point toward the Amazonian. "And that's *my* desk." Damn all the men in my life for taking my safety nets from me.

He rolls his lips in over his teeth like he's trying to stop himself from laughing at me.

The fucker.

"I didn't know if you were coming in today, and I needed help. Scarlet let me borrow her yesterday." He says this calmly, like it made sense.

Newsflash: It didn't.

I feel smaller and more insignificant than I already did. My family used to own this building, and now I feel like Oliver Twist, begging for scraps at the table. Not a great way to start the day.

She steps into Max's office. Stops next to me and looks down.

Not like she's better than me, more like she's tall enough to have to look down at me.

No lie, this woman has to be at least five-foot-ten to my

five-foot-three. Even her heels are higher than mine, and I'm a heel kinda girl. She's wearing a cream pantsuit, and her chocolate-brown hair looks like it belongs on a shampoo commercial. Seriously, I'd do her if I swung that way.

Maybe I should give up on men and give it a try.

Men are assholes.

"You must be Daphne." She offers me her hand. Great. She's more professional than me too. "I'm Taylor. Nice to meet you."

I shake her hand, albeit begrudgingly. She's got what my grandpa would have called a good shake. Strong. Firm. No weak wrist. "Nice to meet you. Thank you for filling in while I was gone. But I'm back now."

She doesn't hide her smile like Max did earlier. Instead, she turns toward Max, and her perfume wafts my way. *Dammit.* She even smells good. Probably did my job ten times better than me too. And again, I need this job now more than ever.

"You good with me heading back to the King offices, boss?"

He nods. "Thanks for your help, Taylor. I appreciate it."

He *appreciates* it.

Why does that burn like a bitter pill?

"No problem. Scarlet told me you owe her lunch for a week." She turns her eyes back to me and doesn't hide her quick appraisal as her eyes drag over me from top to toe. "I like your dress. Chanel?"

"Vintage." Lucky for me, I moved all my mom's old clothes over to Dixon's house before I started this job. At least I'm not standing before her in one of my favorite thrift-shop finds. And damn, if I don't want to smack myself for thinking that. Lord. What is wrong with me? I can't get out of my own head today.

"Daphne?"

I look up to see Max staring at me.

Guess I zoned out for a moment. "Sorry, what were you saying?"

"Glad to have you back, Ms. Brenner." His dark blue eyes twinkle with the laughter he's smart enough to keep to himself. I guess he can read a room after all because, boss or not, amused or not, if Max Kingston laughed right now, I may scream . . . or hit.

I'm not a violent person by nature, but a girl can only take so much before she explodes.

And annoyed or not, that's not the type of explosion I'd like to explore with Max Kingston.

I may not want this job, but I certainly need it, so I flash him a smile. "Glad to be back, Mr. Kingston."

MAX

SATURDAY, MY SIBLINGS AND I ALL GATHERED TO SUPPORT Scarlet's boyfriend, former MMA champion, Cade St. James, and his gym, Crucible. They hold a fundraiser each year to support local veterans' programs. Hudson, who Cade now trains, is the current US MMA Champion. His next title fight is in a few months, so he wasn't able to fight tonight. But according to him, he was the perfect MC for the event.

According to Scarlet, they were able to raise more money tonight than ever before.

Luckily for me, Cade kept his word and didn't tell my sister I matched all his other donations and then some.

My little assistant isn't the only one who believes in giving back, even if I failed to share that with her. I may have been lucky enough to be born into generational wealth, but I don't take the responsibility that comes with it lightly. I would have started a charitable division of the Revolution with or without Daphne bringing it up. But seeing the fire in her eyes when she talked about it left me with no doubt that she's the one to run it.

Though, she needs to show me she's capable of building this foundation from the ground up. I need her to do the leg work if she wants to run it one day. She needs to understand every aspect of it to make it a success.

And I have no doubt she will.

Daphne hasn't hesitated with anything I've asked of her.

She may be a little feisty, but she's very good at her job.

And I enjoy her attitude . . . maybe a little too much.

"No luck on the home front?" Becks piles into the back of the Range Rover after the final fight of the fundraiser, and Sawyer and I take the two captain's chairs in the next row. Somehow, these two asses convinced me to head to Kingdom for a drink with them.

"The home front?" I look between the two of them. "What the hell are you talking about?"

Sawyer shakes his head. "I think what our idiot brother is asking is how's the house hunt going?" He turns around to face Becks in the row behind us. "Becket, you're a lawyer, for fuck's sake. Aren't you supposed to be able to speak circles around the rest of us?"

I let Luka know where to go, then relax into my chair and listen to my brothers argue before stepping in. "I don't remember looking for a place sucking this bad when I bought the penthouse. I went out with the realtor once last week and didn't like anything."

"Is she hot?" Becks kicks his feet up on my arm rest, and I shove them down, ignoring his question.

"You looking at another penthouse or thinking about a house this time?" Sawyer pulls something up on his cell phone, then hands it to me. "This just went on the market. It's not too far from Sam and Amelia. I saw the sign on the gate the other day."

I scan over the screen, then send myself the link. Maybe it's time to think bigger.

"Thanks, man. I hadn't really thought about a house, but maybe it's the way to go. More space. More privacy." I wish I could just have one of them do this shit for me. But not taking the time is how I ended up being thirty-two and still living at Dad's.

We weren't inside Kingdom ten minutes before Sawyer ended up behind the bar. It's close to midnight, and the place is packed. Luckily, Becks and I are seated at the back of the bar, tucked into a corner. When one Kingston is out, it's not too hard to avoid being noticed. Add a second or third, and flying under the radar gets harder.

Especially somewhere that bears our name.

The thumping beat of the bass is like a heartbeat throbbing through the crowd while the packed dance floor moves in time, singing along with the band. By The Edge is doing a reunion tour, and Sawyer was lucky enough to get them to agree to stop by for a set tonight since they're in town.

Pretty sure they're Lenny's favorite band.

She's going to be so pissed she missed them.

Sawyer places two beers in front of Becks and me just as his name is squealed from behind us, and a tiny brunette squeezes in next to us.

"Sawyerrrr . . ." The obviously intoxicated woman screeches to a halt next to me and reaches across the bar to squeeze my brother. "How are you?"

I move over to make room, and she quickly turns to look at me.

"Wow. It's a whole mess of Kingstons." Carys Murphy stares back at me with her blinding smile. "Hey, Max." She looks around me and waves. "Hiya, Becks."

Sawyer leans across the bar and squeezes her hands. "Hey, Carys. How long are you in town?"

A group of women approach, and another familiar voice answers before Carys can.

"As long as we can keep her." Daphne is standing in the center of two other women. One I recognize. She's been in the Sinclairs' suite during the Kings games. Her brother was just drafted to Baltimore and just married Coach's daughter.

The other one looks familiar, but I'm not sure why. I can't place her face.

Daphne's holding her hair twisted up on top of her head. Her skin is flushed from dancing, and a tiny drop of sweat drips down the front of her sparkly shirt, where it disappears between her cleavage.

"She's home for good," the taller woman with pink hair replies.

Carys turns to face the woman. "Shh." She raises her finger to her lips. "My mom doesn't know I dropped out of school yet."

Oh shit.

Yeah, I know Coach's wife enough to know that's not gonna go over well.

The other blonde with the three women announces she's running to the ladies' room, and Chloe grabs her hand to go with her.

I take advantage of the distraction to catch my little assistant's attention, taking a step back so I'm next to her. "Hello, Miss Brenner."

Shocked, her pale blue eyes fly up to meet mine. "Max Kingston . . . in a bar? I thought you'd be way too uptight for a place like this."

Becks throws his arm around my shoulder, butting into the conversation. "You mean a bar our brother owns? Even Max isn't that uptight." He reaches his hand out in front of her. "Becket Kingston. Nice to meet you . . ."

I shrug Becks off. "Becket, this is Daphne Brenner." I wait for him to fill in the blanks but can tell he's clueless. "My assistant."

"My friends call me 'D.'" She gives him her hand, and the fucker kisses her knuckles until I elbow him in the gut.

He stumbles back a step but recovers well. "Oh. You're the poor woman in charge of my brother? I think we need to get you a drink. Max is a dick." Becks turns back to Sawyer and tells him to add the ladies' drinks to his tab.

Daphne leans into me, and the clean, crisp scent of pears invades my senses. "Does he actually pay his tab, or does your brother let him drink for free?"

Her white-blonde hair falls forward, and I tuck a lock behind her ear on instinct.

It's as soft as I've imagined since the day we met.

Maybe it's the relaxed atmosphere because I'm actually enjoying a night out with my brothers. Or maybe it's because I've fought the pull toward Daphne since the first time we met, but giving in feels natural.

She shivers, but steps into me. "I didn't really picture you as a bar kind of guy."

"And why is that?" I take a pull from my bottle of beer and watch as Daphne takes it from my hands and holds it up to her pouty red lips, the movement tempting me with promises I'm not sure she's ready to keep.

"It's kinda hard to imagine you relaxing, I guess."

With that bottle up against her lips, teasing me, I imagine what it would look like to have them wrapped around my cock, while I wrap her silky hair around my fist and angle her just where I want her.

I'll just keep that thought to myself. "You're playing with fire, Miss Brenner."

"I'm in the mood to watch something burn, Mr. Kingston." She sips the beer, then hands it back to me, and my cock jumps in my pants at the forbidden idea.

I'm tracking an escalating argument happening behind us when I grab her waist and spin the two of us, holding her between me and the bar to keep her safe. Sawyer catches the move and whistles for a bouncer, who flies around the corner of the bar. The sound of flesh on flesh can be heard over the music as chaos ensues in the immediate area.

Daphne's fingers grasp my forearms, icy blue eyes wide and trained on me as her friends fight to see what's happening from behind Becks.

"Hey, you okay?" I bend my knees and look into her eyes.

She nods, a little shaken. "Thanks to you." Her tongue darts out and wets her lips.

Our eyes lock, and something passes between the two of us. It only takes a second for me to memorize every emotion flickering in her pale gaze.

Desire.

Want.

Need.

I grab the empty stool next to us and sit her on it before I do something stupid.

"That was intense." Carys moves next to Daphne and calls out over the music, "We're gonna dance. You coming?"

Daphne shakes her head without breaking our stare. "You go ahead without me."

Out of the corner of my eye, I catch Becket being drug out on the dance floor with the girls, but my eyes are locked on the beautiful woman sitting in front of me. Her chest rises and falls with each stuttered breath she takes. "Are you sure you're okay?"

She nods, then slowly reaches out and grabs at my shirt, pulling me toward her hesitantly.

My hands grip the bar on either side of her, caging her in, and we stand locked in this bubble.

The thick tension-filled air grows heavier with every heavy beat of the bass.

Neither of us are willing to break the spell of this moment.

She tugs again, trying to get me where she wants me. But this time, I don't budge. "Daphne . . . You're a beautiful woman."

A gorgeous, pink flush colors her chest, working its way up to her cheeks, and I desperately want to see how far down her body it goes.

"We shouldn't do this, Miss Brenner. You work for me." The words feel like acid leaving my mouth as everything south of it rebels at the idea of rejecting her. But I refuse to be the guy who takes advantage of the situation.

She untangles her hands from the front of my shirt and runs them up my forearms. Her fingers trace the lines of my tattoo. Her dark-purple nails are a stark contrast to her pale skin.

Nails that would feel amazing scouring my back once we're both stripped of our clothes.

"I do work for you, Mr. Kingston. And you know what the one good thing my piece-of-shit father did for me was?" Without giving me a chance to answer, she leans closer, bringing her lips to the shell of my ear and dropping her voice. "He gave me a twelve-month contract. You can't fire me for an entire year. We might as well have some fun. I promise you, nothing needs to change. You'll still drive me crazy Monday morning."

"I'm not looking for a girlfriend, Daphne." She's saying all the right things. But when something seems too good to be true, it usually is.

"Good. Because the last thing I need is someone else who thinks they have a say over the way I live, Max. I've had enough of that to last a lifetime." Her eyes dance between mine. "And I'm not looking for it now."

I move closer, erasing any space between us. "Are you sure?"

My entire body riots at the idea that she could change her mind. But I ask it anyway because it's the right thing to do.

Daphne nods her head with a beautiful smile on her lips.

"Words, Miss Brenner. I need to hear the words."

Excitement is hot.

But consent is fucking sexy.

Her fingers tighten on my arms. "I'm sure, Mr. Kingston. Now get me out of here."

I reach into my pocket and pull three hundred-dollar bills from my wallet and throw them on the bar. "Hey, Sawyer." I wait for him to look up. "Can you tell Becks to catch an Uber back?"

Sawyer looks between Daphne and me and raises a brow. "Yeah. I've got ya covered."

I frame Daphne's face in both my hands. "Do you need to text your friends?"

"I'll do it from the car."

"No, baby. You're going to be doing other things in the car. Text your friends."

DAPHNE

WITH TREMBLING HANDS, I PULL OUT MY PHONE, NEARLY dropping it.

Daphne: Leaving for the night. Don't wait up.

I don't bother waiting for a response. With my task complete, I shove my phone back into the pocket of the jeans I might as well have painted on my body earlier tonight and take the hand Max extends for me as I stand up from the bar stool.

Hungry eyes run over my body, and my stomach clenches in anticipation of what's to come.

Hopefully me.

More than once.

He pulls me behind him, blocking me from the crowd with his big body as we move in sync toward the exit. Kingdom is packed tonight, and when the band says they're taking a break, there's a mass exodus from the dance floor as everyone rushes toward the bar, jostling us. I grip Max's hand tighter to stop myself from falling flat on my ass, and he spins around faster than I expected and backs the two of us into a dark corner, hidden by one of the old steel beams left behind when the building was converted from a warehouse to what it is now.

I may never have met Sawyer Kingston before tonight, but Maddie and I spent plenty of our college nights in this bar. And yet, this is my first time hiding in the shadows here with a hot man. His arms cage me in for the second time tonight, and goosebumps break out over my already heated flesh. "Why, Mr. Kingston, you seem to like trapping me in your arms."

"Trapped implies you don't want to be here, Daphne." He leans in, and his lips capture mine in a kiss that sears me to my soul and removes all brain function. One big hand slides along my jaw. His thumb caresses my cheekbone while the other glides down my body and dips under my tank to rest on my lower back.

The heat of his palm brands me.

Melting me as it claims a part of me that makes me shiver.

I wrap both arms around his shoulders and resist the urge to climb him like a jungle gym right here inside Kingdom. I'm sure I wouldn't be the first person to do that here, but I still have enough composure to know better. Even if it sounds like fun.

He licks the seam of my lips until I open for him.

The taste of beer and bad decisions mix together like a cocktail of pure sin as our tongues clash, leaving me aching for more.

Max pulls back slightly and skims his lips along my cheek up to my ear. "I know you like being trapped by me, Miss Brenner. I can smell how turned on you are." His tongue runs along the shell of my ear, and I squeeze my thighs together, already desperate for relief. "I bet if I slid my hand inside your pants right here, you'd be soaked for me, Daphne."

I lick my lips, knowing he'd be right. "Maybe . . . But you're going to need to get us out of here to find out."

In another swift move, he wraps an arm around my shoulders and guides us the hell out of Kingdom before anyone else can get in our way.

Thank God.

Because I'm about two seconds from stripping myself naked and begging Max Kingston to make me come. Common sense is great, but it only goes so far when your brain is short-circuiting from a lust-induced haze.

Once we step outside, the muggy July heat surrounds us like a heavy blanket as Luka ushers us into the back of his gleaming black Range Rover. The cool interior chills my skin, but when I attempt to sit down in one of the two captain's chairs, the firm squeeze of Max's hand on my hip warms me right back up.

I glance over my shoulder at him, guessing the tilt of his head means he wants me to move to the third row. I slide my heels off and climb onto the bench seat of the third row, giddy with anticipation.

Considering Luka is driving us, and there isn't privacy glass in here, I'm guessing we'll need to stay pretty PG.

What a disappointment.

When Max climbs in next to me, his big body crowds me until I'm tucked further behind a captain's chair while his long legs are sprawled out in the aisle.

"Where to, sir?" Luka asks from behind the wheel, his eyes watching us through the rearview. And it dawns on me that Max moved me here to keep me hidden from view.

So it's gonna be like that?

My earlier disappointment in what I assumed was our PG car ride evaporates as excitement starts building in its place.

"The estate. And take your time." His eyes never leave my face, his big palm resting on my knee, scorching through my jeans as he leans further into my space. "Unless you want to go to your place?"

I shake my head, my hair falling into my face again.

"Words, Daphne." Strong fingers move my hair away and hold my face. "This only works with words."

"Take me to your place, Max. I don't want to go home." I

shiver as the word *home* leaves my lips but push the emotions accompanying it out of my head easily when Max grabs my face and pulls me toward him.

He's on me in an instant, swallowing my moan as his tongue tangles with mine. His hand presses up the length of my thigh, then traces the seam of my jeans, rubbing my core and driving me wild, and we haven't taken off a single piece of clothing.

I need more.

I want everything.

My pussy pulses with need, and I shift, trying to give him better access.

But Max doesn't stop.

He doesn't change tactics.

He works my pussy through my jeans with one hand, whispering filthy words while he plays me to perfection. "Your pussy is so hot, Daphne. I want to feel it on my tongue. On my cock. I want to taste you when you come."

I angle my body toward him, aching for more.

He trails a finger back and slides it along the seam of my ass. "How bad do you want to come?"

Jesus Christ.

Everything about this moment has me on the verge of losing control.

His words. His actions. My body is on fire.

My head lolls back against the cool leather seat, my eyes closed as the lights of the city fade into the dark streets of the suburbs. Chasing a wave that's not far from reach. And he hasn't even touched bare skin. I might actually explode when that happens. "So bad."

Max grazes his lips over mine before biting down and tugging on my bottom lip. "Eyes on me, or this stops."

My eyes fly open, and I run my hands through his dirty-blonde hair. My fingers sink in where it curls against his collar and tug. Hard. "I want you to make me come," I whisper. "Don't you dare stop." I'm silently praying the words are as quiet as I want them to be, so I don't die of embarrassment the next time I have to be in a car with Luka.

But when Max's big thumb rubs a circle around my clit, I see stars burst into the night's sky behind my eyes and couldn't give a flying fuck what Luka hears.

Max's mouth is back on mine, muffling my moans.

But nothing could dull the ecstasy coursing through my veins.

Holy shit. That was the hottest moment of my life.

Of. My. Life.

And that was with all our clothes *on*.

I throw my leg over Max's lap and straddle him. Grinding my now hypersensitive sex along an impressive bulge in his pants I can't fucking wait to get in my mouth.

His hands run up my thighs and squeeze the curve of my ass as the car slows down.

I turn my head to see Luka reaching through an open window and punching a code into a metal box outside of a black wrought-iron gate. A massive mansion looms in the distance. Max grabs my chin and pulls my face back to his. He kisses me until the car stops, then gets out first, shielding my body from Luka when he helps me out on shaky legs.

The lights are all off in the monstrously big brick home, the only illumination coming from the landscape lighting. But that's enough to showcase its beauty. Three wings are visible from the front, but more come into view as we take a stone path toward a black wrought-iron gate. The stars twinkle in the inky night's sky. It's a beautiful night to be outside of the city.

I stop and take it all in as my bare feet sink into the soft, wet grass. "Where are we going?"

Max places his palm on the small of my back. "Eyes on

me, Daphne." When I bring my gaze back to him, he smiles. "We're going to the guesthouse. I don't want to wake my little sister up later when I make you scream my name so loud, you won't have any voice left tomorrow."

"I think I met enough of your family tonight," I tell him, dazed and wondering how many times I'll be screaming his name before dawn.

MAX

I LEAD DAPHNE DOWN THE STONE PATH AND AROUND THE BACK of the house. The heavy scent of the magnolia trees in bloom hangs thick in the air. The white blossoms glow in the moonlight, and I feel like I'm sixteen again and trying to get laid without getting caught bringing Daphne back here.

The fact that I know my younger brothers have done this for the same reason doesn't escape me. But it's better than having to explain to anyone what I'm doing. In the six years since I've moved back here, I've never brought a woman home.

To a hotel, yes.

To this house, where my family lives? No.

But Daphne's not just anyone.

This is going to complicate things.

Question is, will it be for the better or worse?

Complications can be fun if you let them, and I've always loved a challenge.

The bombshell next to me tugs my arm when she sees the pool hidden behind the scaled-down version of the estate. Swinging around in front of me, she stops and drops the heels she's carrying to the ground. "Can you see that pool from the main house?"

"No, you can't." I think I like where this is going.

Daphne smiles at my response and tugs my belt free of my jeans. "It's really hot out here." Her head tilts to the side coyly. "Don't you think?" Her slim fingers unbutton my jeans and tug them down before she flattens her palms under my shirt and slides them up my sides.

I kick off my shoes and pants, then my shirt as Daphne slips out of the slinky, sparkly, strappy shirt she's wearing, then unclasps a lacy strapless bra. I just about swallow my tongue at the view. Her breasts are a perfect handful with the prettiest pale-pink nipples I've ever seen.

She shimmies her jeans down her legs in a way that only women can. It's enough to drive a sane man straight to a padded room, and my cock tries to push free of my boxers, eager to get to her. With a smirk, Daphne adds her jeans to the growing pile of discarded clothes, leaving her in the tiniest pink lace panties.

"You are gorgeous." They're the only three words my brain can formulate as I drink in the sight of all her creamy skin.

Her smile grows. "I'm fast too. So, you better catch me quick if you want me."

She spins on her heel and takes off toward the pool. She's light on her feet until she trips on one of the sprinkler heads buried in the lawn. I'm faster and manage to grab her from behind before she goes down and hold her still for a moment. My erection presses against the cleft of Daphne's ass. My hands trail down her body, skimming over her delectable curves as she trembles in my arms.

I press my lips to the heated skin of her neck and work my way down her spine until I'm on my knees behind her, easing her panties down over the ass of my fucking dreams and leaving them in the grass. With one quick smack to the iridescent skin of her ass, I stand and scoop her into my arms before I finish her sprint to the pool and jump into the deep end, taking Daphne with me.

When we surface, she laughs and pushes my head back

underwater, and she's still laughing when my head bobs back up. I could get addicted to the sound of her laughter. "I've always wanted to do this."

"Skinny dip?" I question, as I pull her toward me, her legs wrapping around my waist while her hands push the wet hair from my face. My head dips down, and I drag my tongue around one pale-pink nipple, then suck it into my mouth.

"Mm-hmm." She grinds her center over my cock and arches her back. "Among other things," she adds with an air of mischief in her voice.

I palm her other breast, flicking my thumb over her already hardened nipple, and my cock strains within the confines of my boxer briefs. "What other things?"

"How about you sit on the side of the pool, and I'll show you?" Her pale icy-blue eyes sparkle as she asks the question only an asshole would ignore. I move us so we're on the slope of the pool, standing around four to five feet deep, then drop her legs.

Daphne dips down under the water and peels my boxers from my legs and flings them into the grass when she surfaces, then pushes me back to the edge.

With both hands on the coping surrounding the pool, I pull myself up and lean my elbows back on the cool pavers surrounding the pool and watch Daphne. The water breaks over the tops of her full breasts, leaving everything else hidden under the water. Long blonde hair hangs wet over her shoulders, framing her gorgeous face as she grips me and drags her hand up and down my dick before her thumb glides over a pearl of precum at the tip. She slowly sinks back under the water before she licks my cock from root to tip, swirling her tongue around the head and looking up at me through her dark lashes before swallowing me to the back of her throat.

Something about this . . . the water, her body, those

eyes . . . *her eyes.* It's the most erotic thing I've ever experienced.

Little moans leave her lips, and I look down and watch her mouth slide up and down my cock. She hums, and the vibrations pull at something deep in my spine. My balls tighten, and the familiar sensation catches me off guard. "Daphne. You need to stop."

When she ignores me, I reach forward and gather her hair in one hand and pull.

Her eyes fly up to mine. And she smiles, then swallows me back down her throat.

"Jesus, Daphne." I come on a long, low groan and lay back on the cool brick. "Holy shit, D." I open my eyes to see her standing over me.

"So it takes an orgasm to get you to call me 'D'?" One hand is resting on her curvy hip, and my eyes trail down her body to the bare lips of her sex. But I want to lay this woman out on my bed and get comfortable before I make her come again.

I hop up to my feet and pull her naked, wet body against mine. "No. That erotic little show you just gave me limited my active brain cells. I still don't like your nickname."

Her hands smooth up my chest and over my shoulders as our lips collide. Reaching down, I lift her legs and wrap them around my waist, then carry us both into the guesthouse. I kick the door shut behind us before lying her down on the bed and crawling across it to wedge my shoulders between her splayed legs.

"My turn," I groan once she's laid out before me. I pepper kisses along her bare pussy lips, then spread her wide with my thumbs. Licking a line up her center, I circle her clit and flick it over and over until she's writhing beneath me.

Daphne moans, the sound throaty and guttural, and my

spent cock again grows hard against the cool sheets of the bed. A cocky grin grows across my face. I may be thirty-two, but Daphne brings out my inner fifteen-year-old. Constantly horny and ready for round two. I lift one smooth leg and throw it over my shoulder, opening her to me, and fuck her with my tongue as her back bows off the bed.

"God, *yes*. Right there." She rides my face with desperate pleas. "Don't you dare stop."

This bombshell is my every fantasy come to life.

Taking what she wants

Commanding it.

It's fucking sexy to be with a woman who knows what she needs to get off, especially when she isn't afraid to be vocal about it.

I'm a man with a singular purpose: to make this woman come so hard so many damn times tonight, she'll never look at another man again without wishing it was me.

I want to own her body.

When her walls flutter and clench, I throw her other leg over my shoulder and grab her ass in my hands, pulling her closer as I plunge my tongue into her core over and over until she shatters beneath me.

Nothing has ever tasted sweeter than Daphne Brenner's pussy.

Reaching over, I grab a condom from the nightstand drawer where I know Hudson stashed them.

Daphne sits up, her boobs bouncing with the movement, and my cock fucking weeps with the need to be inside her.

"May I?" She reaches out for the condom.

Who am I to tell her no?

She tears the packet open with her teeth, then smiles at me.

"Put the condom on me, Daphne."

My little assistant sits back on her heels and pouts. "And then what?"

I fist my dick and pump it once, enjoying this little tease more than I should. "Then you get your ass in the air. I've been dreaming about getting you on your knees for weeks."

DAPHNE

Without missing a beat, I crawl across the California king bed until I'm centered on my hands and knees, ass in the air, fully exposed. An air of excitement envelops me as fingertips dance gently down my spine and over the curve of my ass. Turning my head, I look over my shoulder and watch Max.

With heavy-lidded eyes, Max watches as he runs his cock through my drenched sex, only lifting his head moments before our gazes collide and he enters me.

Slowly.

Stretching me. Teasing me.

Making sure I'm ready for him.

My hands grip the blanket, and my lids flutter closed. "It's not nice to tease, Mr. Kingston."

"I don't want to hurt you, Daphne." He pulls out of me completely, leaving me empty and wanting.

"I won't break."

One side of his mouth tips up in a cocky smile, happy to accept my challenge. Max slams into me in one beautifully rough thrust.

My head drops down to the mattress as I cry out and push back, meeting him thrust for delicious thrust.

"You are fucking perfect." Thrust. "So hot." Thrust. "So tight."

With each snap of his hips, my core tightens, and my pussy pounds.

Strong arms wrap around my chest and waist and pull me upright.

My back arches against his chest, my heart beating frantically.

Needing to be closer, I throw my arms up and around his neck.

His fingers skim over the lips of my sex, and I clench around his dick when they graze my clit. "Oh, God." My orgasm is so close, but I'm not ready for this to end.

"Not God, Daphne." He nips at my neck, and I can hear the smug smile in his voice. "God doesn't have a damn thing to do with this."

My muscles burn, and my legs shake as I drop my head against his shoulder for support. "I need to come," I beg him, dragging out the words.

"Yeah, baby. I've got you." He turns my head and licks into my mouth. His deft fingers firmly circle my clit. "Come now, Daphne."

As if I have no choice but to obey his command, I shatter in his arms. The power of my orgasm wrecks my body. My voice goes hoarse as I scream his name.

Max lowers me flat to the bed and pulls my knees up higher. He eases out of me, and I almost relax until he slams home with such force that I'm pushed up the mattress. My sensitive nipples rub against the decadently soft blanket with every thrust of his hard body.

"Max . . ." I plead. I'm not sure I can take much more. I'm still trying to catch my breath from that last orgasm, and I already feel him chasing me up another peak.

He pulls out long enough to flip my limp body over to my back, like I'm a doll for him to use and position at his pleasure. He drags his lips over my stomach and swirls the tip of his tongue around my nipples before settling himself between my thighs.

"Oh, I think you've got more in you, baby."

I was never a fan of pet names until the word "baby" fell from his sinful lips.

He wraps his arms around me, bringing our bodies close to each other. Our faces are barely an inch apart, his breath fanning across my cheeks. He slides into me slowly, taking his time as he drags his dick along my walls before hitting something deep inside me. Something that's never been touched before and makes my entire body pull taut.

"Oh. My. *God.*"

Max stills, half out of me, and I want to scream in frustration. "What did I tell you, Daphne?"

My hands scour down his muscular body, sliding over his lats and gripping his ass with my nails as I pull him into me. "I'll call you whatever you want, Max. Just do that again." I lick the pulse thrumming in his neck. My lips graze the underside of his jaw as I whimper, "Please, Max. *Please.*"

His blue eyes darken to almost black before he drives into me, hitting that spot over and over again until I'm finally screaming so loud, I may have woken his entire family. Honestly, I can't bring myself to care.

This time, when my walls flutter and my body clenches at the crest of my orgasm, Max topples over the edge with me. Groaning, he strokes me longer, harder, until we're both reduced to a tangled ball of sweaty limbs and racing hearts.

Max gets up to dispose of the condom, and I look over in surprise when the door to the guesthouse opens, and he leaves without a word.

A minute later, he walks back in, completely naked and carrying all our clothes, before kicking the door shut once more.

I lean up on an elbow to watch him, barely able to resist the impulse to lick my lips. "Good thinking. It would suck if the sprinklers came on and my phone got drenched."

Max Kingston is a work of art that should be on display in some foreign museum. Hard lines of solid muscle cover his big body. His entire right arm is covered in tattoos down to his hand. Mix that with those too-long blonde locks of his, and he looks more like he should be one of the players on the field rather than the president covered by an expensive suit behind a desk all day.

But damn, does he look pretty in those suits.

The bed dips as he joins me, taking time to pull a blanket up around us before tucking me into his strong arms against his chest. "Close your eyes, Daphne. Get some sleep. I'll take you home in the morning."

I trace the dark lines of a tattoo on his left pec. "Okay. But we need to talk about this before we're back in the office Monday morning."

"We do . . . What are you thinking?" Max's fingers run through my hair, and I purr like a content kitten.

Lordy, that feels nice.

But we need to make sure we're on the same page when we step back into our roles at the Revolution. I pull away slightly from his touch because I can't think when he's doing that. "Well, I'd like it if this is something we could keep between the two of us. Not something the entire organization is privy to."

"I agree. My question is, do you want to keep doing this? Because I'd like to. But like I said earlier, I'm not looking for more than sex. Friends with benefits is about all I can offer right now." His finger, clearly needing something to pet since I removed the temptation of my hair, circles my nipple, and I shiver. "But those benefits will be plentiful."

Oh my God, his *voice*. It shouldn't do things to me. But it does.

Focus, D.

"I get that. My life's a mess. I definitely can't handle

adding anything or anyone else to my plate." I squeak when he rolls my nipple between his thumb and finger, then tugs on it. And like he's pulling an invisible cord straight down to my clit, I nudge my leg between his as I drag my body closer. "But if you're sleeping with me, you're not sleeping with anyone else."

"Same goes for you, Miss Brenner. Mutually monogamous friends with benefits." His fingers go back to stroking my hair with a wicked gleam in his eye. "I'd say let's shake on it, but I think I have a better idea."

"Max," I laugh as his mouth trails down my neck. "Aren't you tired?" Even as he speaks, I feel his cock stirring against my thigh.

"Sleep is for the weak, Daphne. And I promised you benefits." He sucks the spot between my neck and my shoulder, and my entire body melts into him. A girl could get addicted to this.

And when he scrapes his teeth along that same spot, I can't help but wonder what I've gotten myself into.

MAX

My eyes crack open the next morning when the obnoxious ring of an incoming text wakes me. I reach over carefully to silence it, not wanting to wake the siren currently sprawled across my chest. The platform bed in the guesthouse may be a California king, but you'd think it was a twin with the way Daphne slept on me all night—her head on my chest, hair tickling my face, and legs tangled between mine.

The arm I've got around her body fell asleep hours ago, but for some reason, I haven't moved it or her, until now. Slipping it carefully from under her body, I slide out of bed and search for my clothes among the myriad of condom wrappers littering the floor before stuffing them in the trash can. I pull my jeans up my legs and search for the extra clothes we all stashed in the closet over the first few months of the summer, throwing one of Hudson's black Crucible t-shirts over my head.

I don't do this.

Not the whole sleeping *together* thing. I mean, actually *sleeping* with another human beside me.

Not in a long time.

The act of sleeping in bed with another person is a level of intimacy I don't typically allow. Plus, I usually sleep like shit alone, and adding another person to the mix never helped. At least, not before last night.

Not ready to delve into why last night was different, I

check my phone and read over the incoming text from my realtor, Holly.

Holly: Got your text last night. That house just went on the market two days ago. If you want it, you need to act fast. It won't last long. I can get us in there today at ten a.m.
Max: I'll meet you there.

I pocket the phone and sit back down next to Daphne. It's already nine-thirty, so we should probably get moving. I brush her soft blonde hair back from her cheek. She looks peaceful and relaxed. I almost hate to wake her up. *Almost.* "Time to wake up, Sleeping Beauty." But I enjoy feisty Daphne too.

"Go away." Guess she's not a morning person.

My hand dips down under the cool, white sheet and slides down to her hip, tracing the naked skin of her soft curves, wishing I had more time but knowing I'm already cutting it close. "Daphne . . ." My nose nuzzles her ear, and she hums in appreciation, turning her head toward me.

"It's Sunday morning, Max. Go back to sleep." Her long lashes fan against her skin before she slowly opens her sleepy eyes. "What time is it?"

"It's time to get up. I've got to meet Holly in thirty minutes. If you don't mind coming with me, I can take you home after." I push to my feet, knowing if I don't get up now, we aren't going to make it to meet the realtor. And as much as my dick loves that idea, I've got things to do today.

Daphne throws the sheet from her body and sits up, stretching her arms over her head. She looks around the room, cataloging the mess we made last night. "Any chance you've got a t-shirt tucked away somewhere around here?"

I walk back into the closet and look through the mostly men's clothes folded on shelves, and my stomach sours, not at all happy with the idea of seeing another man's clothes on Daphne. I search through the hangers before finding a yellow cotton sundress that one of my sister's probably used as a swimsuit coverup at some point. *Jackpot.* Once I'm back in the bedroom, I hand her the dress, and a coy smile takes over her face.

"Wow." Her lashes flutter. "You use this place so often there's a need to stock extra clothes?" Daphne stands from the bed and slides the soft fabric over her softer skin, her perfect tits sway with the movement, as a single finger goes up in the air. "Give me five minutes, and I'll be good to go."

I take a minute to scroll through my texts while she's in the bathroom.

Becks: Seriously Maxipad? You ditched me for the assistant?
Sawyer: In Maximus's defense. Did you see her? She's hot.
Becks: I saw her. She looks Like Julianne Hough with bigger tits.
Sawyer: Who the hell is Julianne Hough?
Becks: The Dancing With The Stars chick.
Sawyer: Who the fuck are you?
Becks: Whatever. Like you've never watched it.
Sawyer: I haven't because I don't have a vagina.
Sawyer: How about you stop smoking so much weed, fuckface.
Becks You're just jealous my dick is bigger.
Sawyer: In your dreams.
Becks: She's still his assistant. You don't fuck the assistant unless you want to get sued.
Sawyer: Shocking, but he's got a point.
Becks: WTF is shocking about that?
Sawyer: He's not answering us.
Becks: Fine. Don't listen to me, asshole. It's your funeral.

My brothers are morons. Becket is one of the top attorneys in the state, and Sawyer runs one of the most successful bars in the city. Yet somehow, they revert to children when a woman is involved.

When the bathroom door opens, Daphne's long blonde hair is pulled into a messy bun sitting on top of her head. Her face has been washed clean, leaving no remnants of the smoky eye or red lips she had last night. She looks younger. Fresher. She looks fucking gorgeous, and my cock strains behind my zipper.

"Ready?" I place my palm at the small of her back and usher her out of the guesthouse and back up the stone path to the garage.

The sun is already sitting high in the sky, the warm rays licking my skin. I love summer. Always have. There's something about the heat, the heaviness of the air, and the scent of the freshly cut grass. Growing up, it signified the few months during the year where we could be carefree. No school. Less responsibility. More fun. That may not be the case now, but the memories still linger with my love for the season.

We walk inside the large garage, and I grab my keys off the hook on the wall where we all keep our keys.

Daphne looks around, wide-eyed at the display of cars.

Hudson must be home because his jeep and Ashlyn's SUV are both here. As are my cars.

"No Luka this morning?"

I shake my head, and Daphne eyes the Mercedes for a minute before moving to the convertible, excitement shining in her pale blue eyes. "Do you even know how to drive yourself or do I get to drive one of these pretties? If so, my vote's the Vette."

"Feeling feisty this morning?" I open the passenger side door of my 1960 cherry-red-and-white Corvette roadster and smack her delectable ass as she gets in. "Or were you hoping for a repeat of what we did in the backseat last night?"

When her cheeks grow hot, I've got my answer.

She liked what we did last night, and she liked the threat of being seen.

This little fact is going to be so much fun to explore.

DAPHNE

Whipping through the streets of Kroydon Hills with the top down on Max's Corvette and the warm wind in my hair isn't exactly the way I imagined spending my Sunday morning. But there are worse places to be. Last night was . . . unexpected.

Not that I regret it.

We swing through the drive-thru of my favorite bakery and get two coffees from a young girl who might as well have hearts in her eyes when she lays them on Max. She thanks him by name, and I swear her squeal follows us as we pull away.

"Come here a lot?" I tease.

His lips tip up into a crooked, carefree grin. Definitely not a look I've seen on his face in the office before but one I could get used to in a heartbeat. "Yeah. My sister Amelia owns the shop. She recently added the drive-thru to the building and some new teenagers to the staff for the summer break. I guess they know me by now. I come through most mornings on my way into the office."

"What's it like?" I sip my salty caramel latte and soak in the warm sun on my face.

Max raises his brow and waits for clarification.

"Growing up with so many siblings? You're the oldest of like, ten, right?"

He turns down a familiar street. Relaxed, his left arm rests on the open window frame. "Not quite. There's nine of us. We didn't even find out about Amelia until a few years ago, and I was in my late twenties when Madeline was born. So growing up, it was just the seven of us. Hudson, Lenny, and Jace are a lot younger than me. But Scarlet, Becks, Sawyer, and I are closer together in age. I guess we're a bit of a handful. There was always someone around to get into trouble with. We were never alone. But being a Kingston meant a lot was expected of us at an early age. I remember I couldn't wait to get as far away as I could for college, just to see what life was like without constantly feeling smothered."

"You went to college in California, right?" I prod. I can't help it. He's opening up, and I want to know it all.

"You've been doing your research." His smile is beautiful when he teases me like this.

"It's where I played football for Joe Sinclair. And why I brought him onboard as the head coach for the Philadelphia Kings. I wasn't a Kingston there." He makes another turn and pulls down a winding tree-lined driveway, leading to a whitewashed brick colonial with a high-pitched black roof and black shutters. Lush green ivy is growing up one side of the massive estate, curling around the shutters, and a beautiful sunroom, covered in floor-to-ceiling windows, runs the length of the other.

Max parks the car behind a familiar BMW before getting out and rounding the front to open my door.

I'm excited to see the inside once Holly opens the front door. She's dressed in a pristine red skirt suit with a tight black tank underneath that dips deep down into her abundant cleavage. Her greedy eyes drink in the sight of Max, who's next to me in dark jeans and a relaxed green Crucible t-shirt. The short sleeves showcase the tattoos on his forearm, and his hair is messy from the drive over . . . and from the way my fingers gripped it all night while he fucked me. Not that I'll be sharing that with her.

Her face transforms instantly from a gorgeous smile to an annoyed glare when her eyes slow their perusal of Max and she realizes I'm standing next to him. She zeroes in on his hand at my back, and if she could incinerate me with her eyes alone, my ashes would be blowing down the driveway. She is *not* happy to see me.

Oh, game on, honey.

Game. Freaking. On.

We might not be anything more than a fun distraction to each other, but that doesn't mean I'm willing to let him go just yet. And definitely not to her.

"Max." Holly forces a smile back on her overly made-up face and steps aside to let him in. He simply nods in return. The man of few words from the office is back in play. Undeterred, she begins telling him the highlights and rundown of the house.

Over five thousand square feet of living space.

Six bedrooms.

Nine bathrooms.

Five acres, so there's plenty of room for security.

The house was recently decorated by the top company on the East Coast, and the owners are willing to sell with or without the furniture. I've only known Max for a short amount of time, but I'm betting that the idea of buying it as-is without the hassle of having to furnish it after is appealing to him.

But when she gets to the outdoor swimming pool and then mentions the indoor lap pool, Max's handsome face turns toward me, a cocky smirk playing on his lips. I swear to God, if I had panties on, they'd be incinerated from how sinfully sexy that look is. I have no doubt we're both thinking back to last night in his pool, and now I desperately want a repeat. "Hear that, Daphne? *Two* pools. Double the fun."

I bite down on my lower lip, trying to hold back my snicker. "Imagine that."

He quickly reverts to work mode and reaches out, pointing to the tablet in Holly's hand. "If it's all right with you, can I take that? I'd rather we just walk around than be sold to."

Holly looks like she swallowed a lemon, but she hands Max the device and tells him she'll be waiting in the kitchen when he's ready.

Oh, I can bet I know what she's hoping he'll be ready for.

Max and I walk through all three levels of the house. Each room is more stunning than the last. Original dark hardwood flooring. Custom built-ins. High ceilings. The bedrooms are all gorgeous, and the master is absolute perfection. It sits at the back of the house with a balcony overlooking a stunning garden and an even more beautiful pool. A double-sided fireplace opening to both the room and the en suite is to die for. There's a gorgeous canopy bed in the center of the room with fluffy white linens just waiting to be spoiled.

I spin to ask Max what he thinks, but he silences me with his lips on mine, coaxing them open until his tongue tangles with mine. I wrap my arms around his neck, but he stops me. He drops the iPad on the bed and grabs both my hands, then spins me around and places them on the bed.

His palms skim under the hem of my borrowed dress as his body leans over mine, and hot breath tickles my ear. "Can you be quiet, siren?"

I peek over my shoulder. "Siren?"

I'm silenced when Max drops to his knees, and shivers ripple down my spine as he exposes my naked skin to the cool air blowing in from the vents. "Max . . ."

"Shh." The heat in the depths of his fathomless blue eyes holds promises I have no doubt he'll deliver on, and I lay my chest flat against the duvet and grasp it with both fists as he drags his flattened tongue up the length of my sex.

Oh *God*.

I buck back against him. My head turns toward the open door, checking to see if we've been caught, but after a moment, when he drags his finger down the curve of my ass and circles that virgin hole, I stop caring. He adds one blunt finger to my pussy. Then another. A web of color bursts behind my eyes as I fight to control the silent scream escaping from my throat.

I collapse against the bed and let Max fix my dress before I attempt to make my legs work. Once I push up, his arm encircles my waist, and his lips caress the shell of my ear. "Your cunt is delicious, Daphne."

I lean back against his chest and soak in his strength since I don't know whether I could stand on my own right now.

He wraps my hair around his fist and nips my neck. "Let's go buy a house."

And for one solid second, I imagine us doing that together.

This man may be more dangerous than I thought.

Max informed Holly he'd take the house, furniture and all. He also said that he'd pay 10 percent over the asking price, in cash, if he could settle in less than thirty days. She's going to get back to him with an answer, but I can't imagine anyone saying no to that offer.

Holly might not have gotten the guy, but she's going to get one hell of a commission. I think she may believe *I've* gotten the guy, but she's wrong there too. The words *mutually beneficial friendship* play over and over in my head with every touch of his hand and secretive smile given this morning. I may have to remind myself a few hundred times that I can't get involved in any kind of relationship while my life is falling apart around me.

But that's just fine with me.

At least, that's what I'll try to convince myself of later.

When I'm alone.

In the comfort of my own room.

Once we're back in the car, it's Max's turn to probe. "How's your dad been since the acquisition? I can't imagine retiring at his age. I think I'd be bored out of my mind."

I shrug, not wanting to get into this now. And especially not with him. "I haven't seen much of him lately."

He glances my way with concerned eyes. "Everything okay?"

"Of course," I bristle. "Why wouldn't it be?"

"No reason. Just something Sam mentioned a while ago. Our dads were friends once upon a time, Daph. If there's anything I can do to help, let me know. Okay?" The hand that was resting on my thigh squeezes, and I inch away, not wanting the contact now.

Max follows my directions to Dixon's house. It doesn't feel right to call it my house. It was never supposed to be permanent, just a place for Maddie and me to use as a stopover on our way to our new place. But I think our stay may last longer than we anticipated.

He pulls his hand away from me. "Have you been working on the information we need for Start A Revolution?"

I preen at the fact he called it by what I want to name it and not just *the foundation*. "Actually, I have." I turn in my seat and contemplate putting my feet up on his dash but choose not to piss off the sleeping lion, so I tuck them under me instead. "I'm working out a few ideas for a massive kick-off event to raise the first round of capital. I'd like to throw a fundraiser before the season starts in September."

"Oh yeah? What kind of fundraiser are you considering?"

"I want to do a bachelor auction with the team members. Bid on a date with your favorite player kind of event. Their date can consist of four hours of a mutually agreed upon activity. Dinner, dancing, ice skating. Something like that. We'll have cocktails and hors d'oeuvres. A silent auction with baskets of donated items the guests can bid on as well. Maybe early September."

"That's less than two months from now." Max pulls into the driveway of Dixon's place and turns the car off. "Can you pull that together, Miss Brenner?" He pulls his sunglasses off and tosses them onto the dashboard. "We could allocate one of the interns to help you."

"I thought I needed to bring you everything and *then* you'd decide whether I could move forward, Mr. Kingston?" I flutter my lashes coyly. "I don't want special treatment because I'm sleeping with the boss."

He reaches across the car, and I'm not sure what I thought he was going to do, but unbuckling my seatbelt was not it. I was expecting something much less tame. "Oh, you still have to make your presentation, Ms. Brenner. But I've watched you for a few weeks now. And I have no doubt you can do this."

Well . . . shoot. Knowing that Max Kingston thinks I'm capable tugs at a heartstring I didn't even know was even there. This man, who is the master of his own universe, is ready to give my dream a chance. And damn, I don't want to let him down.

He gets out and rounds the car, opening my door. "I don't beat around the bush, Daphne. And if I want something, I make it happen. If you want this, make it happen. Bring me what you've got tomorrow, and we'll discuss allocating resources. And I want you to plan on a long meeting.

Because after that, you're going to help me get O'Doul on board with my plans for the team."

"O'Doul is a puppy dog once you get to know him. But he doesn't like change. Never has. I can help with that."

He nods. "The stronger the team, the more financially sound, and the more funds to put toward Start A Revolution. Works out for both of us."

I grab my clutch and heels from the floor of the car, then lift up on my toes and kiss his cheek. I put a little extra sway in my step as his eyes burn into me while I walk to the front door, then turn my head and smile. "See you tomorrow, boss."

DAPHNE

THAT NIGHT, I'M SITTING AT THE DINING ROOM TABLE, earbuds in, listening to a new audiobook that Carys's stepsister just released. A spiral notebook, my MacBook, and a whiteboard are all spread out before me, along with an assortment of colored pens and markers. Cinder lounges on the chair next to me, a bored look on her face, while Dixon and his friend, Watkins, play *Madden* on the Xbox in the adjoining family room.

Watkins is the starting tight end for the Kings with Dix. You'd think these two would get enough football, playing professionally, but you'd be wrong. Watkins and a few of the other guys from the team are here a few times a week, and they're always playing video games. I don't know how Mads manages to make them look cool on social media.

When Maddie gets home, she drops her dance bag by the door and smiles like the Cheshire freaking cat when she sees me.

I pop my earbuds out, knowing I'm about to get grilled. "Hey. Where've you been?" The best defense is always a good offense, and just maybe I can skate by without an interrogation if I get her talking about herself. "I didn't realize you had class this late on a Sunday." I eye her makeup pointedly, knowing that she doesn't wear any to teach dance or yoga.

Mads's eyebrows shoot up and dart toward Dix to see if he heard me. Once she's satisfied he didn't, she drops down into the chair on the other side of the table. "I could ask you the same thing, Goldilocks. Whose bed did you sleep in last night? Because it certainly wasn't yours."

My cheeks heat in response when flashes of last night run through my mind. I lower my voice. "Don't act like you didn't know where I was. I texted you guys."

"Yes, you did." She reaches across the table and steals my glass of water. "You texted to say you were leaving . . . with your boss."

"What?" Dixon yells over the game before he pauses it and hops over the giant couch to join us at the table. "You went home with Bobby O'Doul?" Eyes pinched and mouth open, he's not trying to hide his disgust before he shuts his mouth and curls his upper lip.

Watkins joins what's quickly becoming a shit show. "Dude. He's old enough to be your grandfather, D."

Dixon groans, "You're fucking gorgeous, D. You don't need to be playing with shriveled up balls just yet."

My life, ladies and gentlemen.

Water comes out of Maddie's nose as she laughs at her idiot brother before she shoves him away from her. "What is wrong with you two? She didn't go home with Coach O'Doul. She went home with Max Kingston."

Dix and Watkins look at each other with wide eyes before they both turn to me with matching shocked expressions firmly planted on their chiseled faces. Dixon's morphs into something else, but I can't put my finger on it. "Max *Kingston*? You slept with Max Kingston?"

I close my laptop and stand from the table, so I don't have to hurt my neck to glare pointedly at Dix. "That is none of your business, and this conversation is over."

With lightning-fast reflexes only a professional athlete possesses, his fingers encircle my wrist and stop my retreat before it can start. "I'm sorry. That was out of line. I just . . . I was surprised."

I tug my wrist away from him as Maddie moves in front of her brother. Big blue eyes beg me to stay calm. "We're sorry. Don't be mad, D. We're just worried about you. I mean, it sounds like fun, but are you ready for the consequences of being with Max Kingston?"

"I'm not with him, Mads. It's just a little fun. Pretty sure I deserve it after the last few weeks."

Maddie pushes harder. "D. I've listened to your plan for Start A Revolution for the past four years. Do you want to risk that on a hookup with your boss? It would've been hard enough to be taken seriously as the owner's daughter. I think it might be worse to be the owner's *girlfriend*."

I lift my eyes to see anger shining in Dixon's. "Just be careful, D. You've lost a lot over the past few weeks. The last thing you want anyone thinking is that you're going after him for his money or the safety he can give you."

Maddie throws her arms around me. "We just don't want to see you get hurt."

I squeeze her back. "Will you trust that I know what I'm doing? Please. I appreciate your concern, but I'm good. I swear. I just want to make sure everything is perfect for my Start A Revolution presentation tomorrow."

"Anything we can do to help?" Dixon offers, and a new idea begins taking shape.

"Actually," I look between the three of them. "I think I have an idea."

After staying up all night, perfecting my presentation, I'm a nervous wreck the next morning. I'm finally going to get the chance to present Start A Revolution the way I'd always envisioned. Only instead of my father sitting on the other side of the desk, it's the man whose name I screamed all night Saturday.

The way his eyes looked up at me from between my legs is seared into my soul. Never to be forgotten.

"Good morning, Miss Brenner." His blue eyes stay completely impassive. He's in business mode. Thank God. I'm so nervous I don't know if I could do this any other way. Things got a little weird for a hot minute during the ride home yesterday. "Are you ready to begin?" He opens a leather-bound folio and grabs a pen.

I blow out a breath and run my sweaty palms over the front of my gray pencil skirt, trying to get my heartbeat to slow down to an acceptable rhythm instead of continuing to gallop away like a prized racehorse. The sleeveless baby-blue blouse with little ruffles at the arms and collar is one of my favorites, and my mother's pearls hang delicately around my neck. I can't resist touching them, reminding me I've always known I was going to run this foundation, just like my mom did before she met my dad.

Max sits across from me, elbows resting on his desk, with an expectant look on his handsome face.

I go through my entire presentation, stopping to answer the few questions Max asks along the way.

He's quiet the majority of the time, absorbing everything with the same brooding intensity I've become accustomed to with him.

I finish with my pitch for the first big charity event to launch the foundation. As I go over the details I was able to tentatively organize yesterday, I see the interest glinting in his indigo blue eyes. "I've already secured commitments from ten Revolution players and ten Kings players, who have all generously agreed to be auctioned off if I'm able to move forward."

"Kings players too? Really?" Max places his pen down,

seemingly intrigued. "You were able to get twenty professional athletes to agree to be auctioned off less than two months from now? You found a night that worked for everyone and a venue? All on this short of notice?" He seems astonished.

And I can't tell if that's a good thing or not.

"You seem surprised." I try to make it seem like it was easy, but the truth is, I worked on this all day, and it wasn't until Dixon pissed me off that I was able to get him to agree to be in the auction and to help me recruit the others. The Revolution players were easy enough. They know me. I might not have worked for the team for long, but this arena is my home. I've been around enough over the years that none of the guys I reached out to would dare say no.

"Not surprised, Daphne." He closes his folio and crosses his arms over his chest. "Impressed. And maybe a little annoyed."

"Annoyed?" What the hell? My stomach rolls, wondering what I could have done wrong. "Why annoyed?"

He stands and rounds his desk. "Because I was just getting used to you as an assistant, and now I'm going to have to find a new one to take your place once you get this up and running."

"Oh my God." My hands fly up to my mouth, trying to hold back my excitement. "Does that mean . . . ?" I don't want to finish the question. What if I'm wrong?

He leans back, resting against his desk, and his hands grip the edge. Only inches separate him and the chair I'm sitting in. Heat pools deep in my belly, remembering just how those hands felt on my body before I can shove those inconvenient thoughts back into the box where they belong while we're in this building. No matter how much I want to blur those lines.

A vein in his jaw ticks before his lips tip up in a crooked smile. "It means I think it's time to Start A Revolution."

I don't think. I just react. Jumping up from my chair, I throw my arms around him.

Max catches me with ease, his strong arms circling my back.

We've been here before, but not like this.

The last time I hugged Max in this office, I didn't know what he felt like inside me.

He holds me tightly to him momentarily, then lowers his face to my hair. His erection grows hard and thick between us until he places me back down on my feet, his hands gently holding my shoulders. "I can't let you go from your position just yet though. So, you're going to have to do double duty for a while. I need you here while we get everyone on the same page. I'm assigning you an intern to help you for now. I want you to consider what staff you're going to need to get started and send it to me. We'll see what we can do."

"Sure. Absolutely. I'll do whatever we need." I can't believe my dream is about to be a reality, and my dad isn't even here to see it.

Turns out, I didn't need him or his pull with the organization to make it happen after all. And I can't hold back a bittersweet smile when I realize I did this all on my own. Not because I wanted to, although I did.

But because I had to.

I don't have a family anymore.

They're all gone.

MAX

Holly got back to me later in the week, letting me know that the owners accepted my offer, and the house was mine. We can sign the contracts as soon as I want, if that works for me, which means I need to call Becks.

I don't want to. I know he's going to give me shit for ditching him Saturday. It's what we do. My siblings and I are tight. And if we made ballbusting an Olympic fucking sport, Becket would be the gold medalist every time.

Son of a bitch.

I pick up the phone from my desk and call his cell.

Asshole picks up on the first ring.

"Maxipad . . ."

I grind my molars, reminding myself it's illegal to kill your brother. "Hey, man. Can you look over a contract for me?"

I hear movement on the other end of the call, then he slow claps.

Fucking slow claps me.

"Maybe you're not as dumb as I thought. Having her sign a contract could work." Becks sighs, and I resist the urge to crush my phone in the palm of my hand. "Would have been better if you did that before you fucked her. Seriously . . . What were you thinking? She's your assistant. And from what I'm hearing, Daddy's financial troubles are bigger than we knew. To her, you look like a big old—heavy emphasis on *old*—juicy whale she's got in her net, asshole."

"I swear to God, Becks. Do you ever listen to yourself?" I rub my temple. "And what the hell are you talking about, anyway?" I look up when Daphne knocks on my open door.

"I'm heading out for the night. Talk later, okay?" She's half-whispering while she looks at the cell phone in my hand, and I pray she didn't hear what the asshole was saying.

"See ya tomorrow." I watch her pull her bag up higher on her shoulder and turn away. And damn, I wish I was leaving with her. If I'm honest with myself, I was hoping to get her to grab dinner with me. I hadn't realized what time it was. We've been so busy this week, we haven't exactly discussed what happened or when it can happen again.

"Helloooo? You still there, Maximus?" I squeeze the phone again and take in a deep breath through my nose.

"I'm buying a house and need you to look over the contract."

A silence lingers, before Becks answers, "So, no Christian Grey contract for you?"

"Christian who?" It's like he has the attention span of a fucking toddler, which is an insult to toddlers.

"The movie, dude. *Fifty Shades.*"

"Why the fuck have you seen that movie? Porn's free online." I drag my hand over my face and miss the days I could just walk down the hall to his office.

Becks laughs at me.

Asshole.

"Because I have a girlfriend who made me watch it one night. Wasn't my thing, but it got her excited as fuck, and she let me do all sorts of things to her afterward. Don't knock it till you try it."

Becks's girlfriend, Kendall, is a grade A bitch. None of us like her. And we can't figure out what the hell he sees in her. But they've been together for a few years now.

Jesus, I hope he doesn't marry her.

"Listen, I just emailed you the contract. Can you look it over?" I'm over this conversation, my mind still hung up on Daphne leaving. I guess dinner would have been a date. And we're not dating. My idea sounded better in my head Saturday than it does now.

I can't actually date my assistant.

I don't date.

I may bring someone with me to an event and fuck them afterward. But we both know what we're getting out of the night, and a call the next day isn't it.

That's not an option with Daphne.

"Yeah. Whatever. You going back to Dad's tonight? I'll look this over and meet you there. The food's better there anyway."

"Thanks, man. I'll see you then." I disconnect the call, and another knock on my door has me looking up. Coach O'Doul stands in my doorway. Waiting. "Evening, Coach."

He walks in, and hands me a legal pad, which I look over quickly. It's a list of names. "What's this?"

"You say you want this team to succeed. Here's your chance." O'Doul leans over the desk and points at the yellow pad. "That's a list of unrestricted free agents, and a few trades I'd like to make happen. The last two years should have been rebuilding years, and Brenner didn't invest the way we needed him to. I picked up a few good guys in the draft, but they're young. We need to stack our depth chart with more seasoned players. That list will help get us there."

I lean back in my chair and eye the numbers we'll need to get some of these guys here. "A few of these guys won't come cheap." I've already had my sister Lenny run numbers on a couple of free agents. She's the numbers genius and works her magic for the Kings. A few of the guys on this list are already on my radar.

"Did you buy this team because you're bored? Or do you

actually want to win? Because I want to win. I've only got a few more years of coaching before I promised my wife I'd retire. I want to bring home the damn Cup." He straightens and stares down at me. "I've read up on you. You like to be the best, Kingston. You did some impressive things with the Kings after you stepped up, and you weren't afraid to put your money where your mouth is. You gonna do that here?"

Disrespectful O'Doul and I are never going to be on the same page. But this . . . this I can work with. I understand how a man can be driven by the desire to win. To leave your mark on something that's going to last longer than you will. "Wanna walk me through your plan to win the Cup?"

Coach leans over and flips to the next page on the notepad. When he sits down, a devious grin spreads across his face. "I thought you'd never ask."

And that's how we spend the next two hours.

Working through O'Doul's plan and who he needs to put it in motion.

Calls are made.

Emails sent.

And finally, a plan begins to take shape.

By the time the two of us walk out to our cars late that night, we're on the same page.

Luka opens the car door for me, and I stop to shake O'Doul's hand. "Nice working with ya, Coach."

"You too, Kingston." He takes a few steps before I stop him, the question that's been bouncing around in my mind since he showed me his notepad, demanding an answer.

"Hey, Coach. If you don't mind me asking, what changed your mind? Last week, you thought I was the enemy."

"I had lunch with Daphne the other day. Don't know if I've ever met someone with as pure a heart as that young woman has, and she thinks you're the real deal. She seems to think you're the only person who might actually want the Cup more than me. I figured I had nothing to lose. Have a good night, Kingston." Bobby O'Doul gets into a massive Ford truck and pulls out of the lot while I'm still stuck in place.

There goes my little assistant, surprising me again.

When I walk into my father's house that evening, I'm greeted by my giggling sister. The youngest one. I never really thought I wanted kids until Ashlyn had Madeline. Growing up and constantly surrounded by people, I always imagined a quieter life . . . when I thought about it. Which wasn't exactly often in my teens and early twenties. But by the time Madeline was born, Dad was already gone, and it was up to the rest of us to step in and help.

Help Ashlyn, who has no other family.

And be there for Madeline, since Dad couldn't be.

I was twenty-seven when she was born. She could have been mine. I think most of us look at her as ours. But she's a clone of her mother. Cornflower-blue eyes, curly blonde hair the color of straw, and tiny little features like the porcelain dolls that used to line a shelf in Lenny's room. And she's currently upside down, dangling by her feet in Becket's hands.

"Where is it?" Becket asks teasingly, and Madeline's giggles grow louder.

Her upside-down eyes meet mine, and she squeals with glee, "Save me, Max." Her arms stretch in front of her, so I steal her away from Becks and hold her close to me. "Quick, Max. To the kitchen. Momma's in there, and he won't yell at me in front of her."

This kid has had every one of us wrapped around her tiny little fingers since the day she was born, so I do as she says and steal her away to the kitchen where Ashlyn is cleaning up after dinner.

"Momma . . . Becks is after me." She twirls her fingers in my hair with one hand and squeezes the life out of me with her little legs.

"What did you do, baby?" Ashlyn wipes her hand on a towel and stifles a laugh when Becks follows us into the room. The delicious scent of fajitas fills the air, and my mouth waters. My eyes scan the room for leftovers until I eye my brother. Fucker probably ate them all.

"She was playing on my phone and forgot where she put it." Becks tickles Madeline's sides. "Can you please go look for it for me?"

She sighs like a teenager and pushes to be let down. "Fine." Once I place her on her feet, she sulks away, and Becket points at Ashlyn.

"If she can't find my phone, you owe me a new one."

"Sure, Becket. I'll get right on that." She finishes her glass of wine and adds it to the dishwasher. "There's leftovers in the fridge, if you're hungry, Max."

"Thank you."

"I'm going to help look for your phone, Becket." She walks around the two of us and follows after Madeline.

While I get the leftovers out of the fridge, Becks drops the contract on the marble island. "Everything looks good. Price seems high, but you can afford it." He thumbs the corner of the pages between his thumb and forefinger like a blackjack dealer would shuffle cards. "You really want something this big?"

I throw a fajita in the microwave and grab two beers, passing one to Becket. "It's not so much about the size as it is about the privacy. We looked at a few penthouses, but they really weren't doing it for me. This place worked." What I don't mention to Becks is that it's easy to imagine a life there. A family filling it. A little girl, Madeline's age, who looks like Daphne.

Becks clinks his bottle to mine. "We, huh? Who's we? You and the assistant?"

"It wasn't like that. I brought her with me so we could work in the car." I grab my plate from the microwave and try to ignore the idiot while I eat, but it's like those damn ants we couldn't get rid of after Jace left a slice of pizza under his bed last year.

You can't get rid of them, no matter what you fucking do.

They're just there.

Just everywhere.

Annoying you.

"Don't get wrapped up in this girl, Maximus." His tone grows unusually serious. "She's bad news. Her father fucked away his company and all their money. Chick's gonna have major daddy issues, maybe even *sugar* daddy issues. It can't end well. And we've both been there before, when they're more interested in our last name than us. Don't put yourself through that."

I bite back the angry response sitting on the tip of my tongue and try to pacify him. "Thanks for the advice, man. But I'm good. I've got it handled."

"Maximus—"

Madeline comes running into the kitchen with Becks's phone in her hand. That is, until she falls, and the thing goes flying across the floor, coming to a screeching, screen-cracking stop against the leg of one of the counter stools.

He looks down at the broken phone, then at our baby sister who has tears in her eyes, and I take the Get Out of Jail Free card I was just handed and get the hell out of the kitchen. "Thanks, man. Good luck with that." I nod toward the phone and slink away.

No way Daphne's that girl. She's not that kind of person. I know she's not.

Right?

DAPHNE

THE DINING ROOM TABLE HAS BECOME MY NEW SANCTUARY.
Some nights, I'd probably be better off just staying at the
office and working late there instead of coming back to
Dixon's. But I refuse to be that person, and I'd rather be
comfortable than sitting at my desk. Even if the view there is
better.

The last few days have been intense.

Max and I finally found our rhythm and have been
working well together.

Working being the key word there.

It didn't hurt that he assigned one of the interns to me.
Willow is a fresh-faced eighteen-year-old whose mother
works in our payroll department. She's willing to do whatever I need but doesn't really know how to do anything
just yet.

Hey, beggars can't be choosers.

I can teach her what she doesn't know. The problem with
that is it actually takes more time than doing it myself. So,
my days have been long. Like, really long. Even then, I still
leave before Max each night.

He's working so damn hard to get everyone in the organization on the same page, I think he may have slept in the
office all week.

When I asked him what he was trying to do, he told me,
*"A winning team starts with a winning culture. And we don't have
either right now."*

It's been days since our night in his guesthouse, and other than the hug we shared on Monday, he hasn't touched me once. Neither of us has said a word about it either. If it weren't for the way he watches me, I'd think I was insane and had imagined the whole thing.

But my imagination has never been that good, and those memories are vividly burned into my brain.

I'm not sure what I expected. This is my first go at a friends-with-benefits thing. But I guess I'm a little disappointed we haven't managed to grab any time together this week. I'm not sure if he changed his mind. Or maybe it's the whole boss/assistant thing that got to him. Either way, I think something must have gotten to him. I mean, what the hell? One day, he was eating me out on someone else's bed, and the next, we were back to being coworkers. And I didn't like it. Not one bit.

If Max is the sun at the center of his universe, when he shines his light down on you, it's glowing and warm and feels so damn good, you want more. It only took me a few hours to figure that little nugget out. And I want more.

So here I sit at the massive black dining table with my laptop open as I finish up my to-do list. Max didn't come into the office at all today. Just sent me a message saying he was going to work from home in the morning and had something personal to take care of in the afternoon. Kinda cold. Definitely formal. Nothing friendly about it.

I guess our boundaries have been reset.

He's my boss, and I'm the assistant.

Maybe I should be glad that we managed to avoid the complications that would come with a workplace relationship. Even if it wasn't supposed to be a real relationship. Maybe it's better this way. And maybe, if I feed myself enough maybes, I'll be able to cover up that tiny place in my heart that sighs a dreamy sigh at the idea of a real relationship with Max Kingston.

I figured there was no need to stay late on a Friday night if I could get the same thing done here. At least here I can take my bra off. And that's exactly what I did when I got home.

Which brings me to now, sitting in my new sanctuary, wearing a red cami and pink cotton boxer shorts with tiny red hearts embroidered all over them, sans bra and panties. Because seriously, what's the point?

Cinder decided to grace me with her presence tonight and has been batting a ball between her white paws under the table, providing me with a distraction every time she decides to bat my ankle instead. My cell phone vibrates against the table with an unfamiliar number, and butterflies take flight in my chest with hope. "Hello?"

The connection is bad, and the static hurts my ear before the call drops.

This is the second one of those I've gotten this week, and I can't help but wonder if it's got something to do with my dad. Maybe he just wants to hear my voice, like a bad hallmark movie or something. Maybe he's regretting his choices.

Or maybe I'm seriously stretching, and it's just a wrong number.

I shake myself from my runaway thoughts and catch Dixon walking into the room. Freshly showered, having just gotten home from practice, he stops dead in his tracks, and I check to make sure I don't have a boob popping out or something.

Nope. All tucked in.

Here's the thing, Dixon has seen me in a bikini. He's seen a whole lot of my skin. So I have no idea what in the actual hell is up with this deer-in-the-headlights reaction I'm getting now. Dix shoves his hands in the pockets of his camo cargo shorts. "Hey, D. What are you doing home?"

"Working." Then it dawns on me. "Oh shit. Did you want the house to yourself?" I close my laptop and start pulling my stuff together. "I can get out of here if you've got a date coming over." I mean, I've never seen him with a girl, or a guy for that matter, but it's only been a few weeks.

His long legs cross the room, and his big palm on my notebook halts my movement. "No. No date. I was going to ask if you wanted to watch a movie. We could order dinner."

I straighten. "Sounds good. I ate dinner already, but I'm down for a movie. I need to call it a night on work anyway. It's been a long week, and I feel like I haven't stopped. But the inaugural event for the Start A Revolution Foundation is a go. I've got the location and the catering." I tick off my list on my fingers and smile up at Dixon. "The band. The athletes for the auction. Thanks for your help with that, by the way. I'm working on donations for the silent auction and the guest list now. It's really coming together."

"D." Dixon tucks a lock of hair behind my ear, and the world stands still as his pupils dilate.

No. Don't do it.

Just as the thought stops me dead in my tracks, the doorbell rings.

Dixon looks over his shoulder like he's expecting someone else to answer the door, then groans, "Don't move."

I don't know that I could even if I wanted to.

That was the strangest interaction, and I think I'm losing my mind because I could swear he was going to kiss me. Brandon Dixon. My best friend's older brother, who I've known since I was eighteen. Who I live with. Jesus Christ. I haven't been in any kind of relationship in years, and now, it's like every forbidden romance book ever written is falling into my lap. *What the hell?*

"D," Dixon calls to me. "The door's for you."

I move down the hall and come to a stop when I see Max standing just inside the door. Glaring hard at Dixon, who's doing his own glaring right back at Max. *What the hell?*

"Hey, Max." I nervously smooth my hair behind my ear. The same thing Dixon just did. Both men track the movement, and I'm suddenly extremely uncomfortable. "What are you doing here?"

Max's eyes drag over my body, and the urge to cover myself wars with the need to be touched by this man.

He pulls a small bouquet of hydrangeas from behind his back and offers them to me. "I bought the house today and wanted to say thank you for your help. I was going to ask you to go out to dinner with me."

"She already ate dinner," Dixon answers for me, and the look on Max's face is less than thrilled.

I fight the urge to scowl back at my roomie. "I did eat dinner already. Dixon and I were going to watch a movie. Want to join us?"

As the words leave my mouth, Dixon walks away, clearly not thrilled at the idea of our guest. "I'm going to order pizza. Let me know if you guys want anything."

Once he's out of sight, Max shuts the front door behind himself and steps closer. "Why is my center here?"

"Pretty sure he's not your center anymore. He's your sister's now. And this is his house. His sister is my best friend, and we moved in with Dixon after we graduated." I take the pretty flowers from his hands and bring them to my nose. They smell heavenly. "Thank you for these. They're lovely."

Not satisfied with my answer, he pushes for more. "Why do you live with Brandon Dixon? I thought this was your house."

A ridiculous laugh bubbles up. I can't help it. "Max, I don't know why you'd think that. This is Dix's house. It's the perfect house for two point five kids and a Golden Labradoodle. Why would it be my house?"

"I just assumed." Max reaches out to take my hand, and I step into him, tipping my head back. "I've fucking missed you."

The declaration is my undoing. "I've missed you too."

His hands grab either side of my face and pull my lips to his, forcing me to my toes. A warm wave of want washes over me as he licks at the seam of my lips until I open and suck his tongue into my mouth. Sighing. Relieved. Wanting so much more than this kiss. My hands wrap around his waist, aching to smooth the skin under the soft t-shirt blocking me.

He pulls away and nips my chin, then whispers in my ear, "I've been dying to do that all week. Seeing you . . . being near you every day but not being allowed to touch was fucking excruciating."

I capture his lips with mine, needing more. "I thought you just weren't interested." I gasp, and fist his shirt, desperate. "That we were a onetime thing."

His fingers slide under the straps of my cami, plucking them like the strings of a guitar. "I'm interested, Daphne."

A throat clearing makes me jump back before Dixon tells us the pizza is on its way and heads into the other room.

Heat creeps up my cheeks like I've just been caught in the act. I guess, in a way, I was. I look up through my lashes at the handsome man in front of me, who definitely had better things to do tonight, and bite down on my lower lip. "Wanna watch a movie?"

Cinder joins the two of us in the hall, winding herself through Max's legs, trying to decide if he passes the test before she flicks her tail in his direction and walks away with cool indifference.

He glances down at her, then back to me. "Is that what you really want to do tonight?"

"No. But it's what I need to do first." I lift up onto my toes and kiss the bottom of his chin.

"Guess I'm watching a movie then."

MAX

Daphne's roommate came home just as the mini-marshmallow men came to life on the shelf of the grocery store, and she made us rewind the movie to the beginning, appalled that they'd watch the new *Ghostbusters* without her. It was funny and definitely nostalgic. But as I sit on the couch with Daphne's bare legs draped over mine, forcing my hands to remain as PG-13 as the rating of the movie, I wish we were anywhere but here. I've skimmed my fingers up her soft thighs, occasionally dipping under her shorts enough to know she's not wearing panties, but nothing further.

Her cat keeps rubbing itself up against my leg, like it's trying to mark its territory and claim me as hers, the way I wish her owner would.

But not with one of my players sitting with his feet propped up on the other side of the sectional, throwing pissed-off glances our way.

He wants her.

It's obvious to anyone with eyes.

But I think Daphne is oblivious.

Brandon Dixon has played for the Philadelphia Kings since we drafted him out of Kroydon University five years ago. He's a great center. A beast on the field. He and our quarterback, Declan Sinclair, have a shorthand most centers only dream of having with their QB, and they've won us back-to-back championships.

And I fucking hate him.

At least right now.

Maybe not hate *him*.

But I hate that she lives here with him. I hate that Daphne's in that thin, little red tank top with her creamy breasts spilling over the top and shorts that will definitely give you a show if she bends over. And I hate that he's here to see it. That he's been seeing it for weeks before I did.

These aren't feelings I should have about someone I'm in a casual relationship with.

But there's very little that's casual about the feelings she stirs in me.

And even less casual is the way I've had to fight the urge to bend her over my office desk all week. Or my desire to cover her skin, so Brandon Dixon doesn't get the chance to see it. I've never been possessive about a woman before, but Daphne's different. And apparently, I'm a jealous asshole because I hate the fact that while I was trying to stay away from her at the office all week, he got to spend time with her every night.

And I dislike this little revelation even more because I don't do jealousy.

It's pointless.

If someone wants to be with you, they should be.

If they'd rather be somewhere else, they were never yours to start with.

I learned that lesson the hard way in college, like most idiots do. I was eighteen and away from home. I went to a West Coast college to escape the notoriety that comes with my family. And I did. At least, I thought I did. I also thought I was in love with a beautiful, sweet girl. Until I found out she was only in it in hopes of landing a Kingston and all the money she thought would come with that. Turns out, she was screwing my fraternity brother the entire time. He told me everything one night in a drunken stupor after she ditched both of us for some English duke.

But where the fuck does all this lead me?

Because this woman sure as fuck isn't supposed to be mine.

We both said casual.

Mutually beneficial.

Can't offer you more.

These were my words. My idea. I have no right to be possessive of this incredible woman, who was late to work the other day because one of the dogs at the shelter where she volunteers got loose and she just had to help get him back in his cage. Her heart's as big as her brain. And her brain seems pretty damn big. Between helping me search for a new assistant, she's been updating me daily on her progress with Start A Revolution, and it's nothing short of amazing.

I have no claim to her, yet the pride I feel for what she's accomplishing is immense.

Basically, I'm screwed.

And by the time the original Ghostbusters show up on the screen, I'm hornier than a teenager who just fingered his first girl. Probably because the last time I sat and watched a movie with a raging hard-on, I was a teenager fingering his first girlfriend.

When the movie ends, Dixon stands and quickly says goodnight without sparing us a glance. He must have spared them all during the movie. His sister grabs the bowl of popcorn from the table and stands too. "I've got to teach baby ballerinas all day tomorrow, so I'm also out. Night, guys. Good to see you again, Max."

"You too." Two down.

"Night, Mads." Daphne watches her friend leave the room, then throws her leg over my lap and straddles me. "I feel like I just had chaperones on a date or something." Her silvery-blue eyes sparkle as she runs her fingers through my hair. "Want to come upstairs?"

"Daphne." I wrap my hands around her wrists and hold her still. "I'm not going to fuck you in another man's house."

"What?" She pulls back, the hurt clear in her beautiful silver eyes.

And I don't like being the cause of it.

I cradle her cheeks in my hands, smoothing her hair back from her face, the smell of her pear shampoo enveloping the two of us. I never knew I'd associate pears with sex. But I'll never be able to smell them without thinking about it again.

She gasps when I lean in and suck her bottom lip between mine, and my cock swells from the sound.

"Have dinner with me tomorrow night at the new house. Just you and me. And pack a bag because you won't be coming home after."

She wiggles her perfect peach of an ass against my already rock-solid cock, and I groan. "Daphne . . ."

"Just come upstairs, Max. I don't want to wait until tomorrow." Her voice is breathy. Needy. And so fucking sexy. "Please."

My hand glides inside the leg of her pink cotton shorts and traces the seam of her bare, hot pussy. "I'm not fucking you here, Daphne." I circle her clit as she tries to get me to give her what she wants. "You're not coming on my cock in another man's house, but I'll take care of you if you can be quiet." I drag my tongue up the column of her throat and swallow her gasp as I push two fingers into her wet heat and rub the heel of my palm against her clit. "Can you be quiet, Daphne?"

She rocks her hips against me, breathy little moans escaping from her pink lips.

"Shh. Not a sound or this stops."

Her fingers slip under my shirt, scoring my skin with her

nails. And I swear to God, my balls draw up like I'm gonna come in my pants. I mentally go through everything I've got to do tomorrow while I work her faster, making sure she's the only one who comes on this couch. And when I push my thumb down on her clit and bite her bottom lip, my siren comes on a silent cry. Eyes closed and mouth open in a perfect O. Fucking beautiful. The scent of sex mixes with the clean, crisp scent of her, cementing my newfound love of pears, and I pull my fingers from her and place them against her bottom lip. "Suck."

Daphne's eyes widen in surprise, and she wraps those pouty, soft lips around my fingers and hums as she sucks.

Jesus Christ.

She pops her lips off me and smiles. "Are you sure you don't want to come upstairs? Pretty sure I owe you one." Her hips circle my dick, and this little siren smiles a wicked smile, full of promise.

"Dinner tomorrow. My house. Luka will pick you up." I wrap my hands around her tiny waist. This woman is all soft curves and even softer skin that my hands ache to touch. I lay her back against the couch and trail my fingertips over the satin piping of her red tank. "I want to make you dinner. Then I want to eat you for dessert."

Her eyes crinkle with confusion. "That sounds like a date."

"I guess it does. Do you have a problem with that?" The words leave my mouth before I consider what I'll do if she says yes.

She shakes her head. "I thought we weren't doing the dating thing."

I move my face close to hers and drop my lips to her forehead. "You deserve more than our little arrangement." I stand and right my clothes, then hold my hand out for her to take. "We'll talk about it tomorrow. Now, walk me out."

I've never been a man afraid to work for what I want. And I want this woman.

Daphne's white-blonde hair falls in soft waves around her flushed face but does a shit job at hiding her frustration. "You're really not going to come upstairs?"

I gather her silky hair in my hand and tug her head back as I crowd her. "No. I'm not. I'm a man, Daphne. Not a boy. I want you in my bed. In my house. I thought I didn't have time for a relationship, but I think what I don't have time for is games. I don't want to fuck around. I want you. But not here. Not down the hall from your roommate, who clearly wants to fuck you."

"He does not want to fuck me, Max. He's my friend." She takes a defiant step into me, and I tilt her head back.

"Oh, he wants to fuck you. Have you looked in a mirror?" I tug harder on her hair. "Any man with eyes would want to fuck you, Daphne. And that man knows you. So he knows you're gorgeous, and smart, and have a giant heart. You're the entire package. And I'm an ass for not telling you that sooner."

When she stares at me without answering, I kiss her lips and back away. "Tomorrow night, Daphne."

I close the front door behind me, leaving her in a sex-dazed haze before I drive back to spend my last night at my father's house, alone in my bed.

Getting myself off while I think about my siren sleeping under another man's roof.

Not what I was planning for the night.

But it'll have to do.

MAX

By noon on Saturday, the moving company has brought everything in, set it up, cleaned it up, and left.

Efficient and effective.

Just how I like it.

There wasn't that much to be moved, considering I bought this place fully furnished, but anything I didn't want, I had them move into the guesthouse in case I changed my mind. But something is still missing. I guess I should order some groceries. And a meal service. And a cleaning service. Maybe I can combine the two and get a house manager like we have at Dad's house. Wonder if Mrs. Burns wants a change of scenery.

If I stole her away, I think I'd have a Kingston sibling riot on my hands.

It'd be worth it for her cooking skills alone.

I add the task to the Notes app on my phone just as the doorbell chimes.

When it chimes a second time, like an impatient child keeps hitting it, I know one of my brothers is standing on the other side of the door. Turns out, it isn't just one of them. It's all of them.

Everyone.

I don't have time to be annoyed before my sister Amelia walks in, kisses me on the cheek, then hands me my nine-month-old nephew, Maddox. She grabs two bags full of

Sweet Temptations pink bakery boxes from her husband, Sam, and holds them up triumphantly. "Where do you want these? I brought your favorite."

Madeline, and Cade's daughter, Brynlee, race by us into the house with Ashlyn following more slowly behind the two of them. "Coffee, Max. We need coffee." She disappears among the commotion.

Jace takes the bags from Amelia's hands. "Strawberry shortcake?"

"They're *your* favorite, and I send them to your dorm all the time. Max's favorite is lemon-raspberry." She plants her hands on her hips and smiles.

Jace pouts, just like Maddox, and Amelia shoves him away, then follows. "There's strawberry shortcake in there too."

As the rest of the family follows her in like a swarm of bees, I shake my head and laugh. This is what was missing.

Chaos.

"Wherever you want," I yell back to Amelia, who's halfway through the house already, then blow a raspberry on Maddox's chubby neck and whisper, "Your mom's nuts, kid." He slaps his drooly, wet hands against my face and giggles uncontrollably.

Yeah. He knows his mom's crazy.

He better be careful because she's a perfect shot too.

Lenny and her fiancé, Sebastian, follow behind Amelia with a new, stainless-steel espresso machine still in the box. "Which way to the kitchen? I need a cup of coffee."

I look between her and Bash. "Are you allowed to have caffeine, Len?" My sister is pregnant. Not as far along as Scarlet, but the next generation of Kingstons is coming. I guess they're destined to love caffeine as much as this generation.

Bash makes an *oh shit* noise somewhere deep in his throat. "Don't even try to separate your sister from her coffee." He kisses the crown of Len's head, then smacks her ass.

I've learned to ignore the two of them.

"Watch it. I have decaf too." Len reaches her hands out for Maddox. "Come to Auntie Len, sweet boy." Already a lover of all the ladies, the little man throws himself at his aunt before they disappear down the hall with Bash following dutifully behind them.

Their wedding is next week.

She wanted something small and intimate at Dad's house.

Something perfectly Lenny.

And I was happy to make it happen for her.

I have no idea when we all grew up, but somewhere along the way, we did.

Well, most of us anyway.

"What up, Maxipad?" Hudson throws his arm around me and hands me a bottle of Johnny Walker King. "Don't let Cade see this. I'm in training mode and not allowed to drink before the next fight." He looks around for Scarlet's boyfriend, Cade *The Saint* St. James, the former MMA champion, who also happens to be Hud's trainer, and grins when he's nowhere to be found.

"You're an asshat, Hud." Sawyer smacks the back of Hud's head, then holds up a magnum of champagne. "Congratulations, brother. This place is perfect for you."

"Thanks." I nod as Scarlet walks in with Cade, his arms full of grocery bags.

He shifts them to his side and looks around. "Anyone see which way Brynlee ran?"

Hudson moves to stand in front of the Johnny Walker, like a kid afraid to get caught by his teacher. Brynlee comes running back into the room, headed straight for Hud. He grabs her mid-run and throws her on his shoulders. "Let's go see what kind of trouble we can get into, Brynnie."

Little-girl giggles echo around the room, and I watch them take off to explore.

A pang of jealousy hitting me in the chest.

A silent wish that Daphne was here too.

What the fuck is wrong with me?

"Okay, Maximus. Where's the kitchen?" When I stare at Scarlet, she waves her hand in front of my face. "Hello? Earth to Max. We've got food for your fridge."

"Straight through there." I point in the direction Lenny went earlier. "Thanks, Scar."

Becks moves around all of us with a case of beer in his hands. "I win. I brought the beer."

Scarlet groans. "And thankfully, you left your girlfriend at home."

He ignores her as we all enter the kitchen, and my sister instructs everyone on what needs to go where, just like the general she was born to be. Before long, the food is put away. Takeout's been ordered. There's a cupcake smashed on Jace's face, and I'm not sure who did it. And laughter is filling the house.

I take it in.

Everything.

All of them.

The noise.

The love.

The complete chaos.

And goddamn, I'm so grateful.

I sit down at the kitchen island next to Scarlet, who passes me a piece of paper. "What's this?"

She points at the names and numbers with her pen. "The first one is the food service I use. The second is the cleaning service, and the third is the staffing service you need to call to find someone who's going to do it all for you once you're ready. Use one and two for now while you're looking for three."

I fold the paper carefully and put it in my jeans pocket. "Thanks, sis. For everything."

Scarlet regards me with a tilt of her head. "Like we were going to let you do this alone. You've taken care of us all for years, Max. It's our turn to take care of you." She rests her hand over the top of mine for a minute, then moves my hand to her baby bump and pushes down.

My niece kicks me. Hard. And it blows my mind a little.

"You're the glue that holds us together, Maximus. You always will be. But it's your turn to be happy. And don't try to tell me you have been because content and happy, *truly happy,* are two completely different things." She watches Cade squat down to talk with Brynlee and Madeline, and a serene smile plays over my sister's lips.

"I guess they are."

She takes a deep, soothing breath, then holds me with her eyes. "What are you going to do about it, Max?"

"I'm working on it, Scar." Getting out of the shadow of Dad has been the first step. Finding my footing with the Revolution and building the foundation for them to be an even greater team than the Kings is another. But getting out of his house has been the most freeing. I guess it's the real start to finally working on my own life instead of worrying about everyone else's.

And I think I'd like to explore this thing with Daphne.

I have this sense the two of us could make each other happy.

Brynlee runs to us, holding her hands behind her back. "Daddy says to give you this." She hands Scarlet a dandelion she must have picked from the backyard, then runs off with Madeline.

Scarlet watches wistfully, then turns back to me, holding the weed in her hand as if it were the most precious gift she'd ever been given. "Happy, Max. You've gotta try it. It's pretty amazing."

DAPHNE

"Carys." My best friend sits cross-legged on the bed, completely lost in whatever she's looking at on her phone.

She pops her head up, clearly distracted.

"Come on. You're supposed to be helping me pick something to wear to Max's tonight." I stomp out of my closet in my bra and panties and snatch her phone away. "What are you looking at, anyway?"

It only takes a second before I feel like an ass when I see the screen, immediately understanding why she's ignoring me. An up-close selfie of her and her ex fills the screen. She's looking right into the camera, but he only has eyes for her. She's been in love with him for a long time, and while I've learned to keep my mouth shut on why they broke up, I still think I've been a shitty friend.

I sit next to her on the bed and give her phone back to her. "Have you heard from him?"

"No." A sad smile stares back at me. "Not since he left." She throws herself back against my mattress. "I really screwed it up this time, D. I pushed him away because I thought it was the right thing to do. Now . . . I'm not so sure."

I lay down next to her and link my pinky with hers. "He loves you, Care Bear. You need to talk to him," I say, her childhood nickname slipping from my lips. "Have you called him?"

A fractured breath escapes from her as her voice cracks. "He didn't answer." She rolls to her side, facing me and shoves her hands under her face. "I don't know if he's going to call back this time. I think we're really done. I know that's what I thought I wanted, but maybe . . . Maybe I was wrong."

I've got to tread carefully here because I told you so's aren't what she needs right now. Instead, I roll over, mirroring her. "He'll call back. Just give him time."

"Maybe." She closes her green eyes, then smacks her hands against the duvet and wipes at her face. When she opens her eyes, they skim over me in horror. "*What* are you wearing?"

I shove her away. "Like you haven't seen me in my underwear before."

"Just because I've seen you naked doesn't mean I want to see you in granny panties." Carys rolls off the bed, then pulls me up too. "Please tell me you aren't considering wearing those panties or that bra to get naked in front of Max freaking Kingston. I mean, come on . . . That man looks like a Greek god. You need to up your game, D." She bends down and picks up a small bag from the floor and shoves them into my hands. "Go try these on, then let me see."

"Carys . . ." I peek inside the bag and finger the delicate blue lace. "These are stunning." Carys and Chloe have been quietly working together on an upscale lingerie line for the past two years, and I've been the beneficiary of quite a few of their original pieces, but none have been as lavish as this set.

I step into my bathroom and slip into the sheer, crystal-blue demi-cup bra and matching French cut panties. They're trimmed in a slightly darker blue silk with a small bow between my breasts and at my hips. And they feel luxurious against my skin. Plus, they look great against my late summer tan. Sometimes, I long to be as naturally thin as my best friend. I wish I was as delicate and petite. But wearing these, I want to celebrate my curves instead of envying someone else's.

"I want to see them on you, D," she hollers from the other side of the bathroom door.

The two of us have been changing in front of each other for years. This isn't new. So I don't even hesitate to walk back into my bedroom nearly naked.

"Damn . . ." Carys walks a circle around me, adjusting the straps of the bra and tightening the tiny silk ties at my hips. "Perfect." She takes a step back and smiles to herself. "Now let's find something that he can rip off of you without messing up what's underneath." She holds me with a glare and a finger pointed at my face. "Do not let him take your panties off before he takes off your dress. I want this man to see you just like this."

I laugh at her. "See me or see the lingerie?"

She tilts her head and thinks about it. "Both. The lingerie is perfect, but you're spectacular. Now, let's find you something to put on over it."

My anticipation has been building all day, and with it, so has my anxiety.

Max has said one thing, but his actions and words painted a very different picture last night. I'm not sure which Max I'll get tonight, and the harder I think about it, the less sure I am of which one I want more. Mutually beneficial sounded great last weekend. Less stress. Less chance of heartbreak.

But more . . . Is he worth the risk?

And can I survive the inevitable fall?

When your best friend is a designer, it's easier to willingly hand over control of what you're wearing to her because she's going to take over anyway.

Carys picks a black-eyelet sundress with thick straps that's fitted to the waist before it flares out around my knees, along with a pair of hot-pink strappy sandals. My white pedicure pops against them.

I spin around and check myself out in the mirror. "Not too bad."

She smacks my ass. "Not too bad . . . Please. That man is going to be eating *you* instead of dinner. I'm calling it now."

I raise my brows and swallow my laugh. "Yeah. He's good at that."

Her eyes widen in surprise. "You like him, don't you?"

I spritz a little body spray in front of myself, then walk through it, playing down the question. "It's not like that." But even I don't believe my own words.

"You can lie to yourself all you want, D. But I know you. You like him." Her eyes strip away any smart comeback I may have had, waiting for the truth.

Even if I'm not ready to give it just yet.

"I could like him . . . if I let myself. But I don't know if I'm ready to let myself. And I don't think he knows what he's looking for either. So why push it? This summer has sucked, and I want to have a little fun. Let me have my fun, Care Bear." I tug at her arm, hoping she'll drop it.

Praying she won't start pushing me more about my dad.

Losing myself in work, I can handle.

Having fun with Max is a no-brainer.

But I'm not prepared to deal with the fallout of my relationship with my father just yet.

"Fine. But Max Kingston's a keeper, D. You forget I've known him for years. I've seen him with his sisters. I've seen him with my family. I've watched the way he treats people. He's not some boy you fuck around with. He's a man you fall in love with. And I don't want to see you get hurt like me. At least, don't be the cause of your own hurt, like I am." She grabs her cell from my bed and shoves it in the pocket of her jean shorts. "You look beautiful. Go. Have fun." She hugs me, then pulls away. "And for fuck's sake, call me tomorrow and tell me all about it."

Carys turns and walks out of my room before I call after her. "Love you, C."

Max Kingston is all man, and for as long as we're doing this thing, he's all mine.

Those are the only promises I'll make.

Luka pulls up to the house not long after Carys leaves, and I force myself to not think about what I did in the backseat the last time this man drove me somewhere. My face flames, thinking about what he must have seen. Once I'm tucked safely in the car, I think he expected a quiet ride to Max's new house, but I've never done especially well with quiet. "So Luka, how long have you been working for Max?"

His dark eyes meet mine through the rearview. "Three years."

"So, you're his bodyguard? Like Kevin Costner?" Smooth, D. Real smooth. And this is why no one will ever accuse me of being cool.

"Something like that." He doesn't look up, but I catch his smirk in the mirror.

"My father never had a bodyguard. He said it was too intrusive. He was happy with the security team at the arena." I never really thought much of it before now.

Luka gives in and turns the music down a touch. "Then your father was taking unnecessary risks. No one gets to the level he was without drawing attention, and not all attention is good. I don't have to be intrusive to be effective."

"I'm sorry. I didn't mean—"

"No need to apologize." He turns the music back up, effectively ending the conversation. And I sit with my hands clasped in my lap, trying to figure out how to remove the foot that's firmly planted in my mouth.

The drive takes less than ten minutes and passes quietly with songs from *The White Album* by The Beatles playing softly in the background. The man has great taste in music.

As we pull down Max's winding driveway, I have another chance to really study the exterior of the house. I like that it's older. It's got character. It's not a cookie-cutter mansion in an over-priced neighborhood. It reminds me of an old English estate.

Regal.

Perfect for Max Kingston.

Once the car stops, Luka opens my door and offers me his hand. He already has my leather overnight bag grasped in his other hand. "Have a lovely evening, Ms. Brenner."

Before I can even consider where Luka is going, Max is at my side, and *oh my*, he's delicious. Old, well-worn jeans hang perfectly from his hips. They're frayed at the knee from time, not style, and the hem lightly brushes the stones beneath our feet.

Oh my goodness. Beneath his bare feet.

Why are men incrementally hotter when they're barefoot in jeans?

What is it about that look? A soft-looking deep-blue t-shirt, the color of his eyes, stretches across his chest and arms. If suit-and-tie Max is hot, relaxed Max is a five-alarm fire. "Thanks, Luka. We won't be going anywhere tonight." He takes my bag from Luka, then presses his hand to my back and lowers his voice. "You look fucking incredible."

A chill runs down my spine with his unspoken promise.

He guides me through the open door, drops my bag at his feet as he closes it, then cages me in against it with his strong arms. One hand is above me, flat against the door, the other grips my hip as his lips crash down on mine.

I open for him on a gasp, and his tongue invades roughly.

I welcome it. Relish in it.

Needing more. Wanting him.

When Max pulls away, he runs his hand over my hair, tugging gently. "I've been thinking about doing that since I left you last night."

"Just that?" I swear, I don't know where I get the confidence I have when I'm with this man.

His pupils darken, and there's no mistaking the desire in his eyes. "No. Not just that. But I'm going to feed you before I fuck you, siren."

Oh, yes please . . .

MAX

Iᴛ's ᴏɴᴇ ᴏғ ᴛʜᴏsᴇ ʟᴀᴛᴇ Aᴜɢᴜsᴛ ɴɪɢʜᴛs ᴡʜᴇʀᴇ ᴛʜᴇ ᴡᴀʀᴍᴛʜ of the sun still warms your skin long after it dips down behind the trees. Daphne and I ate outside on the blue stone patio. The vaulted roof, and sheer white curtains blowing in the breeze give an extra air of privacy to the space, and with that, an extra layer of comfort to the evening. A bottle of wine and a plate of cupcakes sit between us, thanks in part, to my sisters.

Getting rid of the family earlier was difficult enough.

Making sure they were gone in time for me to have this gorgeous woman to myself, without giving them any hint I had other plans, was what I imagine a negotiator's wet dreams are made of. Kind of appropriate because this woman has been giving me wet dreams for weeks.

Daphne kicks her shoes off and places her feet next to my legs on my chair as she sips her wine. And I just watch her. Liking that she's comfortable in my space. Reveling in the realization that I like her in my home. "Why Start A Revolution?"

She flutters her inky-black lashes and eyes me over her wine glass. "What do you mean?"

"You're young, and intelligent, not to mention beautiful and wealthy with a degree from a top-tier university. Why start the foundation instead of taking over the team? Why not keep the mantle of your grandfather going? I met him with my dad once or twice when I was younger. It was obvious he loved his team the way my dad loved ours." I want to know what makes this woman tick. What pushes her? What makes her happy?

I pull her feet into my lap and run my thumbs along her arch.

She moans, and the sound makes it hard to think.

"I don't remember ever *not* wanting to run the foundation. You know there was one before my grandpa died. My dad shut it down years ago, and it always bothered me. My grandpa was a big believer in giving back to the community that gave so much to him. He took me to volunteer with him when I was little. He'd put on a baseball hat and his old jacket with the little crocodile on the pocket."

She smiles wistfully to herself, lost in the happy memories that thought must bring her. And the urge to make sure her life is filled with happiness hits me hard.

"He'd never give people his last name. We'd work for a few hours in the food bank or the animal shelter. But my favorite was always when we'd go to the Boys and Girls Club. He'd always bring stuff with him, usually sports equipment." She rolls her pretty eyes and runs the tips of her fingers over the top of her glass. "Some of the kids were older than me, some weren't. But they'd all get so excited when he came. They had no idea who he was. They just appreciated his time and generosity. And afterward, he'd always play with them. Throw the football. Hit a baseball. He was really bad at soccer. But he was really good at hockey." She looks off to the side, seemingly lost in her thoughts, and I stare at her, loving this side of Daphne. Appreciating getting this piece of the puzzle that is this woman. "He made a difference, but so did those kids. I'm not sure who enjoyed those days more. Them or him."

"You will too," I tell her. And I mean it. "Start A Revolution is going to make a difference in a lot of kids' lives." And she's going to be the heart of it.

She might even end up owning mine in the process.

Funny thing is that doesn't scare me.

Daphne's cheeks flush, and she places her empty glass on the table. "Tell me something about yourself." I dig my knuckle into the arch of her foot and enjoy the responding moan. "Something I can't find out from *Philly Magazine* or some internet article."

"Been reading up on me again?" The soft breeze catches her long hair, and her delicious scent wraps around us.

She slowly shakes her head from side to side. "Nope. Why read what other people have to say when I can get it straight from the source. My friend Carys says you're a good man. Are you? Or do you have everyone fooled?"

"Carys Murphy?" I rub my thumbs against the pad of her foot. "Yeah, I was surprised to see you with her at Kingdom. I didn't realize you two know each other."

Daphne hums her approval deep in her throat, and my cock jumps behind the zipper of my jeans.

"She's been my best friend for years. And she likes you. Now, stop evading." Her other foot gently presses against my cock as her lips tip up, daring me to ignore her.

I run my hands up her legs, kneading her smooth skin. "I guess that depends on who you ask. My family would probably say I'm a good man. I don't know if anybody else would, and I frankly don't give a fuck what they think anyway. They all think I'm happy to walk in my father's shadow. To sit back and watch the company do well. And I guess a lot of people would be content with that. But I want more. I want to make my own mark on the world. I'd been actively searching for what that was going to look like when your father approached me about buying the Revolution. I'd never considered expanding into hockey, but once I started thinking about it, I realized this was exactly what I wanted to do. I've already been given an empire. Now I want to make my own legacy. I want the Revolution to be the greatest team in the league. Not just the best, but the greatest."

She tilts her head and examines me. "What do you mean?"

"I want people to love coming to work. I want them to feel like they're appreciated. I want them to know they all matter. I want my players to know we respect their skill and their health. That their value is not just how many goals they score or shots they take. Your grandfather taught you the importance of giving back. My father taught me the importance of valuing every single person within your organization. It's the only way to win. And I don't lose."

She swirls her finger through the vanilla icing on the cupcake in front of her, then sucks it seductively. Then she asks coyly, "And what about me, Max? Do I get to be let in? Or am I just something to be won before you move on?"

I lean over the table and slide my finger through the icing, then hold it up to her lips. Daphne runs her tongue around the tip and sucks it into her mouth, pulling on an invisible string that's already on the verge of snapping. "You're already in, Daphne. You're in further than I've ever let anyone before. And I'm not sure if I'm going to be able to move on."

Innocent eyes flash back at me. "Thanks for letting me in."

As if I had a choice.

She's like water.

A force of nature slipping past even the strongest barriers and wearing down your walls without you even realizing it's happening.

She stands from her chair, her pale blue eyes holding mine hostage. "Do you know your confidence is contagious?"

I wait to see what she's going to do next, but she just stands before me, waiting for an answer. "No. No one's ever told me that before."

"It is. I feel more confident when I'm with you." She leans over me, hands braced on the arms of my chair, and her blonde hair is a curtain around her face. "When I'm with you, I feel like I can do whatever I want." Her pale eyebrow arches. "Well . . . anything within reason."

Knowing this beautiful woman feels more confident because of me is a humbling thing. I wasn't expecting it. But the need to make sure she always feels that way is strong and enticing.

I run my hands under her pretty black dress and up the backs of her soft, bare legs. "And what do you want to do?" The fact that she's so willing to take control and take what she wants might be the sexiest thing I've ever seen.

It's her. She's just . . . She's everything.

She lowers herself slowly to her knees in front of me, her eyes locked on mine. "I'm going to take what I want." She unbuttons my jeans, taking my cock in her hand and never taking her eyes from mine as she teasingly licks the head, like an ice cream cone she wants to savor before swallowing me.

I gather her hair in my hand and wrap it around my knuckles.

Can't have anything fuck with the view of the bombshell in front of me.

"I like you like this, siren." Her moan of approval vibrates through my spine. "That pretty fucking mouth on me."

Daphne Brenner is quickly becoming an addiction I don't want to kick.

She looks up at me, then swallows me deeper, adding a hand to encircle my shaft. Her beautiful eyes water, and my entire body tightens.

"You trust me, Daph?"

She nods her head and moans around me.

"Touch yourself, siren. I want you to dip your fingers in your pussy, then rub them around your clit." I pull her hair tighter. "But don't come. Don't touch your clit, Daphne. Circle it. I'll know if you don't."

Her eyes sparkle as she spreads her legs and does as she's told. Her fucking dress is in the way, and I can't see her pussy, but I don't want to stop.

Standing, I take her head in my hands and gently thrust my hips, making sure she can take me. "You okay, beautiful?"

Daphne hums happily around my cock as her hand moves faster.

So I follow her lead and fuck her face.

She takes it. She takes it all. Moaning and working herself harder than before.

And when her entire body starts to move on her hand, I pull back. "Don't come, Daphne."

She rips her hand from her body, then grabs my ass with both hands, taking me all the way into her mouth and swallowing.

The orgasm rips through my body like a raging fucking rapid. I come on a loud fucking groan. And the siren in front of me swallows every last drop.

When I open my eyes, she's on her knees. Legs pressed tightly together. Flushed cheeks and hazy, needy eyes.

Something inside me snaps.

I lift her from her knees, holding her against me as I sweep the contents of the table away. Glass shatters and the bottle of wine tips over, its contents dripping down over the edge of the teakwood table.

When my hands reach under her dress and grab the sides of her panties, she places her palm against my chest. "Stop."

One word.

One of the most powerful words in the English language.

My body trembles as I take a step back and look around. "Fuck. I'm sorry. Did I scare you?"

Daphne laughs. Thank Christ. She laughs, then shakes her head, and I relax.

"Sorry, but I made a promise to my lingerie designer." She reaches around to her back and lowers a hidden zipper, then slips her dress over her head and drops it on a chair. "I need you to get the full effect." She's mouth-watering in sheer, pale-blue lace and silk. Her perfect fucking breasts, heavy and full. And her rose-colored nipples are two hard peaks my mouth aches to taste.

I hesitantly take a step closer, before she places a hand on my chest. "Any notes for the designer?"

"You're fucking perfect." I run a hand down her face as my mouth captures hers. Then, with one hand holding the back of her head, I push her back flat against the table and strip out of my shirt.

Her greedy gaze licks my skin.

But it's my turn to play.

I steal an ice cube from the bucket the wine is sitting in and drag it down her body, tracing her curves. Learning them. Loving them. Memorizing them as if they hold the keys to the kingdom and my life depends on getting in. Leaving a trail of water against her hot skin as I go. I circle her tits, one then the other, trailing lightly over her nipples, eliciting a gasp as they harden even more.

Her belly quivers as I slide the ice down her taut stomach, dipping into her bellybutton before tracing the curves of her flared hips. Her panties match her bra and tie in blue silk bows at her hips I ache to untie. But all in due time.

The fabric covering her sex is soft and sheer.

It's also wet.

Instead of pulling them down her legs, I run what's left of the ice cube over the lips of her pussy through the outside of her panties. My girl's back bows off the table, and she screams out my name. With the ice cube forgotten, I lick the lips of her pussy through the fabric, and Daphne whimpers. So I flatten my tongue and do it again. And again. And again. I eat her through her fucking soaked panties until she's screaming my name, begging me for more. Her knees clamp tight against my head, and her knuckles are turning white from her effort to grip the edge of the table. But the tease is too fun to stop.

The taste of Daphne on my tongue is better than any meal I've ever eaten.

And her cries have me achingly hard again.

"Max, please," she cries out as I spear her clit, then suck it into my mouth, and her entire body shakes with her orgasm as she moans my name.

My name on her lips snaps the last string of control I have left.

Fuck me, I need to hear that again.

I stand and grab a condom from my pocket as I shuck my jeans and boxers. I stare down at Daphne laid out before me, her chest heaving and her hair splayed out around her like a golden halo.

Jesus Christ. She's the most beautiful thing I've ever seen.

Needing her naked more than my next breath, I rip the panties from her hips and drop them to the floor.

"Hey . . ." she protests. "Those are new."

I quickly smack her pussy, and she moans as her body shakes in response. "I'll buy you another pair." Then I fist my cock and drag it through her drenched sex. "Tell me what you want, Daphne."

"You." She reaches her arm up and drags it down my chest. "I want you, Max. Just you."

I push into her throbbing heat in a hard thrust, then pull out and do it again.

Her breasts bounce with every movement.

My hands slide up her body and over her nipples.

Tweaking them. Pinching them. Eliciting every moan I can out of Daphne. Then I drag them down to her waist and grip tightly as I pull her body against mine on each snap of my hips.

She wraps her legs around my waist, her feet digging into my ass and urging me on.

"Yes, Max. God, yes." Her lids flutter shut.

"Eyes on me, siren. Watch me fuck you. Tell me what you need." I move my hands to her back and prop her up so I can take her mouth.

The new angle has her vibrating around me as her pussy clamps down on my cock.

I pick her up off the table and pull her down on me as I thrust up again and again.

Daphne wraps her arms around my neck and kisses me fiercely through her moans.

Her thighs clench around me.

And my balls draw up tight to my body before we both fucking explode in a white-hot heat of ecstasy.

I hold her tightly to me.

Not ready to lose the connection yet.

If ever.

DAPHNE

Max and I managed to christen the table outside, the shower, and I'd say we christened his bed, but technically I think we did that before he bought the house. My face flames, thinking about it. The fluffy white duvet and sheets are gone, replaced with charcoal bedding. A touch of Max in a house that otherwise doesn't hold much of his personality yet.

The beautiful night has given way to a gray Sunday morning. The raindrops play a soothing tune against the glass doors of the balcony at the back of the bedroom and nearly lull me back to sleep. Nearly. But I have to pee. When I turn my head to look at Max, I can't hold back my smile. He's asleep on his stomach, his strong arm wrapped around me. Those gorgeous, unruly blonde locks of his are a full-blown sex mess, and I wouldn't have it any other way. When your man's hair is prettier than yours, it'd be a shame not to wrap it around your fingers and tug. I mean, come on . . . It's just so sexy.

Though, I'm not really sure if I can call Max my man.

But I definitely don't hate the idea.

I slide carefully out from under him and grab his discarded t-shirt from the bench at the bottom of the bed, slipping it over my head before I make my way into the bathroom. After taking care of business, I poke around in the drawers and find a box of toothbrushes, stealing one to brush my teeth and run a comb through my hair. My clothes and toiletries are in my overnight bag, which didn't make it upstairs last night. My phone's in there too.

I decide to let him sleep while I pad lightly down the stairs. My bag still sits at the bottom, where Max left it last night, and I leave it right where it is, just grabbing my phone from the pocket and head for the kitchen and what I'm hoping is a functioning coffee pot. The rain continues its soothing song against the roof, and I silently wonder if I open a window whether it would set off the alarm. I decide against finding out and instead find a beautiful stainless-steel coffee maker. Hmm. Now to find the beans.

I'm waiting for the coffee to stop brewing and scrolling through social media when the doorbell rings. At least I think it's the doorbell. I look around the kitchen like someone's going to open the door, but Max hasn't woken up yet.

Shit.

Am I supposed to answer it?

I decide to wake Max up and let him answer his own door, but by the time I walk back through the house, he's already awake and walking down the last few steps. And thank you, sweet baby Jesus. Because I immediately decide the view I'm treated to is better than office Max or relaxed t-shirt and jeans Max. Ladies and gentlemen, I give you Max Kingston, shirtless, with low-slung gray sweatpants hanging from his hips. Every indent of his six-pack abs is on beautiful display, and I'm very confident it is indeed a six pack. My tongue got up close and personal with every single indent last night. His perfectly chiseled V is like a neon sign, directing my eyes down to his impressive erection, and my mouth waters. I slow my steps as he reaches for me. "You're up?" *Genius, Daphne.* Way to be observant.

His hands circle my waist as his lips close gently over mine.

He tastes like mint and desire.

His blue eyes are focused on me, and damn, it feels like the sun is shining directly on me instead of raining outside.

"I was just coming to find you." He tucks my hair behind my ear, and a shiver travels down my back. "I—"

The doorbell rings again, and Max looks up to the ceiling and closes his eyes for a moment before looking down at me and smoothing his hands over my head. "I'm sorry."

He steps away from me and answers the door before I can ask what he's sorry for.

The door opens, and Max leans against the frame. "I was wondering which one of you it was."

A feminine voice laughs. "Took you long enough, Maximus." She pushes by him and stops when she sees me. Eleanor Kingston is standing across from me in her brother's foyer, and I'm wearing nothing but his shirt.

Guess I just made a stunning first impression.

"Oh." Her eyes grow impossibly wide when she spots me. "I didn't realize you had company." She looks between the two of us before finally settling on me and offering me her hand. "Hi, I'm Len." When Len looks back at Max again, she bites her bottom lip exaggeratedly and laughs. "Looks like you didn't waste any time, Maximus."

Max runs his hand over his face, and I bristle at the comment. "Excuse me?" Nothing like getting offended when you're wearing a man's shirt and no panties. Really makes you feel strong and in charge. *Not.*

"Oh my God. I'm so sorry. That did not come out the right way. It's just the whole family has been texting about you." Lenny rushes to fix her faux pas, but that sentence definitely didn't do the trick.

"I'm sorry, what?" I take a step back, but Max moves to my side and wraps his arm around my shoulder.

He eyes his sister warily. "How about you come into the

kitchen, and I'll make us some coffee, Len? Then you can tell me exactly why you're here."

She eyes his hand protectively wrapped around me and smiles. "Sure, Max. I never turn down coffee. Just don't tell Bash. This is my second cup today." She moves toward the kitchen, apparently already knowing exactly where it is.

Max slides his hand down to the small of my back, then further down until he cups my bare bottom. His lips skim over my ear. "Sorry about this. My siblings are a little much."

I duck away from him and pick up my bag. "I'll meet you in the kitchen. I just want to put on a pair of pants." I can't believe this is how I met his sister.

"Leave the shirt on, Daphne. I like you in my clothes." His voice is firm and raspy and does funny things to my insides before he smacks my ass and disappears down the hall.

I grab the black cotton shorts I packed to sleep in, not sure why I thought I'd be sleeping in clothes, but thankful they're in here, and slide them up my legs. I tuck the front of the t-shirt in the front of the shorts, so that you can see I'm wearing shorts. Then I lift the shirt to my nose and inhale. Fresh and clean with a hint of something deep and rich, it's utterly Max, and I don't think he's getting this shirt back when I leave today. I throw my hair up in a ponytail and adjust the shirt so it's not slipping off my shoulder.

Once I decide this is as good as it's getting, I place my bag on the bottom step and join the brother/sister duo in the kitchen.

Wondering exactly what they know about me.

And what they think of it.

Then I ask myself if I care. But I already know the answer. This man's family means the world to him. If I want to consider being *more* with Max Kingston, his siblings are part of the deal. So, I hold my head high, throw my shoulders back, and decide it's time to win over the first one.

MAX

I FOLLOW LEN INTO THE KITCHEN, TRYING TO REMEMBER A time I've been more pissed at her. "What the fuck was that, Eleanor?"

She's already poured herself a cup of coffee and hands it to me. "That was me in shock, Maximus. I don't remember the last time you brought a girl around the family." The little brat taps her finger to her lips and thinks about it for a moment, then holds the damn finger in the air, as if to say *a-ha!* "Oh, that's right. You've never brought a girl around the family before."

I put the coffee mug down on the counter and glare at my sister. "I didn't bring her around the family today either. You walked into my house."

"Yup. I need a key, by the way." She purses her lips and pours another cup of coffee for herself, then sits down on one of the stools at the island. "She's really pretty, Max."

"She's fucking beautiful, Len." I lean back against the counter and watch my sister smell her coffee but not drink it.

"You say 'fuck' too much, big brother."

"Yeah well, you drink too much coffee for a pregnant woman, little sister."

Len lifts her coffee mug high into the air and tilts her head slightly. "Touché. I'm just smelling it this time."

"You are so weird, Len."

A throat clears behind us as Daphne enters the room. She

picks up a mug that had been sitting on the table in the built-in breakfast nook, then tops it off with fresh coffee and joins the two of us at the island.

And I have to fight the urge to wrap my arm protectively around her.

Reminding myself that's not us.

Not yet.

But I can't help but think maybe it should be. Last night didn't just change us. It changed everything.

Having her here.

Having her next to me.

Having her meet my family.

It just *feels* right.

Lenny's entire face lights up as her gaze skips between Daphne and me. "So, Daphne . . . You and my brother?"

I expect Daphne to blanch at the teasing in Len's voice.

But what I'm learning is the only thing I should expect from Daphne is she never does what I expect her to do.

"So, Len. Sebastian Beneventi? Did you know when we were little, he used to behead my Barbies?" She sits back and sips her coffee as my sister cackles. Actually fucking cackles in response.

"Oh my God, no. Tell me more. How did I not know you know Bash?" Lenny leans toward Daphne, and I think she'd shove me out of the way completely if she could.

Daphne's legs brush mine as she swivels her chair toward my sister, and I give in and lay my palm possessively on her thigh. Happy she's getting along with my sister but selfishly wanting to have her undivided attention on me, if only Lenny would leave.

"The Murphys' house was always the hangout house, and Carys has been my best friend since elementary school. Bash and I both spent our summers practically living there when we were little. Mrs. Murphy made the best pancakes, and Aiden always helped her. That gave Bash time to torture Carys and me. My Barbies usually paid the price." She shrugs like it's no big deal, but I'm pretty sure sharing that with my sister somehow won her a friend for life.

Women are fucking crazy.

"I can't wait to torture him with that later. I'll bet you've got way more dirt than that." Len smirks my way. "The little sisters have all the good stories."

"Well, I'm just a little sister by proxy, but Aiden, Bash, and Brady Ryan were always up to something. Carys and I were two years younger, so we never ran in the same crowds. Bash was always a good guy. He was the quiet one of those three." She squeezes my hand between her legs, and damn, what I wouldn't give to be touching her bare skin.

"You know, Bash was insistent that Carys sing at our wedding. He said he'd get chills when she'd sing the National Anthem at their games. She's singing the song we're going to dance our first dance to." Lenny grabs my arm excitedly. "That's why I'm here, Maximus. I have a favor to ask you."

"What is it, Len?"

Lenny's lower lip trembles. "I know we're doing the whole wedding a little smaller than you wanted, and I appreciate you not making it a big Kingston debacle. But I have one more request." Her eyes water, and I have no idea what just happened.

"Hey, hey . . ." I pull my hand from Daphne and wrap Lenny in my arms. "What happened? Who do I need to kill?" And God, if only I were joking. I swear, I'd do anything for my little sister.

She rests her head against my chest and wraps her arms around my back. "Will you walk me down the aisle?"

"I don't know, kid. That means I have to give you away,

and I don't know if I can do that. Bash is a good guy, and he loves you, but I don't know if I can give you to him." I wish I was kidding. It doesn't matter that she's a grown woman. She'll always be that tiny, little girl with pigtails who used to chase me around the house and would only jump in the pool if I was holding her hand. And it's always felt so damn good being the man she looked up to.

"Max . . . Please." She exhales, making a sound somewhere between a sob and a laugh. "It's got to be you."

"Anything, Len. I'll do anything you ask. You know that." I kiss the top of her head.

"Stupid hormones." She wipes her nose and stands up, pushing away from me. "I swear, I cried at a Hallmark commercial last night. I don't know how bad it's going to be by the time I'm ready to have this kid." She takes her coffee cup and shuffles to the sink, then turns around and stares at Daphne. "I'm sorry for interrupting your morning. Although, if you're going to be with him, you might want to get used to it. The entire family has a key to my house, and at least one person uses it every week."

"Oh, well . . ." Daphne stutters, and I'm curious what she stopped herself from saying. "It was really nice meeting you, Lenny. Please tell Bash I said, 'Congratulations.'"

"You should come to the wedding. Maybe you could force this one to dance a little."

And thank you so fucking much for that, little sister. Because every grown man wants his sister to invite a woman to attend a wedding as *his* date. I've been so focused on other things, the thought of inviting Daphne never even crossed my mind. And by the look on her beautiful face, it's easy to see how badly I fucked up.

"Oh. Thank you, but I couldn't. I appreciate it though. You know, I think I hear my phone ringing. I'll just . . . I'll see you later." Daphne practically trips over herself to get out of the room, and the look I give Lenny is glacial.

"Eleanor . . ."

"I like her, Maximus." She kisses me on the cheek, then flicks my ear. Brat. "Don't fuck it up."

Pretty sure she just fucked it up for me.

DAPHNE

IF I THOUGHT MEETING MAX'S SISTER WITHOUT MY PANTIES was bad, being invited to her wedding as Max's date was worse. He knew it. I knew it. The only one who didn't realize it was Lenny. Although I'm pretty sure my quick escape made that obvious. But a girl has to guard her heart around that man and his all too welcoming family members. Well, member—singular. Who knows how the rest of them would react to me?

And damn my heart for caring.

But how am I supposed to guard it from him when he's all . . . well, him? He's bossy, and arrogant, and demanding. But damn, if it's not incredibly sexy. And totally Max. But the way I feel when I'm with him . . . it's more. It's . . . I feel cherished. And I'm not sure he even realizes it.

On that note, I decide it's time to go while I still have my dignity intact.

I grab my bag from the bottom of the steps and take it up to Max's bedroom. It only takes a minute to gather my things from last night and stuff them inside. Once that's done, I pull up the Uber app on my phone and request a car. Thank God, I'll only have to wait seven minutes for it to arrive. Just as I shoulder my bag, the bedroom door opens behind me.

"Daphne . . ." His voice holds an authoritative demand that I both bristle at and want to submit to all at once.

Instead, I tell myself to be strong. No feelings. This is supposed to be fun.

"Hey." I cross the room and lift up to my toes to kiss the stubble on his chiseled cheek. "My Uber should be here in a minute. I had a lot of fun last night." I brush by him in my attempt to escape, but Max wraps his fingers around my arm.

"Slow down." He backs me against the wall and pushes my bag from my shoulder to the floor. "Why are you running away?" His dark-blue eyes search mine for an answer he's not getting.

My hands rest on his hips, and my fingers curl into his sweats. The pull to him is so damn strong, but I hold my ground. "I've got a ton to do for the foundation today. Throwing together the event of the year in less than a month isn't as easy as I make it appear." I brush my lips gently over his. "I'll see you in the office tomorrow." I duck under the arm caging me in and grab my bag.

"Daphne." Our eyes meet, and I wish he'd just let me leave with a little bit of my dignity still intact. "At least let me drive you home."

I force a smile. "Don't worry about it. My Uber should be here in . . ." I look at my phone, "less than a minute. Bye, Max."

He doesn't try to stop me this time, and as I walk down the grand staircase, I don't miss the sound of something hitting the wall in his room. I think it's his fist.

He made the rules.

We both agreed to them.

Now, we just need to stick to them.

It's the only way this can work.

I'm greeted by raised voices when I walk through the front door of Dixon's house. Maddie and Dixon are always yelling.

It's still kinda foreign to me. My dad never yelled. If he was mad at you, he ignored you. If he didn't like something, he removed it from our lives. It was a cold way to handle problems, but in a way, it's what he's done this time too. He removed himself from the problem . . . and from me.

I close the door behind me, hoping I'll be able to sneak upstairs unnoticed.

But no such luck.

Both Dixon siblings turn their heads simultaneously to see who's here. Then they talk over each other in a mad rush to enlist me to their side in whatever fight this is. I raise my hand in the air like a crossing guard telling the kids to stop or get hit by a bus. My head is throbbing like I'm the one who's already been run over by the damn bus today, and I'm not in the mood for that fucker to throw it in reverse and do it again.

Dix stops speaking, but Maddie jumps at the chance to be heard.

"You're not going to believe what this controlling blowhard is trying to do." Her face is bright red as her hands move every which way while she's talking.

"Madison." I stop her. "I'm right here, and I have a headache. Can you please stop yelling?"

She drops her head. "Sorry. I'm trying to explain to my brother dearest he doesn't have a say in who I go out with." Then she spins almost violently to her brother before he can say whatever word is about to come out of his mouth. "It's not even a real date, Brandon. Watkins didn't want to go to the wedding alone and asked if I'd go with him. I seriously don't see what's the big darn deal."

"What wedding?" What's with all the wedding talk today?

Dixon sits on the arm of the couch and crosses his massive arms over his chest. His basketball shorts hang loosely over his legs, and one of those sleeveless tanks with arm holes hanging open to his waist showcases every muscle on his side.

Why can't I just be attracted to him?

It'd be so much easier.

He eyes his sister, frustration evident in his tight features. Dix takes being overprotective to an extreme. "Sebastian Beneventi is marrying—"

"Eleanor Kingston," I cut him off. It's like this damn wedding is determined to follow me around.

"Yeah," he agrees. "They're keeping it small. But Bash has known Watkins since they played together at Kroydon, so he's invited."

Maddie shoves her brother's shoulder, but he doesn't move. "Yup. And Watty invited me. What's the big friggin' deal? You're going to be there."

I drop my bag on the floor and try to hide my growing need to never hear about this damn wedding again. "Why are you going to be there?"

"Because Carys invited him," Mads announces it like she's trumpeting the birth of a new royal.

Oh, Carys. Of all the people to use to get over someone . . .

"As a friend, you little shit." Dixon's words lack real anger, but the annoyance is there, loud and clear. "She didn't want to go alone."

Maddie straightens her spine. "Well, neither did Watkins. What's the difference?"

"Carys doesn't want to fuck me." He stands and marches across the room, flexing his hands like he's looking for a fight. I think I'm a little worried about Watkins tomorrow. "So help me, Maddie. Don't do this."

For a hot minute, I think Mads is going to give in. But I couldn't be more wrong. She stomps to the bottom of the stairs, then turns around and stares her brother down. "Watch me."

And that's exactly what Dixon and I do as she storms up the stairs and slams her bedroom door. Apparently, I'm not the only one whose morning has been ruined by this wedding.

Needing to keep my brain occupied with something other than Max Kingston, I spent the rest of the day working on Start A Revolution. I've managed to narrow down our focus to local after-school children's programs. Some kids need programs like these because their parents have to work, while others need them because their parents just don't care. And it's either this or hanging on a street corner where trouble will, no doubt, find them.

Maddie and Dixon both retreated to their corners earlier and have left me alone. But the weight of the day has worn on me. Apparently, a night spent in Max's arms and a morning spent dealing with conflict and stress turns me into an old lady because I'm pretty sure in some states, it's time for the blue-haired, early bird special diners to be coming out, and I'm considering crawling into bed and closing my eyes when my phone vibrates next to me with an unknown number flashing across the screen.

I slide my finger across the screen and hit the speaker button. "Hello?"

"Daphne . . ." My entire being shudders at the sound of my father's voice.

"Daddy?" My voice cracks, thick with emotion. "Is that really you? Oh my God, where are you? What happened?" I have so much to say I'm practically tripping over my words. My emotions run wild, and I vacillate between tears of happiness that he's okay and fury, now that I finally have the chance to confront him and his shitty actions.

"It's me, honey." The connection is shaky, similar to the random calls I've been getting.

"Have you been calling me and hanging up? Has it been you?" Not sure that it matters, but I still want to know.

His voice is breaking up through the line. "Need you to do something for me . . ."

"What? Dad, I can barely hear you. What's happening? Where are you?"

The static hurts my ears and my soul. This is my chance to get answers. To convince him to come home, and I can't hear him.

"Daph, I need a favor. Do you still have your mother's wedding rings?"

Indignation lights up my body. "Of course, I still have Mom's rings. Why wouldn't I? I'm not the one who sells pieces of our family." I regret the words the minute they leave my lips. "I'm sorry, Dad. Just tell me where you are and how we can fix this."

"We can't fix it . . ." More static cuts him off. ". . . need to sell them and wire me the money." I couldn't possibly have heard him correctly. Could I?

"Wait . . . what? What do you need me to sell, Dad?" No . . . please. Just no. "And before you answer and break my heart, do you even want to ask how I'm doing? How I'm handling a life with absolutely no family here to support me? Or how I'm dealing with my father abandoning me? And that's after he sold my home and did God knows what with all my belongings." The anger starts as a small flame in the pit of my stomach, but each word fans it higher until my entire body is on the verge of bursting into a flaming fucking inferno.

"Daphne—"

"Don't," I stop him. My tentative fury transforming to full-blown rage. "Don't 'Daphne' me. You even closed my trust fund, Dad. You *stole* it." I don't realize I'm crying until my tears trail down over my lips. "I would have given you every penny, but you took it," my voice grows louder, "from me," until I'm finally shrieking on a sob. "Your only daughter. And now you want me to sell Mom's wedding rings?"

He doesn't speak. Doesn't answer. It doesn't sound like he even breathes.

"Well? What do you want to say now?" A knock on my door is followed by it cracking open and Maddie's head peeking through. She waits for me to tell her what to do, and with a nod of my head, my watery eyes silently plead for her help.

She sits down on the floor next to me and laces our fingers together.

My father takes an audible breath. "That's exactly why I called you, Daphne. I took care of you your entire life, and I need your help now. Those rings are a family heirloom worth millions. I need you to do this for me."

"I'm not selling the rings. They're worth more than money to me. They're practically the only thing of Mom's you left me."

"I'm sorry, Daphne. Is that what you want to hear? Is that what it'll take to get you to do what you're told?" His raised voice comes through the line crystal clear, making me want to throw my phone.

I try to take a calming breath, but calm is out of the question. "I'm doing okay, by the way. I'm working on making the foundation a reality. And my friends are making sure I have a place to live and people to depend on. So don't worry about me. But thanks for asking." My lower lip trembles, and I swallow my pride. "I love you. I hope, whatever you're doing, you're safe. But unless you're going to explain everything to me, don't call me again, Dad."

Maddie squeezes my hand between hers, bolstering me with more strength than she realizes.

"I'm sorry, Daphne." His voice is sad but firm. He's not giving in.

"I'm sorry too, Dad." I stare at the unknown number and do one of the most difficult things I hope I ever have to do in my life. I hang up on my father and block his number, removing him from my life the way he taught me to remove all problematic things.

MAX

Bobby O'Doul's office is laid out similarly to mine. But where mine could be called cold, and minimal, O'Doul's is warm and inviting. Pictures of his family fill his shelves. Cards written in crayon are tacked to a special spot behind his desk. His jersey from his playing days is framed and hanging in an opposite corner. And black-and-white photographs cover his walls. They're all close-up moments, captured in time. A puck gliding through the air, making you feel the speed. A stick hitting the ice at just the right angle. The bright silver blade of a skate. I can't quite make out the curling black signature in the corner of each piece, but I think it might say O'Doul.

He's built a life in this office. It reminds me of my dad's office at the Kings Stadium.

I look forward to building that work life here.

I want this team to be a family. And I want to be part of that.

I have time to examine them all Wednesday afternoon while I wait for him to end the call he's on with a friend of mine. Well, as good of a friend as Hunter can be, considering he's one of the top sports agents I know, and he makes it his sole purpose in life to extract as much money out of me as he can for his players and himself. If the fucker didn't make it as a sports agent, he'd have been a hell of a professional poker player.

He's Declan & Sebastian's agent. And we've all done dinner a few times.

But when O'Doul's smile grows just before he hangs up, I think we've finally got a deal. Patrick disconnects the call and slams his hands flat against his desk. "We got him. Hot damn!" He closes his hand into a tight fist that he raises in the air in victory. He and I spent Friday finalizing our plan, and O'Doul started executing it that night. By midday Saturday, we'd secured his number two pick. There wasn't any major movement on Monday, but by the end of yesterday, we'd managed to make two more trades and picked up another free agent. But this call was the key. The hockey gods are smiling on us today. It took a whole lotta luck and our second- and third-round draft picks next year, but we succeeded in getting O'Doul's top pick.

Connor Callahan is coming to the Revolution.

O'Doul reaches into the bottom cabinet behind his desk and pulls out a bottle of bourbon and two glasses. He splashes the bourbon into each glass, then hands me one. "I've got to give it to you, Kingston. You put your money where your mouth is. I think we've got ourselves a team."

I raise my glass to his. "Good." An idea begins to form, a way to keep the positive momentum going. "I'd like to host a team event at my house to kick off the season. These guys don't know me. They don't know what to expect. I'd like to show them what kind of team culture I grew up with and the kind of family I want them to feel like they're a part of."

"Wives and kids too, or just the guys?" O'Doul eyes me warily, like he's not sure what to think.

"Wives and kids. The Revolution is part of the King Corp. family, and that includes everyone."

O'Doul seems satisfied as he sips his bourbon. "When?"

Considering the idea just came to me, I don't *exactly* have a date planned out. "How about the Saturday after preseason practice starts? That gives me a few more weeks to get it together and doesn't interfere with the Start A Revolution event in two weeks."

"Have you found Daphne's replacement yet? She's been pulling double duty for a few weeks now." As much as I wish we had, so I could have her transition to her new position, we've been interviewing for days and haven't seen anyone who she and I both feel could fill her role as my assistant.

"Not yet. But I think we have a few more interviews lined up for tomorrow and Friday."

His shoulders relax as he leans back in his chair. "I can't believe I'm about to say this, but hear me out on this before you say no. My daughter, Quinn, just moved back home from Boston. She finished her first year of law school, came home in May, and told me she doesn't want to be a lawyer anymore." He raises his eyes to the ceiling in apparent frustration, grumbling, "so that's seventy grand I'll never get back," before looking at me. "She has no idea what she wants to do with her life, but she can't sit on her damn ass for the rest of it. She's a hard worker. Incredibly capable. And she's basically run my life and her sister's lives for years. Plus, she knows the organization."

I really fucking hope I'm not going to regret this. "Have her be here tomorrow at nine. I'll talk to her. I can't promise more than that."

"Thanks, Max." Apparently, all it takes to get the old bastard to call me by my first name is to hire his daughter.

I step out of O'Doul's office, having no idea how long that meeting lasted.

Feels like a lifetime.

When I stop by Daphne's desk, she's staring down at the screen of her phone, clearly distracted. I knock my knuckles gently against the corner of the desk to get her attention and watch her mask the look of concern that was there just a moment ago, wanting more than anything to ask her if she's okay.

To find out what's been bothering her for the past few days.

But I don't have that right.

I'm her boss. Nothing more.

So I settle for shop talk instead. "Do you think you could help me plan a season kick-off party at my house?"

"Of course, Mr. Kingston." She bats those damn long lashes at me, and my dick jerks as I picture her doing that spread out beneath me. My sexy bombshell is dressed like a naughty librarian today. Her hair is piled high on top of her head, and a starched, white-tailored shirt is tucked into a curve-hugging black pencil skirt with a bright red belt accentuating her tiny waist and drawing my attention to curves I haven't felt in days, which my fingers ache to touch.

But that can't happen here.

She's been distant since Sunday. But we've been busy, and I'm trying to keep it professional between these walls. "Anything else?"

I plant my hand down on her open notebook and lean in a little too close. "We're back to Mr. Kingston?"

She blinks up at me, a knowing smile dancing across her beautiful face.

But she doesn't respond.

"I'll email you the details. Oh . . . and we need to add a nine a.m. interview for tomorrow. Quinn O'Doul is coming in."

She jots down a note on one of her fluorescent pink sticky notes and adds it to her notebook. "Gotcha, boss."

I walk away, wondering what the hell's gotten into her today.

It's after seven that night when a knock on my open door has me looking up from my computer. I'm not sure what she's still doing in the office.

She usually leaves around five.

"I didn't realize you were still here." We haven't crossed the line here, but I'm tempted to change that as she closes the door behind her.

She glances around my office, her eyes lingering on my closed blinds. "It's just the two of us here now."

My mouth waters as her crisp, citrusy scent hits my nose.

"I was working on organizing your kick-off party. I've lined up the catering, waitstaff, and DJ." She crosses the room toward me and fingers the pearl buttons of her shirt seductively. "I think we should get a face painter too. A lot of these guys have families they'll bring, and you want something to keep the kids occupied, maybe even a bounce house. You have enough room for it." She walks around my desk and leans against it, facing me.

I rest my hands on her hips, looking up at her. She's every fucking fantasy I've ever had come to life. My sexy siren calling me to my destruction, and I'm willingly jumping in.

"I made sure to keep your Friday afternoon free this week, like you asked. You got a hot date?"

My brain tells me we shouldn't be doing this here, in my office. In any office. This isn't smart or thought-out. But my brain's losing the fight as I lick my lips with anticipation, want and need battling for control. I'm close to crossing a line that, until now, I had no intentions of crossing. "Thanks. We're getting together for Sebastian's bachelor party that night."

"The night before the wedding? Cutting it close, aren't you?" She scrapes her fingers along my scalp, and it feels good.

So fucking good.

"Yeah well, everyone has practice and preseason games. Two of his friends play for Baltimore and couldn't make it up before now."

Daphne loosens my tie, then her fingers trace the lines of my chest before her lips brush my ear, and she whispers, "You forget I know his friends better than you do."

My phone vibrates on my desk with Lenny's face flashing across it, and I groan.

Daphne's eyes dart down. "Take the call, Max." She straightens herself, then trails her fingertips along the tattoo on my arm. "I'm heading home. I'll see you tomorrow, boss."

I grip her wrist. "Come home with me."

"I can't." Something in the mask that's just slipped back into place tells me she's lying.

The call goes to voicemail, and I stand to follow her out when my office line rings.

"Daphne . . ." I call after her, but she doesn't turn around.

"See you tomorrow, Max."

I ignore the voice in my head telling me to chase her and answer the damn phone. "Max Kingston."

"Oh, thank God, Max. I need your help." Len's out of breath and sounds frazzled, which is not at all normal for Lenny. But it is three days before her wedding.

"I'm here, Len. What do you need?"

One of us might as well get what we need.

My need just walked out the fucking door.

MAX

"I'm out." Bash throws his cards down on the table on Friday night. He's the last of us gathered in his dining room to fold his hand.

We're all here at Sebastian and Lenny's brownstone in the city, while Len spends the night in her old bedroom at Dad's with her best friend, Juliet. Amelia and Scarlet planned to stay with them for a while before they head home.

Lenny decided Bash wasn't allowed to see her until she walks down the aisle tomorrow. So, she's there, and we're here.

Bash wanted low-key tonight. Poker, top-shelf liquor, and a small group. He's not one to enjoy the spotlight, something we have in common. And with the group gathered here tonight, anywhere we went, we'd have been in the spotlight.

Ten of us are sitting around a mid-century modern dining table, while Bash's dog, Butkus, snores in the corner of the room. An old-school playlist of songs you'd hear at the bar Lenny and Bash met at a few summers ago has been playing all night. I keep catching Bash quietly mouthing the words. It's funny to see and is in direct contrast to the way his best friend, Murphy, sings the entire seven minutes of Billy Joel's "Italian Restaurant," at the top of his lungs. He's gotten more words wrong than right.

It's a good thing his sister is the singer in the family.

Aiden Murphy and Brady Ryan both drove up from Baltimore with their wives, and the three guys fall into old habits right away, reminding me of Jace when he was sixteen. It's funny to watch Bash revert to his inner teenager. He's always so damn serious.

Sawyer reaches out and gathers all the money in the center with an asshole grin plastered on his face. "Thanks, guys. I think you've just paid my rent for the month." Fucker's won the last three hands of Texas Hold'em.

Jace is drunk. He's been chasing beer with shots of whiskey all night. Not my finest parenting moment, but the kid's nineteen, and he lives in the hockey house on his college campus. No way he's not drinking there too. At least here, he's surrounded by us. And as he does another shot, I have a bad feeling about the state he'll be in tomorrow.

When he slams his empty shot glass down on the table and demands another, Becks pushes back from the table. "I call *'not it'* when Jack-off pukes later."

Sawyer, Hudson, and I all simultaneously chime in, "Not it." Guess we all revert back to our younger years when we're together.

Everyone else laughs, but Hud points a finger at Bash. "You're the newest family member. I think it's a rite of passage."

Bash scans the room, trying to gauge how serious we are.

He must not like what he sees. "Dude. I'm the groom. I need my beauty sleep."

Murphy throws his head back and bellows out a deep laugh. "Aww . . . Pretty boy needs his beauty sleep. You're not getting any prettier, man. Might as well hold little Kingston's hair while his head's buried in the toilet."

"How about you do it and tell me all about it tomorrow?" Bash picks up a piece of pepperoni bread and throws it at Murphy's face.

Murphy catches it midair and pops it into his mouth. "No thanks. I'll be going home to my very pregnant, and therefore, very horny, wife tonight. And my head will be buried somewhere way, way better. Where's your girl sleeping again? Oh, that's right. Not in your bed."

"Dude, that's my sister." Hudson's lip curls up in disgust, and Jace gags. I think it's a fake gag, but he's a little green, so I'm not 100 percent sure about that.

Declan jumps to Murphy's defense. "I hate to break it to you, but your sister's three months pregnant. I'm pretty sure they've had sex."

"Kinda like your dad and his mom. Right, Murphy?" Bash ducks his head when the food flies his way. This story circulates whenever you get these guys together. We've all heard about the time Murphy walked in on his mom bent over the table while Coach Sinclair plowed away with his pants around his knees. It was before anyone knew they were together. I can't even fucking fathom how bad that had to be.

Hudson covers his face with his hands. "No talking about my sister and sex. Seriously fucking gross."

"Sister jokes aren't the same without Coop here, anyway." Bash stands from the table and raises his beer in his hand. "To Cooper. The only single one left. Wish he could be here with us tomorrow."

Brady, Murphy, and Declan all raise their glasses, followed by the rest of us.

Cooper Sinclair is Declan's little brother and Brady's wife, Natalie's, twin brother. From what I've heard and seen through the years since his dad started coaching the Kings, he was the fourth musketeer for these three guys. He's a Navy SEAL now. I heard he wouldn't be able to make it to the wedding.

Bash's older brother, Sam, comes into the room with a box of Cuban cigars in his hand. "Anyone care to join me?"

Sebastian points toward the backyard. "Outside, Sam. If Lenny smells that shit in here, she'll have my head."

"Sounds like she's already got you by the balls." Jace smirks, thinking he got a good dig in. Poor drunk bastard.

"She does. You should see what she likes to do to them." Bash sips his beer and watches Jace cringe. Again. I swear, he's fallen on the ice too many times.

Becks grabs a bottle of Johnny Walker Blue, and Sam and I follow him outside. The three of us sit around a blue-flame firepit as cigars are passed around.

I sink into the overstuffed outdoor sectional and kick my feet up on the edge of the firepit. Relaxed. Everything went smoothly today. Lenny's rehearsal took less than thirty minutes, then she kicked us all out. My sisters are having a girl's night while we're here. Pajamas and a movie, they said. A flash of Daphne on the couch last weekend, laughing at *Ghostbusters,* crosses my mind. And for a moment, I wonder what Daphne would think of them if she actually had the opportunity to spend time with them.

What would she think of my big, crazy family?

Somebody always needs something.

We yell too much.

Sarcasm is our love language, and revenge is a Kingston sibling's sacred weapon.

But I never wondered if I'd have someone standing by my side when I needed them. Most of the time, I wish they'd take a few steps back, but I like them there.

I think they'd like her too.

I should have asked her to come with me to the wedding.

And as if the motherfucker read my mind, Becks exhales a perfect circle of smoke from his cigar and kicks my foot with his. "You bringing the assistant tomorrow? Or are you worried she'll trade you in for Jace since she's closer to his age than yours, old man?"

Annoyance burns through my veins.

With him and myself. "No. I didn't ask Daphne."

Sam lifts the bottle of whiskey to his lips, then passes it to Becks. "You with Daphne Brenner, Max?"

"Is she the only Daphne in the city, Sam?" I grab the bottle from Becks and take a drink, then hand it back.

"That's a yes, in case you weren't sure." Beck passes the damn bottle back to Sam. These two were lifelong friends before Sam married our sister Amelia, and right now, they're both pissing me off.

Sam laughs it off. "No, dumbass. But your sisters like to gossip. And you people text each other every time someone takes a shit." The cherry of his cigar burns brightly as he inhales, then leans back against the sectional. "She tell you her father left town? Took the money you guys paid him for the team and fucking ran like a scared little bitch. Didn't pay a single one of his debts."

My brain explodes at his words. "What the fuck are you talking about?" That can't be right. She hasn't said a word. Is this why she's been distant?

Concern tugs at my heart. My girl has been hurting, and she felt like she couldn't share it with me. Because I basically told her she couldn't. That we were just scratching a fucking itch.

Becks steals the bottle back and passes it to me. "Here, Max. You look like you need this."

"Who'd he owe money to? I figured the company was in bad shape, but I hadn't considered he was fucking around in your world." I grab the bottle from Becket and stand to pace the patio. "Is Daphne safe?" I start to spiral, thinking of all the ways this asshole screwed over his own daughter. If Sam knows about this, her father got himself into some bad shit. Our brother-in-law *is* the Philadelphia mafia. He runs the whole damn thing.

And when he merely looks ominously at me in response, I know the answer.

The visceral reaction I have to that look makes me want to kill her father. Not just say it but do it. Self-centered piece of fucking shit. "I'll pay it."

"The fuck—" Becks blows up, but Sam cuts him off.

"She's safe. I don't hurt women who have nothing to do with their father's debts and who happen to work for my wife's family." He snubs out his cigar. "His debt to me is paid, but he's been racking up new debts in New York for a few weeks now. He tried Atlantic City first. The dumb fuck didn't realize I own that town too."

I drop my cigar in the fire, hand Sam the damn bottle, and pull my phone from my pocket to let Luka know I'm ready to go. "Will you guys tell Bash I left?"

"Don't, Max. Don't go to her. If she didn't tell you, she didn't want you to know. And I still say there's a reason for that. She wants something from you, and you're playing into it." Becks turns to Sam. "Come on, man. Back me up."

Sam looks less than eager to agree. "Your girlfriend is a society-climbing bitch, Becket. I don't think you're in any place to be giving relationship advice."

I head for the back gate. "Just tell Bash I'll see him tomorrow." Then I stop and turn back to my brother. "And make sure somebody takes care of Jace. Don't let him fuck anything up for Len." For once in my goddamn life, I'm taking care of my own shit before anyone else's.

DAHNE

WHAT THE HELL? A LOUD NOISE COMING FROM DOWNSTAIRS wakes me up from a good dream. Like really good. My skin still tingles where Dream Max's fingers were branding my skin the way his eyes were searing my soul. And now, I'm awake instead of blissfully lost in a dream where I was about to have my fourth orgasm.

But as my eyes adjust to the darkness and Cinder slinks off the pillow she was hogging, it's like I can still hear his voice.

And after a minute, I realize why.

Those raised voices filtering into my room aren't from a dream.

They're coming from downstairs, and they belong to Dixon and Max.

I throw my blankets off and hurry down the hall, passing Maddie, who pops her head out of her bedroom door. "D . . ." her sleepy voice cracks.

I stop and look back at her, awake but just barely. "What?"

"You don't have on pants." She points at my bare legs.

Oh well. My shirt covers my ass, and both men have seen me in less.

Okay, that sounds bad. But it's not like Dixon's seen me naked.

Oh my God. I'm justifying my own inner thoughts.

I need more sleep.

Max's voice bounces off the walls of the house, but

Dixon's voice is louder. He sounds feral. "She's asleep, like we all were until you started banging on my door at one a.m. I don't give a shit if you're my boss or not. You need to leave. Now."

"I don't care whether I'm your boss either. I'm not leaving till I see Daphne." Max's voice sounds lethal, with a sexy as fuck, authoritative quality to it that sends a chill down my spine. I *almost* wish I didn't like it.

As I pad down the hall, Dixon's big body comes into view in the dim light. He's shirtless, with only dark-gray boxer briefs covering an ass anyone with eyes would want to bounce a quarter off. Guess I'm not the only one who didn't waste time throwing on pants.

A different woman would at least get a tingle in her stomach in the presence of such a beautifully built man with so many hard-earned muscles on full display. But not me. No matter how much I wish it was that easy, it's not Dixon who makes my belly quiver. It's the jackass waking up the whole damn house in the middle of the night. "Dixon . . ."

He turns around to face me, giving me my first chance to get a good look at Max.

His hair is mussed, and his face looks tense. Coiled. Like he's ready to snap.

"Go back to bed, D. I've got it handled." Dixon turns back to Max, thinking that was the final word.

Umm.

I think not.

"I'm not your sister, Dixon, and I like you telling me what to do even less than *she* does." I move next to him with my hands on my hips and catch Maddie out of the corner of my eye, peeking around the stairs.

She pokes her head out and jumps into the argument. "She's right, Brandon."

"Go back to bed, Madison." Dixon's face contorts at the sound of his sister's voice.

My frustration continues to grow by the damn minute. "Dixon, I've got this handled. Thanks."

A smug smile slides into place on Max's chiseled face. "You heard the lady."

"Oh, he's not the only one I'm mad at, Max Kingston. I wouldn't start getting cocky just yet." I move my pissed-off glare between the two men until Dixon relents and takes a step back.

He runs his hand gently down my arm, and I swear to God, Max growls.

Actually fucking growls.

But Dixon ignores him. "Fine. Just yell if you need me."

"Thank you, but I've got this." I watch him walk down the hallway, then add, "And take Maddie with you," before I take a step away from the door and finally let Max into the house. "What are you doing here, Max? It's the middle of the night."

"You walk around without pants on in front of your roommate often?" His eyes focus on where the hem of my shirt hits the top of my thighs as he takes a step toward me.

I push back against his chest with my hand, halting him. "You don't get to ask me questions like that in the middle of the night. Not when I was woken up by two men arguing, one of whom is you. Sorry if I didn't stop to think about pants. I wanted to find out what the hell was going on."

His body deflates, and he cups my face in his big hands. "You're wearing my shirt."

His anger may have subsided, but mine hasn't, so I choose not to tell him it's become my favorite shirt to sleep in.

But I stop thinking about it completely when his lips crash down over mine. Teeth clashing, tongues tangling. Both of us fighting for control that slips further away by the moment. He tastes like cigars and liquor, and it's a heady combination. Fanning the flames of the fire growing between us until they're licking up my legs.

I wrap my arms desperately around his neck, my anger momentarily forgotten.

Clinging to him until his hands slide down over my ass and lift me in the air.

I swear it's like this every single time I'm with him.

My legs wrap around him, and my pussy aches with need as I'm slammed back against the door. His erection grows thick against the seam of my silk panties, and I grind down against it, desperate for relief.

Begging to get closer.

"Jesus, Daphne . . . I want you so fucking bad."

His words are like a bucket of ice water thrown over us. Dousing every last flame.

I force my head away from his and push back at his chest. "Max, stop."

He pulls his face away, and his deep-blue eyes dart between mine. "What is it? What's wrong? Did I hurt you?" His words are rushed, his voice hoarse and raspy. He sounds like a man on the verge of losing his tightly held control.

I don't think that happens to Max often.

Still pinned against the wall, I stare into his eyes. "Why are you here? What's changed?"

"Changed?" He grips my wrist and brings it to his lips. "What are you talking about?"

"Last week, you didn't want to touch me in another man's house. But tonight, you show up in the middle of the night, ready to rip my panties off in the hall. What's gotten into you?" I drop my legs down, but Max doesn't release his hold of me.

I wish I didn't like it, didn't crave his touch.

Wasn't desperate to take him to my room and not let him

leave until we both come so many times, we lose count. But my pride refuses to let that happen.

He studies my face, and I force myself to stay strong under his penetrating gaze.

"Come to my sister's wedding with me tomorrow. I should have asked you before tonight. I don't know why I didn't."

Are you fucking kidding me?

I shove him back with more force this time and wiggle for him to put me down until my feet are flat on the ground. "No." There's no hiding my barely controlled anger kicking back up to the surface.

"What?" He squints his eyes as if he's confused by my answer.

I push him back with both hands. "You heard me. You didn't want me at your sister's wedding, so you didn't invite me. I can respect that. You aren't my boyfriend, Max. You made the rules, and we both agreed to them. You don't owe me an invitation to a family function, let alone something as personal as your sister's wedding. I'd have been fine with that."

I step to the side and grasp the doorknob, needing to get him out of here before the anger coursing through me turns into hurt. Anger is good. I can hide behind a mask of anger. "But you don't get to show up here in the middle of the night, practically coming to blows with my friend whose house I'm living in, and invite me now because you suddenly feel bad and decided, *'What the hell.'* I'm not a charity case. I'm not a second choice, and I'm not your girlfriend. I think you need to leave."

"Of course, you're not a fucking charity case, Daphne. I want you there." He tips my chin up to force my eyes to his. "What if I said I want you to be so much more than my girlfriend?"

"I'd say you need to be sure that's what you want, then try telling me when I can't taste the whiskey on your breath because I deserve better than that. You are an incredibly easy man to fall for, Max Kingston. But my heart can't afford to be broken again." I turn around and open the front door. "Talk to me when you figure it out. Until then, I'll see you in the office Monday morning."

We stare at each other for a few moments before he moves through the door, then turns and runs his hand over my hair. "Daphne . . ."

"No, Max. You told me last week you don't want to play games. But honestly, it feels like you're playing with me, and I don't appreciate it. Figure out what you want."

He leans in to kiss me goodbye, but I turn my head at the last second.

Watching Max walk to his car feels permanent. Like something is ending. And I hate it.

Once I confirm Luka is in the driver's seat, I close the door and slide my butt down to the floor.

Dammit.

"D?" Mads comes around the corner of the stairs, having obviously not gone back to bed. She sinks down to the floor next to me. "What happened?"

"I think I hate him, Mads." I lean my head on her shoulder.

She wraps her arm around me. "Really?"

"No." I wipe the tears away. "But it's easier than admitting I'm falling in love with him."

MAX

THE NEXT MORNING, MY SIBLINGS AND I ALL GATHERED AT THE house before the big event for a light brunch our house manager, Mrs. Burns, put together for us. She wanted to make sure Lenny ate something today and didn't end up being a tipsy bride.

Her words, not mine.

That meant sleeping in wasn't an option, which wouldn't have been a big deal if I hadn't slept like shit last night. But it's hard to sleep when you keep going through all the ways you've fucked up.

Especially when you're not someone who's used to fucking up.

I went about this all wrong. I got so caught up in proving who I was, I forgot who I am. I've never been someone who's okay with hurting other people. And I hurt Daphne last night.

I knew Daphne Brenner was different the first time she opened her smart mouth.

I just wasn't ready for her.

This realization hit me like a Mac truck somewhere around six this morning, and I haven't been able to stop thinking about it since.

"What the fuck, Maximus? You're in another fucking world today. Are you seriously this upset about Len getting married?" Sawyer elbows me, pulling me from my thoughts.

My brothers and I stand at the back of the aisle, greeting guests as they arrive.

Glass hurricane candles line either side of the wooden floor brought in for tonight's ceremony. White wooden chairs frame the space. I swear to God, it's a fire waiting to happen, but Lenny wanted candlelight at sunset. So that's what she got.

Twinkling lights are hung on all the trees and throughout the tent next to us that we'll move into after the ceremony. It's perfectly Len.

And apparently, I don't look happy for her.

Fuck.

I try to ignore Sawyer, but he won't shut up. "Sebastian's a good guy. You need to stop playing dad and just be happy for her."

"You're an idiot. I'm happy for Len. She loves him. He worships her. They're happy. That's all I want for her. Why would you think I wasn't?"

Coach Sinclair and his wife, Catherine, interrupt us to say hello before settling into their seats behind Bash and Sam's grandmother.

"You've been in a shit mood all day, brother." Hudson offers me his flask, but I shake my head. "The only time you've been happy at all is when Lenny's been around. What's up with that?"

Okay, maybe I could use some advice, but neither of these two asshats would know how to be in a relationship if they were hit over the head with one.

I look around for my other brothers, but it's pointless. Jace is nineteen, and Becks is in a relationship with a succubus. So, I don't think he's an option either.

I need to get some fucking friends I'm not related to.

Declan is around here somewhere. He and I have become friends over the years. But I'm not sure we're *talk about your life* friends. When I find him, he's standing at the front of the aisle, off to the side. He's officiating the ceremony today, and his twin girls are two of the flower girls, along with Madeline and Brynlee. One of Dec's girls is on his hip, and he's talking to Brandon *fucking* Dixon.

This asshole is like a fucking nasty case of jock itch, a real pain in my balls who won't go away.

I take a step away from my brothers, excusing myself before the wedding coordinator halts me in my tracks. She's a tiny woman who has a commanding presence, with a clipboard in her hands and a headset on her head. "It's time, Mr. Kingston. Would you like to go get Eleanor, or would you like me to?"

I look over her shoulder and see Brandon's already taken his seat next to Carys Murphy.

Good. Maybe they're together and he'll stay the hell away from Daphne.

Let's see how Coach deals with him dating his step-daughter.

"Mr. Kingston?" the coordinator pushes for an answer.

"I'll get her. Thank you." A pang of sadness hits me deep in my chest as I walk back up to the house along the smooth flagstone path that was brought in just for today. Short shepherd's hooks with hanging candles light my way.

It's my sister's wedding day, and she deserves my undivided attention.

Time to get my head in the game.

When I knock on Lenny's old bedroom door, Amelia and Lenny's best friend, Juliet, filter out, followed by Scarlet, who stops and kisses me on the cheek. "Try not to cry, Maximus."

And as I step through the door, I appreciate the warning.

My little sister is beautiful. We've always been called the kings, but she looks like the perfect princess. Her dark-brown hair is piled in curls on top of her head, and diamond stud earrings sparkle in her ears. She's wearing a pretty, satin, strapless gown with material flowing down beneath a light-lavender ribbon tied under her chest that accentuates her athletic frame. Luckily for me, she's not wearing a necklace.

"Lenny . . ." My words betray my emotions, but I refuse to cry. "You look beautiful."

She showed me a picture of her dress after Scarlet, Amelia, and she picked it out a few weeks ago, and I took a chance and reached out to the jeweler Dad always used and had something made. I pull the deep-red velvet box from my pocket and hold it out to her. "I got you something."

"Max . . . you didn't need to do that. You already gave me this wedding." She takes the box from my hands and slowly cracks it open, and then she gasps, "Maximus." Big blue, watery eyes meet mine. "It's perfect." With shaky fingers, she holds up the purple diamond surrounded by a halo of tiny white diamonds on a delicate platinum chain. "Will you put it on me?"

I take it from her and move behind her so she can watch us in her mirror. "You're an incredible woman, Eleanor. Your mom and Dad would have been so proud of the person you've become. They both would have been thrilled to know you found someone who loves you the way Bash does." I kiss the crown of her head. "And if he ever steps out of line, you've got a bunch of brothers who will happily kill him for you. Or who'll bury his body if you do it yourself."

She turns and wraps her arms around my shoulders. "I love you, big brother." After squeezing me for a minute, she pulls back, vibrating with happiness. "Now let's do this before Sebastian thinks I ran away."

"I can still get the car, if you want." I point toward the door, and she smacks my hand away.

"Not a chance."

When I stand at the bar and watch my sister and her friends dance to a Meatloaf song, singing at the top of their lungs, I can't hold back my smile. I feel content, knowing she's happy and my job is done. I pull my phone out and text Daphne.

Max: I'm sorry I didn't invite you to the wedding sooner. I wish you were here.
Max: Can I see you after?

I watch the little dots start and stop a few times before a shadow falls over me. Brandon Dixon stands next to me and motions to get the bartender's attention. "Can I get a bottle of water and a Jack and coke?"

"Dixon." I pocket my phone and sip my bourbon, trying to appear calm and not show the irrational rage his presence here is causing me.

"Kingston." He nods his head and turns around to lean his elbows back against the bar. His eyes are on the dancefloor, watching the girls, including his sister. "You left quickly last night. Did Daphne finally realize she could do better?"

I place my glass down on the bar and turn toward him. "What the fuck's your problem?"

"My problem is you." His voice raises slightly. "That girl has been dealt a shit hand the past few months. She doesn't need someone like you playing with her." He takes a step closer to me, but I don't back down.

His size doesn't intimidate me.

Bigger men than him have tried and failed.

"I've met guys like you. You think because you own the world, you own her too. But you don't." Dixon's jaw clenches.

"You don't know me." I lower my voice, eerily calm, but there's no mistaking the threat in my tone. "You don't know what's between Daphne and me. My relationship with her is none of your business."

"But she's not yours or she wouldn't be living in *my* house." A cocky grin spreads across his face. And I swear to God, if I wasn't at my sister's wedding, I'd have already smashed my glass of bourbon against the side of this asshole's head.

Instead, I throw it right back at him. "I don't see her sleeping in your bed."

Having obviously struck the nerve I was aiming for, he takes a step into me, bringing us practically nose to nose.

I lower my voice. "Back. The. Fuck. Up. Now. Because this is my sister's wedding, I'll let you save face. But if you ruin this for her, you'll never play another down of football anywhere. Not professionally. Not semi-pro. You won't even get to touch a fucking ball in a flag league. I will destroy you."

Dixon takes a step back, having never seen this side of me but knowing I don't make idle threats. "You know she deserves better than you, right?"

"She deserves better than both of us." My own words ring a little too true in my ears, cementing my determination to fix things with Daphne.

Dixon shoves his hands in his pockets. "Then step up and take care of her like she deserves."

"I intend to." I just have to get her to forgive me first.

I walk away, leaving him behind, and brush by Hudson. "What the hell was that over there? I was coming to see what was going on."

"It's all good, Hud." I look around, making sure we didn't

cause a scene, but no one else seems to have noticed any tension. "Go have fun."

He eyes me funny, probably knowing I'm full of shit, but he doesn't call me on it. "Yeah. Okay, Maximus. Any reason you didn't bring your girl with you tonight? We were taking bets on whether you would."

"Oh yeah? Which way did you bet?" I'm not surprised, but my curiosity is piqued.

Hudson smiles at me so damn big, his dimples pop in both cheeks. "I thought she'd be here."

"Why?" Now, I'm intrigued.

Hudson grabs my shoulder, like he's about to tell me a secret. "Because you've always been an all-in kinda guy, Max. You don't hold back. It's all or nothing. Lenny said you couldn't keep your eyes or your hands off her last weekend. I just figured that meant something."

"Yeah. I guess it did." I think back to last weekend and how fucking happy I was when I woke up Sunday morning and she was still there. And how badly I fucked up last night. Fuck this. "Excuse me, Hud. I've gotta make a call."

"Go get her, Maximus." Fucking douchebag.

I pull my phone back out and open the text from earlier.

Daphne: I think I need some time, Max. You're giving me whiplash.

She's right. I've been all over the place with her, and she doesn't deserve it.

Time to fix that.

DAPHNE

As if it wasn't bad enough that I'm the only one home all night while both my roommates are at the wedding I kinda wish I was at, he had to go and apologize with perfect words to make my heart sing.

Max: Then let me make it perfectly clear. You're mine, Daphne Brenner. I was an ass for trying to keep us in the friends with benefits zone. We were never going to be just friends. We were more after that first night. I'm going to prove it to you.

You're mine.

Yes, he was an asshole. But he owned up to it and apologized for it. But it was the *"you're mine"* that sealed the deal for me. I wanted to yell back that I don't belong to anyone, but I couldn't. That would have been a lie. As much as I may not want to admit it, I *am* his. I think I've known it for a while now. But still, he doesn't deserve to hear it.

Not yet. Max Kingston needs to figure his shit out before I give him my heart.

Well . . . before I tell him it's his.

I seriously stood no chance.

Once I've showered, I throw on a pair of shorts and a tank top to go in search of coffee. When I get to the kitchen, Dixon is standing there, his muscular back facing me, showcasing the tiny pale scars I asked him about once years ago.

He never answered and just changed the subject. His t-shirt is draped around his neck, and he's making his protein shake.

"Jeez, Dix. What time did you wake up this morning?" I move around him to grab a mug, but he doesn't look up.

"About two hours ago." His answer is flat. It doesn't hold any of the warmth I'm used to. And when he turns around, the look on his face is not his normal expression. "Needed to get my workout in early." He leans back against the counter and watches me drop a pod in the coffee maker.

"How was the wedding?" Apparently, I'm a glutton for punishment.

He drinks half his shake, then wipes his mouth with the back of his hand. His eyes rake over me in a way that makes me uncomfortable. It's not sexual. But I can't quite place my finger on what it is. "It was nice. Maddie drank too much." He smirks. "So did Carys. Was she really dating—"

I slap a hand over his mouth. "We don't say his name. Not ever." He licks my hand, and I pull back and squeal.

Dixon cracks a smile before Maddie joins us in the kitchen and drops dramatically into a chair. "I'm never drinking that much again."

"I told you to slow down. But no one ever listens to me." He rinses the blender and his cup with tense shoulders before he turns back to me. "He really cares about you, D."

"What are you talking about, Dix?"

"Nothing." He pats Maddie on the back of her head and walks out of the room.

"What the heck is his problem? Did something die in his protein powder?" She fills the tea kettle and switches on the stove, then hops her butt up onto the counter. "What time do we have to leave?" She yawns and closes her eyes like that simple action hurts.

"We need to leave in about an hour. You think you're going to make it?"

The kettle starts to whistle, and she groans. "I make no promises."

Luckily for all of us, Maddie survived getting dressed, and Carys and Chloe were already waiting for us by the time we joined them at our favorite little place across the street from Hart & Soul, where Mads teaches ballet. The Busy Bee opened about a year ago. It's country chic with lemon-yellow booths and pecan-wood tables spread throughout. Shiplap covers the walls, and they have the best eggs benedict I've ever had. But it's only open for breakfast and lunch, so you need to get here early.

Not something that happens often on the weekends in my world.

"Okay, can somebody please tell me about the wedding now?" I nail Maddie to her seat with a glare. "How did everything go with Watkins? Are we still on cherry watch?"

"Oh, come on." She stirs the ice cubes around in her Diet Coke. "Nothing was ever going to happen with Watty. He was a perfect gentleman. His hands didn't even wander when he danced with me. Not even an inch."

Chloe snickers as she leans back in the corner of the sunshine-yellow booth. "And those are some big damn hands." She holds hers up in front of her face. "Could you imagine what he could do with those hands?"

"Ugh. What the heck ever. Go ahead and rub it in my face, why don't you?"

Chloe's smirk grows. "Might as well rub something for ya, Mads. You don't know what you've been missing."

"Just because I haven't had sex doesn't mean there hasn't been a little rubbing." Maddie's eye twitches, and we all laugh.

"Your own hand doesn't count, Madison." Chloe sticks her tongue out at Mads.

"Whatever. Don't act like we didn't see who you were dancing with last night, Chloe." Mads flings a sugar packet at Chloe, who just smiles back at our sexually frustrated friend.

"Hello . . . ?" I yell at the three of them. "And who were you dancing with, Chloe?" I look across the table at Carys, who bursts out laughing. "Oh my God. Who was she dancing with?"

Chloe picks up her cup of black coffee and sips. Slowly.

"Well," Carys ignores her roommate. "Let's just say that Dean DiPietro looked like a very happy man when he was doing the walk of shame out of the townhouse today."

I slap my hand against the table. "Wait . . ." I try to place the name with a face but come up empty even though I should know who he is. "DiPietro?"

"Yup." Carys pops the "p" at the end of the word and dips her finger into the whipped cream on the top of her hot chocolate. "As in Bash and Sam's very hot, very connected, cousin. Dean."

My eyes triple in size. "Ho-ly shit, Chloe. He's gorgeous."

"Yeah, he is," Mads laughs. "I'll bet you got a good rubbing."

Chloe steals the cherry from Carys's whipped cream and bites down with a big, mischievous grin on her face. "He's also got a really talented tongue, and a great big . . ."

We're interrupted by the waitress, who passes out our food before asking if we need anything else, blushing the entire time. She scurries away once we tell her we're fine, and the four of us break into peals of laughter. Carys takes the cherry from the top of her pancakes and adds it to Chloe's waffles. "I think we might have scared the waitress. She looks like she can't be more than fifteen."

Chloe picks that cherry up too, then ties the stem in a

191

knot with her tongue and throws it at Carys. "Like we weren't hearing and doing worse than that at fifteen." Then she looks at Maddie. "Well, everyone but you, Mads. That brother of yours looked like he was going to kill Watkins every time he touched you last night."

She nods her head in agreement. "He looked like he wanted to kill Max Kingston too." My fork full of eggs stops mid-way to my mouth. "I'm sorry. What?"

Chloe and Carys look equally confused.

"How am I the only one that saw them get into it at the bar?" She points her fork at the two of them sitting next to each other on the other side of the booth. "How did you miss it? I swear, I thought somebody was going to throw a punch."

I drop my fork down on my plate and face Maddie. "What the hell happened? And why am I just hearing about this now, Madison?"

She shrugs like it's no big deal. "I don't know. We were all dancing, and the two of them caught my attention. They were at the bar, and things looked tense. Like, *really* tense. I know my brother, and I swear to God, I thought he was going to hit Max. But it was over as quickly as it started, and they both walked away."

"You know that shit was over you, D," Carys mumbles around a forkful of blueberry pancakes. She swallows, then adds, "I think Dixon has a thing for you."

"What?" It's Maddie's turn to look confused. "No way." She looks from Carys to me. "No way. You're like a little sister to him."

Chloe grins. "A little sister he wants to bang, maybe."

Maddie picks up a piece of turkey bacon and points it between Chloe and Carys. "Holy smokes. That would explain so much."

"Oh my God, Maddie." Chloe takes the bacon out of her hand and pops it in her mouth. "Seriously, you give blondes a bad name. Your brother has wanted D for years." Leave it to her to be totally blunt.

Maddie sucks in a breath and glances my way. "Did you know this?"

"I had no idea until recently. Even then, he didn't do anything or come out and say anything directly. It's just an impression I've gotten. And we both know he doesn't love the idea of me and Max. I don't think Max's middle-of-the-night drop-in Friday helped matters much." I hate the weird tension between the two of us lately.

"Well . . ." Chloe leaves the word hanging for a moment. "What is going on with you and the oldest, possibly hottest, Kingston?"

"No way. Hudson is way hotter than Max." Maddie's brows shoot up, like she can't believe she said that out loud. "Whatever. Don't look at me like that. I like his muscles."

"Yeah well, you can have Hudson. I'm not sure what's going on with Max and me right now. He wants more. I don't know if I'm ready to give it to him yet." Even if I want to.

"Men suck." Carys shoves a big piece of pancake in her mouth.

"Here's the thing though. I don't think Max sucks. I just think he needs to figure out what he wants." My roomie has hearts in her eyes as she says it, ever the romantic.

I look down at my plate. "He told me he wanted me to be his last night."

No one says a word while they wait for me to continue until Maddie urges me on. "And then . . . ?"

"And then nothing. I'm scared I'm about to get my heart crushed. And no offense, but I don't have Carys's metabolism, so eating my feelings wouldn't go over well for me."

Carys points her fork in my face and swallows. "Heartbreak sucks, D. But I wouldn't change anything about these past two years, except how they ended. Not one single second. I'd do it all over again because it was amazing." Her voice trembles. "Scared is healthy. Guarding your heart is smart. But seriously . . . loving someone. Being loved by them." She takes a quick breath and straightens her spine. "It's better. It's worth the risk. It's worth the pain. It's worth binge eating pancakes. Why do you think I run around Boathouse Row every morning? Because my ass would be the size of the Kings Stadium if I didn't. But I still wouldn't change it. You just have to decide if he's worth it. And not for nothing, but you already know the answer to that."

"If you need big-girl panties to put on right now to deal with your shit, I've got some really pretty new designs back at the townhouse." Chloe sips her coffee, totally serious, while she lightens the mood.

I laugh at her. "How big are we talking?"

Carys stabs a chunk of waffle from Chloe's plate and drags it through the maple syrup.

"I mean, we might need to make hers bigger at this rate." Chloe elbows Carys. "So, I'm sure we can work some magic." Chloe eyes me as she grins. I'm grateful for the break in our serious conversation. I think we've had enough this morning.

DAPHNE

WHEN I GET TO THE OFFICE MONDAY MORNING, IT'S WITH A little extra pep in my step. I made sure to get in thirty minutes earlier than normal because Quinn O'Doul is starting today. It wasn't hard to notice that Coach O'Doul's daughter came in last week less than thrilled at being here for the interview. But by the end of her interview, she seemed slightly more interested. Lucky for her, she only showed interest in the job. I don't know if this is something she'll be doing for the long term, but Max offered her the job, and she accepted.

Either way, I can't hide my excitement that soon I'll be able to focus solely on Start A Revolution, even though I'm a tiny bit bothered that I won't be Max's assistant anymore. I feel like we just found our groove.

Okay, so maybe that's a lie. We still haven't found our groove. But while I like the idea of starting my new job, I kinda hate the idea of a beautiful woman doing my old job.

And Quinn O'Doul is gorgeous.

I've known her for a few years. She's got the whole fiery, sexy red-head thing going on. And I'm not too proud to admit I'd hoped his new assistant would be ugly. I mean, maybe not hideous, but less than stunning would have been nice.

But when I sit down at my desk, I quickly realize my things are gone. The picture I keep on my desk of my grandfather with his arm wrapped around my mom, who's holding me. My Revolution mug. My hands begin shaking as I open my drawers to find nothing inside.

Oh my God.

Have we been robbed?

Have I been fired?

Has my father come in and taken away everything from my work life the way he threw away everything from my home? My monitors are still here, but there's already a laptop hooked up to them, and I brought mine home with me last week so I could work over the weekend.

What the hell?

I pop right back up from my chair and hurry to Max's office.

His door is open, but the room is empty.

Okay, am I in some weird *Twilight Zone* episode or something? I never beat him into the office.

"Daphne." The deep timbre of his rough voice tickles my spine, and I spin around. Max stands in the doorway of the empty office between Coach O'Doul's and his, holding it closed behind him. His dark navy-blue suit matches his eyes. The crisp, white shirt is unbuttoned at the collar, and his silver tie hangs loosely around his neck. He looks absolutely delicious, and I'm drawn to him like a moth to a flame.

I run my hands nervously down the front of my box-pleated black-and-white-striped skirt. His eyes follow the movement, then travel back up my body, lingering on my hips for a moment too long.

The bow of my sleeveless, white-collared shirt ties around my waist and just meets the thick waistband of the skirt. I tug at it, making sure it didn't ride up and isn't showing any unwanted skin. Then I snap out of the trance he's already lulled me into. "Good morning. Do you know what happened to my things? They're not at my desk."

He pushes the door open and smiles.

And *oh my*, that smile.

"I had them moved into your new office, Miss Brenner." He steps aside for me to walk into the office. *My office.* There hasn't been furniture in here for as long as I can remember, but it's fully furnished now. And instead of the sleek dark wood in Max and Coach's offices, there's a lovely white wooden desk with matching cabinets behind it. And on those cabinets sits the picture of the three of us. My grandfather, my mom, and me. All in our matching Revolution jerseys. I was around two years old, and we'd just won the division title. There's a huge bouquet of green and white hydrangeas sitting on the corner of the desk and a basket of pears are placed on the table centered between two chairs on the opposite wall.

"Pears?" The question slips before I think better of it. "I meant thank you so much. I really wasn't expecting to get my own office." I turn my back to Max and run my hand over the surface of my desk, admiring my new surroundings.

The skin on my neck prickles as he brushes my hair from my back and drags his lips along my earlobe. "Pears. Because I'll never smell a pear again without wanting to fuck you, Daphne." His teeth tug my ear gently. Then he's gone, leaving cool air in his place.

I turn my head to look over my shoulder and watch him adjust his suit coat.

"The office is because you've earned it, Miss Brenner." He turns quickly and walks out of the office.

My office.

I pick up the picture and stare at my mother.

Knowing she'd be so proud of me. They both would.

Thank goodness, I've never had any desire to go into teaching.

I seriously suck at showing other people what to do.

I just don't have the patience for it.

Quinn picks everything up fairly easily, and I've still had to fight the urge to do it myself.

And right now, Max is leaning over her desk, looking at something on one of Quinn's monitors. I should probably feel bad that, from my new desk, I have the perfect view of his ass while he does that. But I don't. Not even a little bit.

"Okay, so I'm planning to blast the information on Start A Revolution's socials today. Have you asked Max if you can post on the socials for the Revolution yet?" Mads offered to help me with the social media for Start A Revolution as a favor, and I jumped at the offer. She hums for a minute then adds, "And maybe mention to him they need a better social media manager. Their branding leaves something to be desired. Oh, and I also confirmed with the Kings marketing team that they'll be sharing on their pages since you have so many of their players in the auction on Saturday."

As if the man in question can sense we're talking about him, he stands and makes his way toward my office with a sexy smile on his face.

"Hold on, Mads. Max is right here." I wave him in and put the phone on speaker. "Maddie's on the phone. She's volunteering her time and social media skills for Start A Revolution."

"Yeah." Maddie's voice comes through the speaker, and Max drops down into the seat across from me. "And you need some serious help with the Revolution's social media presence, Max. It's kinda boring, especially compared to the Kings. They're posting for us tomorrow and Friday."

"Really?" He stands and moves around behind me to look at my screen. "Daphne, can you pull up our social media accounts?" He leans over me, and goosebumps break out over my skin when he grabs my mouse and scrolls down. "I see what you're saying, Madison." He hits the mute button. "Who does our social media now?" He looks down at me from the corner of his eye with a crooked grin.

"I'm pretty sure one of the interns is doing it."

He unmutes the phone. "Hey, Maddie? Do you want a job?"

"Umm . . . what?" Her voice cracks, and I hide my laugh. Typical no-nonsense Max.

"The Kings' social media presence is great because we have someone in-house who handles it. The position is full-time, with the understanding they need to be at 80 percent of the games and events throughout the year. Apparently, we don't have that here at the Revolution, but we need it. How about I have Human Resources send you a formal offer letter? Can you look it over and get back to me by the end of the week?" There's silence on the other end of the phone. "Maddie?

"Umm . . . Is it too early to accept?" Maddie's not even trying to hide her excitement.

"Look over the offer, Madison. Check out the salary and the benefits first. Then accept." He kisses the top of my head, shocking me. He's never done that in the office before. "I've got a meeting now, but you should have the paperwork by the end of the day."

Maddie and I both thank him, and I watch him leave.

"D?"

I recline in my chair and sigh. "Yeah, Mads?"

"Your boyfriend just gave me a job. With benefits." She claps her hands with giddy excitement. "In case you weren't sure, I'm officially Team Max now, D. I'll make t-shirts if I have to. Don't let that man go."

Maybe that needs to be the plan, Mads. Maybe . . .

Willow buzzes my phone a little later, and my smile grows. Going from the assistant to having one, even if she's just an intern, is pretty damn cool. "Hey, Willow."

"Daphne, a man is on hold for you. He says he's your dad but didn't have your number. Should I put him through?"

"Yes," my heart hammers in my chest. "Please put him through."

Even knowing who she was connecting, I'm still not prepared when I hear, "Daphne?" from my father on the other end of the phone.

I don't respond.

"You sure managed to go from assistant to director in record time."

I try to swallow down my anger. "How did you know?"

"The directory listed your new title. Congratulations. I know it's what you've always wanted." My father's disdainful tone, combined with his words, breaks the final string connecting us. He should have been the one here for this.

"If you want me, you know where to find me, Dad. Don't call me back here." I hang up on the man I'm no longer sure I ever knew and ask Willow to block any future calls from him. I refuse to let him affect me anymore.

MAX

Daphne knocks on my door at the end of the day, then stuffs her hands into hidden pockets in her skirt and waits. She's barely been out of her office this afternoon. I wanted to check on her, to make sure she was okay, but I don't think she'd appreciate that here.

She waits for me to look up from my computer before stepping through and shutting the door behind her. "You do know that it's acceptable to leave the office before seven, right?" She strolls over to my desk and carefully sits on top of it in front of me, her legs dangling down between mine.

I roll my chair closer to her but resist the urge to touch, wanting to see what she's up to. Curious to see if my siren is planning to tease me and run again like the last time.

When she leans over and loosens my tie, my cock jumps. "You don't have to be the first one in every day and the last one to leave every night, Max." One side of my silk tie is slipped out of the knot and tugged free from my collar before she runs her nails through my hair, and I groan, instantly relaxing into her touch.

It feels so damn good.

"There's always more to be done," I tell her honestly.

"I'm sure you're right. But it'll still be there tomorrow."

She kicks off her red heels, and I grab her smooth calf and wrap my hand around it. "If I go home, I'm just going to work there instead of here. Unless you'd like to grab dinner with me?"

Daphne ignores the question. "Did you offer Maddie a job today for me? Not that it wouldn't have been a lovely way to get in my good graces, but . . . that's going above and beyond." She massages my scalp, and I turn my head and kiss her wrist.

"No, Daph. I offered her a job because she pointed out an area where we're deficient. And you must think she's good at what she does if you're using her for the foundation. So, I offered her a job for the entire organization. Now, you can continue to use her, and we'll get the benefit of using her for the team too, and she'll be paid for it. It's a win, win." I drop my chin to my chest and let her work her magic on my head.

She runs her nails over my scalp, then massages the base of my neck. "She already got the offer letter from Human Resources, and I'm pretty sure she accepted it."

"Good." That's as much as I want to talk about anyone else besides the sexy siren in front of me right now.

Her silvery-blue eyes sparkle back at me as she slips slowly from the desk to her knees.

Her small hands glide up my thighs, tugging on my belt.

"Daphne . . ."

She lowers my zipper and takes me out of my pants. "Hmm?" She lifts her eyes to meet mine, then drags her tongue along one of my balls, then the other, and I forget every fucking thought I ever had. "We're alone, Max. No one's left in the office." Her voice is breathy and so fucking sexy. "And I'm hidden by your desk." Her fingers wrap around me and pump me once before she teasingly swirls her tongue around the tip of my dick.

Fuck.

I give in to temptation, letting my siren lead me anywhere she wants.

Fuck salvation.

I'll welcome my destruction if it's at her hands.

I run my hands through her soft, blonde hair, holding her head with just a touch of pressure. And she purrs. Fucking purrs. Then she pops her mouth off my cock. "Show me what you want, Max. Tell me how you like it." She drags her tongue along my shaft, then licks her lips. "Fuck my mouth, Max."

I groan and guide her head back down as I thrust in. "You liked that?"

Her nails run lightly under my balls, and a wave of pleasure curls down my spine.

"I did like that," she pants around my cock. "I like everything you do to me." She swallows me into the back of her throat, and I lean my head back and raise my eyes to the ceiling, needing to gather my composure so I don't shoot my load right away.

I lower my eyes after I count to ten, and my breath is stolen from my chest. Daphne is the sexiest thing I've ever seen. Her hair is spread out over her shoulders, her cheeks pink and her lips wrapped tight around my dick.

And she's fucking mine.

I thrust my hips and fuck her face like she asked for. Daphne gags, and her eyes water, but she works me harder instead of backing off.

When one hand drops between her legs, I warn her, "Don't touch your clit, Daphne. I want your orgasm tonight. I want all your fucking orgasms." She grabs my dick and squeezes a little harder, and I come on a fucking roar.

Daphne swallows every drop.

Pumping me. Licking me until I pull back and stand up from my office chair.

I reach under her arms and pull her up to her feet, then reach under her skirt and rip her panties from her body, and my mouth seals over hers. And Jesus, it's like my body settles. Everything in me settles.

This woman is everything I ever wanted. Ever needed.

I gather her up in my arms, then walk over to the door and hit the switch to lower the blinds.

"That little show was just for me, siren. But I want to make sure nobody sees what I'm about to do to you."

Her arms tighten around my shoulders, and her lips move to my neck and suck. "I need you, Max."

I sit us down on the couch with her straddling my lap. "Am I forgiven?" My words are hoarse. The consequences of her answer scare me. And nothing fucking scares me.

"Max," she mewls against my ear, then shoves her face back into my neck. Her small hands fist my shirt. "As if I had a choice. My heart is yours, Max. I've been yours. Even when I didn't want to be. Even when you didn't deserve me."

My blood roars in my ears at her declaration. *Mine.* I wrap my fingers around her throat and take her mouth in mine. "I'll never deserve you, Daphne. But I promise to never stop trying." I tug her bottom lip between my teeth. "Everything, Daphne. Every fucking piece of me is yours."

She leans her forehead against mine. "Just you, Max. I don't need anything else, but I do need you."

Her words are a soothing balm to my hardened soul.

"Now take me," she demands as she grinds her soaked pussy against my cock that's already hard again.

My hands slip to the globes of her ass as I drag her up my body.

Daphne places the head of my cock at her entrance, then sinks down slowly. "Ohmygod." She sets a slow, torturous rhythm, taking what she needs while I watch the vision in front of me. Committing it to memory.

My lips find hers as my hands untie the big white bow at

her waist and shove her shirt from her shoulders. Her crisp scent wraps around us, cocooning us. She's got another lacey bra on, the same shade as her skin. Her dark, rosy nipples are hardened tips, poking against the lace of her bra. I suck one into my mouth while I massage the other with my hand, loving her skin. Her sounds. How fucking fantastic her tight, hot pussy feels wrapped around me. Shit. "Daph . . . I don't have a condom on."

She drags her body back up again and slams back down onto me.

A white-hot heat thunders through me.

"I'm on the pill. God . . ." She repeats the move, and I tug her nipple. "Don't stop." She gasps, "Please don't stop."

I slide one hand to her ass and cup her sex from behind. "I couldn't if I wanted to." My middle finger slides to her pussy, gathering her juices. She's fucking drenched. I trail it back up the line of her ass and play with her puckered hole. Circling it. "Has your ass ever been fucked, Daphne?"

"No," she keens. Moving faster. Chasing her orgasm. Her hands circle my wrists as her mouth crashes down over mine. "Oh, God."

I push the tip of my finger into her ass, and Daphne rockets to an orgasm on a silent scream. Her pussy clamps down so hard when she comes, I see fucking stars as my orgasm tears through me, and I spill into her on a powerful thrust.

Our combined juices dripping down my legs.

Her head drops to my shoulder as she wraps her arms around me, panting for air.

I run my hand up and down her body, needing to touch her. To feel her. Needing her. "You okay, siren?"

She whimpers against my skin and presses her lips to my neck as I kiss her temple.

"Words, Daphne."

Her arms tighten around me, and her warm breath tickles my ear. "You're mine too, you know? I'm yours, Max Kingston. But you are mine too. And I'm never letting go."

Thank fucking God.

DAPHNE

I END UP FOLLOWING MAX BACK TO HIS HOUSE, WHERE WE decided to shower . . . together. Thank you, thank you, thank you, to the person who invented showerhead body sprays. Without whom, I may never have gotten to check a few more fantasies off my list.

Yup.

More than one.

And not for nothing, but the muscles that hide under Max's five-thousand-dollar suits are not just for show. That man moves me around like I weigh nothing.

As I wrap the towel around my chest and ring the water out of my hair, I see Max come back into the bathroom in black-jersey sleep pants. That's it. Just comfy-looking black pants. And, oh my, a girl could get used to seeing him like this. He stops behind me and places a gentle kiss on my neck. "You know, siren, I've got a few empty drawers in here if you want to leave some of your things." He kisses my shoulder, then lays a folded pair of boxer shorts and a t-shirt down on the counter in front of me. "There's plenty of room in the bedroom too. You know, if you wanted to leave some clothes here."

I watch him through the mirror, loving this relaxed version of him.

Relaxed Max is my favorite Max.

"That sounds very girlfriend-y, Mr. Kingston." The teasing tone of my voice comes through loud and clear.

Max wraps his arms around my waist and rests his chin on my shoulder. "Yeah. I guess it does. I'm good with that. Are you?"

I rest my head on his shoulder and melt into him. "Yeah. I'm good with that too."

"Good." He wraps his arms around my waist and squeezes. "Now, the important question. What do you want to order for dinner?"

"Surprise me." I turn my head back toward his and kiss the corner of his mouth. "But let's order soon. I've worked up an appetite."

That's how we ended up binging *Ted Lasso* and feeding each other dim sum from Max's favorite place while we sat on the couch.

"Maybe you should buy a professional soccer team next. You know . . . round out the Kings' sports interest a little." The look he gives me is awful, like he'd rather rip his skin from his body.

"Not happening. Football and hockey are definitely enough for my family. And mixed martial arts too, I guess," he adds, since his brother and sister are part of that world before he feeds me a delicious spicy pork dumpling.

"Can I ask you something?"

Max places his box of dumplings down on the coffee table and kicks his feet up. "Technically, you just did. But go ahead."

"Ass." I poke him with my chopstick. "Why did you buy the Revolution?"

"Your dad came to me. He said he was going to sell the organization and was looking for a buyer. He and my dad were friends, and he thought he'd offer it to me first. The deal was a good one, and I took a chance. King Corp has been synonymous with Philly sports for so long, it didn't seem like a far stretch." He takes a breath and then continues, "We originally planned for Scarlet to be the one to take over the Revolution, but the more we dove in, the more I realized that it wasn't right for her but could be right for me. This was my chance to prove I could build something on my own. Not the way King Corp. or the Kings were handed to me, but instead, something for me to take the reins and carve out my own legacy. To build the kind of organization I want. To take the team to the next level that your dad was struggling with." Max sips his beer, then adds, "How is your dad?"

I'm stuck on the fact that my dad approached Max. All this time, I thought the Kingston's wanted the Revolution. That they pursued it. Not that I should be surprised. If Dad was in trouble, it would make sense that he was the one to look for a buyer. "So he came to you? I still can't believe he didn't tell me first." I place my box of food next to his and lay my head against his chest. "Are you happy you bought it?"

He presses a kiss on the top of my head. "The team could lose every single game this year, and buying it would still be the best move I've ever made, Daphne. Because it brought me you." He wraps his arm around me, and we binge the rest of *Ted Lasso*.

Hours later when we finally go to bed, Max wraps his body around mine from behind and kisses me goodnight.

It's soft and sweet.

It's not supposed to lead to anything.

But the chemistry between us is combustible.

I roll over to my back, and Max pulls my shirt over my head as I shimmy out of my borrowed boxers, then push his pants down with my feet, desperate for his skin on mine. Frantic for his weight against me. Dying for him.

He settles between my legs and drags his cock along my sex, wrenching a needy whimper from my throat.

"Max . . . I need you."

His lips capture mine tenderly as he pushes agonizingly slowly inside me. "You've got me." He pulls out completely before repeating the movement but still not giving me enough. One big hand grasps my wrists and holds them above my head. "You've got all of me." He pulls out again and finally . . . finally slides back in, filling me and rocking his hips against mine. "Completely, Daph."

My legs wrap around his hips, clutching him to me the only way I can.

Needing more.

Wanting everything.

Our bodies are so close, my nipples graze his smooth chest with each movement. His arm wraps around my back, holding me to him as he worships my body with his mouth. Licking up my neck while his thumb brushes over my nipple, causing a tight string to pull straight down to my core.

I throw my head back on a pleading moan, then turn my mouth to meet his. His tongue, hot and ready, tangles with mine. As he begins thrusting harder, I pant against his hot skin, and dots of light dance before my eyes.

My orgasm washes over me with an intensity that steals my breath and sears my soul just as Max whispers my name in the dark and spills inside of me. We cling to each other, breathing hard, but not willing to let go.

Max lays us down and pulls the blanket up over us. "My God, Daphne."

I tuck my head under his and rest my hand over his heart. "Why do you call me that? No one else does."

"Are you familiar with Greek mythology?" He runs his hand down my back, tracing my spine, and I shiver and shake my head. "In Greek mythology, Apollo was the god of the sun, one of the most powerful gods. Daphne was a nymph, one he fell for, utterly and completely. She was the most beautiful thing he ever saw. Ultimately, she was his downfall too. But hopefully, that won't be the case with us." He presses his lips to my head. "Now sleep, my siren."

"I won't be your downfall, Max. Please don't be mine." The words are quiet but still a powerful admission.

"I promise."

Early the next morning, I slip into Dixon's house as quietly as possible, needing to get changed before I go to work and hoping I don't wake anyone in the process. But it doesn't matter how quiet I am because Dixon's tying his shoelace in the foyer when I walk in. "Late night?" He pops an earbud in but holds the other in his hand.

Fan-freaking-tastic. "Umm, yeah. I guess so. You going for a run?"

"Yeah." He pops his other ear bud in and passes me.

I decide now's as good a time as any to woman up. "Dix, wait." I grab his arm until he turns around. "Are we okay? I feel like things are weird between us, and I'm not sure what to do about it." I can't stand the thought of losing his friendship. But I can't change the way I feel about Max.

He blows out a breath and takes out both earbuds. "Are you happy, D? Is Max Kingston who you want?"

"I *am* happy, Dix. I wasn't expecting to fall for him, but I have. And I don't think there's any going back now." I laugh, hoping to lighten the mood, but the attempt falls flat.

He moves like he's going to touch my face but drops his hand at the last minute. "If he hurts you, you tell me, and I'll deal with him. Okay?" His voice is strained and quiet, so unlike the man I've known for years, and I hate that I'm hurting him.

"I'm a big girl, Dixon. I can handle it." I take a step toward him, but he backs up and shakes free of my hold. "That's life. We take the good with the bad, right?"

He takes another step back. "You don't deserve any of the bad, D." He puts his earbuds back in and walks out the front door."

Neither do you, Dix. Neither do you.

DAPHNE

By Thursday afternoon, I realize I'm beginning to thrive on chaos.

It's exciting and exhilarating.

The Kings' first game of the season is tonight, and while Dixon and I haven't spent much time together this week, things have become a little less awkward around the house.

Start A Revolution's first fundraising event is only two days away.

And what will hopefully become the first of Max's annual season kickoff parties is one week after that.

Quinn, Willow, and I haven't had two minutes to spare all week. I love it.

My bachelors are confirmed for Saturday. We have eleven Revolution players and seven Kings players, including Dixon and Watkins. Max's brother Hudson volunteered and brought one of the other pro fighters from his gym, Jaxon, with him, adding two MMA fighters to the lineup for an even twenty bachelors. The silent auction items have all been collected and tagged. Maddie has blasted it on social media as the can't-miss event of the season. And by this morning, I've sold more tickets than I ever dared to hope.

Now, let's just pray it pays off.

When Max knocks on my open office door, I lift my head with a smile as he enters. I've barely moved from my seat all day, and the only time I've seen him was first thing this morning, even though his office is only steps from mine.

He walks into the room, sucking all the oxygen in his wake, then drops a kiss to my head and runs his hand over my hair.

We've agreed that neither of us wants to hide our relationship, but in general, we're not going to flaunt it in the office either. I'd really like to not have it be center stage at the event on Saturday. I want the focus to be on Start A Revolution, not on Max Kingston dating the former owner's daughter, who also happens to work for him.

I've come to realize that Max doesn't consider kissing me in either of our offices flaunting it if no one else is with us.

Not like we were ever going to be able to downplay this thing between us anyway.

Once upon a time, I was the owner's daughter.

People will talk, no matter what. I'm sure they were talking when Dad sold the organization so suddenly. I don't think I even want to know what they were saying.

Can it really be that bad if everyone knows I'm the owner's girlfriend?

A tiny voice inside my head reminds me it can be if this thing between us ends, but I try valiantly to ignore that possibility and live in the moment.

Not everyone leaves.

"Are you sure you don't want to watch the game tonight from the box with my family?" Max has been trying to convince me all week to go to the football game with him. But I've held firm. My date tonight is Maddie.

He walks to the table in the corner of my office and helps himself to one of the few pears left in my basket, then winks at me. His intense blue eyes hold a wicked promise that I wish I could enjoy, but he already knows my answer to this question.

"Maybe I'll be able to convince Maddie to come up there with me at some point. But like I told you last night, we've been watching Dixon's games from our seats on the fifty-yard line for the past four years. Dixon gave us the season tickets before his very first game. He says it's good luck. It's tradition. And you know better than to mess with a player's tradition."

Max pulls two lanyards out of his pocket and hands them to me, his fingertips brushing mine. The electricity sings between us. And just like that, goosebumps break out all over my body. "Just in case you change your mind. These will get the two of you up to the suites. Just text me if you need anything." He lowers his voice. "Any chance you want to come home with me after the game?"

"I wish I could," I pout. "But I'm going with Maddie, and I don't want to bail on her."

His eyes glaze over. "I'll miss you in my bed."

"I was there last night." And what a night it was. My legs clench at the memory of his face between my legs. "The memory will have to be enough." Although I'm not sure I'll ever get enough of this man.

"Tomorrow?" Max asks, hope clear in his voice.

I glance at the planner sitting open on my desk. "I'm picking up my dress tomorrow after work, but I could pick up some dinner and come later."

"Oh, you'll come alright. I'll make sure of it." I watch him leave my office, suddenly needing a cold drink. And maybe a cold shower too. Damn him.

MAX

I'M NOT SURE WHAT SURPRISED MY SIBLINGS AND ME MORE tonight.

Scarlet telling us that she bought a new box suite at Kings Stadium just for the family to relax and watch the game. One completely separate from the one the family owns and entertains in, or when she and Cade announced they'd gotten married quietly by themselves during Lenny's wedding reception last week.

We've been watching the game as a family in the owner's box my entire life. Dad never hesitated to have his family on display. And I never thought anything of it. But the idea of actually being able to relax and not be "on" and working the entire game is enticing. Especially as I look around and watch the next generation of the Kings at play.

Amelia's son, Maddox, is bouncing in some baby-seat thing. Scarlet's stepdaughter, Brynlee, and Madeline play peek-a-boo with him, pulling big belly laughs from the little man.

There are no onlookers or reporters.

No celebrities or businessmen to entertain.

Just the family.

This is what it always should have been, and I'm disappointed in myself for not thinking of it earlier.

I accept my glass of bourbon from the bartender and tap glasses with Scarlet's new husband, Cade. "Congratulations. You're a lucky man."

He eyes my sister, who's talking with Lenny. Len's hand is rubbing Scarlet's beach ball of a stomach. She's due in a few weeks. And she's radiant. "I really am. Your sister's incredible."

Scarlet joins us a moment later and tucks her arm through Cade's. "So what do you think, Maximus? Pretty great idea, right?"

"It might be the best one you've ever had, Scar. Dad did a lot of things really well, but shielding the kids from the media was never one of them." I look out over the field, watching the excitement below while we wait for the players to run in through the tunnel. "You're going to do amazing things with this team."

She tilts her head back to look up at me. "Are you still happy that you gave up the Kings for the Revolution?"

"I am." There's no doubt or hesitation. "It was the right move for you and turned out to be the best move for me."

"Jesus Christ, Max." Becks joins the three of us, clearly annoyed by my statement. "Because of your fucking assistant?"

I drop my glass down on the bar and step into Becket's space as my temper flares. "Really? We're fucking doing this again?"

Scarlet steps between the two of us and places a palm on my chest. "Back up, Maximus." She turns to Becks, and Cade moves her behind him, receiving a glacial glare in return from my sister. "And Becket, you need to keep your opinions to yourself. I think the fact that we've all tolerated Kendall for years means we give everyone a chance."

"At least we know she's not after my money. Fuck this." He turns around and storms away, and Scarlet turns around to stare at me.

"What was that?" Then she presses a finger to Cade's chest. "And you . . . What the hell was that? You don't get to just move me around like that. At least not in public." She kisses his lips, then turns back to me. "What's got Becks's panties in a twist?"

"Nothing. He's just being an ass," I assure her. "He doesn't think I should be dating Daphne."

Cade kisses Scarlet's temple. "I'm going to leave you two alone."

She watches him walk away, then rests her hand on her stomach. "I swear, this kid is going to enter this world kicking and screaming like the Kingston she is." She struggles to sit down on one of the bar stools and breathes a sigh of relief when she finally manages to get settled. "If you tell anyone you just saw that, I will nut-punch you when you least expect it. Got it?"

"Got it." I tried really fucking hard not to laugh because I know she's serious and will absolutely go through with her threat. But yeah. That shit was funny.

"Okay. Now, tell me about Daphne." Scar's big blue eyes stare at me expectantly, like I'm going to spill my guts here with all my siblings within earshot. "Come on, Maximus. Is it serious?"

I look around to see who's paying attention, then lower my voice. "Yeah, Scar. It's serious. She's incredible. I think you'll like her."

"We'll see about that. I reserve the right to hate her if she's a shrew. But if she makes you happy, I'll trust that she must be pretty special. Do you love her?"

I sip my bourbon, savoring the burn. "We haven't gone there yet."

"That doesn't mean you don't love her. That just means you're a stupid man who hasn't told her. Don't wait, Max. Don't hold back. If I've learned anything these past few months, it's that." She picks up a soft pretzel from a plate that was just placed in front of us and moans as she chews.

"And seriously, don't worry about Becks. He'll come around."

"I'm not so sure about that. We've never warmed up to Kendall."

"There's no way he's serious about her. It's got to be convenience and good sex. At some point, someone is going to knock Becks on his ass, and I'm going to sit back and enjoy the show." She pops the rest of her pretzel in her mouth and closes her eyes as she savors it.

"Need me to leave you alone with the pretzel, Scar?"

"Shut up, Maxipad. Talk to me when you're eight months pregnant and crave salt more than anything." She thinks about it for a minute before her eyes drift to her husband. "Well, almost anything."

"Yeah. I'm out." I hug my sister. "I'm going to go stop by the owner's box and a few others."

"Don't hold back, Max." Jesus. Could she be louder?

"I hear you. Now eat a pretzel and try not to get too excited, okay? There are kids around."

Scarlet flips me off, and I leave the new suite to make my rounds in some of the old ones.

I stop by Coach Sinclair's box and check in on his family. Carys Murphy and Chloe Ryan watch me carefully. But they wait until Declan and Coach's wives step away before they descend like vultures, ready to pick at my bones.

"Couldn't convince D to watch the game with you either?" Carys moves next to me while Chloe grabs another drink. "Don't feel bad. I've been trying to get her to sit with us whenever I'm home for years, and she won't."

"She said she didn't want to mess with a lucky tradition."

Carys rolls her eyes dramatically. "Whatever. She'd still be here, just with us. Or with you, I guess. You know, I never pictured her with a guy like you."

"A guy like me?" This is the most the youngest Murphy

has ever spoken to me. For a tiny thing, she's got a powerful voice. She's sang the National Anthem for us a time or two. But I don't know if I've ever had a real conversation with her before.

"Yeah. Bossy. In control. A king." She looks out over the field, and I shift, slightly uncomfortable with how well this wisp of a woman just nailed me. "I always thought D would be the one in control, that she'd pick a guy who'd go with the flow. Not a guy who'd challenge her. She never liked a challenge before."

"Oh, she still has the control." Why the fuck am I telling her this? "Listen, Carys. I have no desire to change a single thing about Daphne, if that's what you're worried about."

The smile she gives me could light up the whole fucking stadium. "Good." She pats my shoulder. "Because D's fucking amazing just the way she is. And I know you're the all-powerful Max Kingston, but I've got my ways. If you hurt her, I will destroy you." This little sprite winks and walks away as if she didn't just threaten me.

What the fuck?

She sits down, then turns back toward me. "Hey, Max . . . See you Saturday."

DAPHNE

I walk out of the dressing room Friday night and ask Maddie to zip up my dress for me before moving to the dais so the seamstress can make sure no last-minute alterations are needed. The deep-blue silk drapes over one shoulder and nips in at my waist before sliding over my hips like a second skin and flaring slightly at the bottom.

It's nearly the exact color of Max's eyes and is pretty damn close to the color of the Revolution uniforms.

My grandfather used to have a picture on the shelf of his office of my mom in this dress. She wore it at an event before I was even born. Thank God, I took her clothes before Dad had a chance to get rid of them too.

I spin so I can see every angle in the mirrors.

It's gorgeous, and I feel like I have a piece of my mom with me.

Watching over me. I know she'd be proud.

"Oh, D. It's perfect." Mads claps her hands. "Now spin and let me see the back."

I do as she asks and spin in a small circle as the seamstress comes out and examines me carefully. "It is perfect," she clips out in her heavy Russian accent. "Go change."

"He's going to throw you over his shoulder and carry you out of there on Saturday when he sees you." She accepts the garment bag that holds her dress and unzips mine, then hugs me.

"I can't thank you enough for all your help with this event, Mads. It means so much to me."

"Nyet." The seamstress raises her voice. "No hugging. Do not wrinkle dress."

I move into the dressing room to carefully slip out of the gorgeous gown and throw my leggings back on so we can head to the tuxedo shop before going home. We promised Dixon and Watkins we'd grab their tuxes while we were out. Considering the way they rallied the Kings players to help with the auction and the baskets, grabbing their tuxes was the least I could do.

Maddie and I took one car to the seamstress, so I need to head back home and drop her, our dresses, and the guys' tuxes off before going to Max's for the night. Once we get home, there's pizza on the dining room table, and the Kroydon Hills University football game is on TV. Cinder is curled up next to Watkins, swishing her tail like a hussy, trying to get his attention as he holds a string out of her reach.

It's funny how much a year can change your life. Last year, Mads and I were sitting in that stadium in Kroydon University hoodies with frayed jeans and Chuck Taylors. Navy-blue temporary Crusaders tattoos stuck on our cheeks, cheering while we watched the team play.

I knew where I hoped I'd be a year from then.

But I had no idea what it would actually look like.

A giddy feeling runs through me as I realize how far I've come.

I couldn't have imagined I'd be organizing a foundation that will help so many people.

A foundation that represents my family. My team. My future.

Continuing the tradition my grandfather started.

Or that I'd be doing it while falling in love.

Maddie takes our dresses upstairs while I hang Dixon and Watkins's tuxes on the back of the powder room door, then move back into the family room to join them. "Thanks again for doing this for me, guys. And for getting the other players from the team to help out. I really appreciate it."

Watkins pats the seat between him and Dixon on the couch, and I drop down between them. "So . . . I know how you can thank me."

Dixon smacks the back of Watty's head.

"What the fuck, dude? I wasn't going to say that." Watkins's smile grows bigger. "Although . . ."

"Watkins . . ." Dix growls.

"Whatever, man. I was going to say, put in a good word for me with your friend Carys."

Maddie dances down the stairs. "Aww, Watty. You're breaking my heart. I thought we had something special."

Dixon grabs the remote out of Watkins's hand and points toward the door. "Out. Get out."

"Oh my god. I'm kidding, Brandon. Seriously, sit back down." She grabs the salad in the to-go container next to the pizza and sits down with her feet tucked under her on the other side of the ottoman.

I take the remote from Dixon and return it to Watkins. "Bad news, big guy. Carys is still in love with her ex. I'm holding out hope they work it out."

"Damn. Well, you can't blame a guy for trying. What about Chloe?" He wiggles his eyebrows, not caring that he looks ridiculous.

Dix throws him a look. "Dude. You couldn't handle Chloe."

"More like she couldn't handle *me*. Come on, D. Put in a good word for me."

Dixon and I look at each other. "Give him her number, D.

It could be funny to see just how badly she shoots him down."

"Oh. Want to make a bet on how long the call lasts?" I pull my phone from my pocket.

"You guys are dicks," Watty grumbles.

"Nope. Not all of us," Maddie adds.

I push up from the couch and smile at the guys. "Well, it's been real, fellas, but I've got to go. I'll see you all tomorrow. Remember to practice your smiles. The more money you go for, the more money we get to give to the kids."

"You heading to Max's?" Maddie knows that's where I'm going. I'm not sure why she's poking the sleeping bear. Dixon usually gets grouchy at the mention of Max's name.

"Yeah. I told him I'd meet him after you and I were done."

"I heard Beneventi saying at practice the Kingstons usually match whatever donations the Kings foundation raises. Hope they'll do that for you too, D."

"Really?" That's news to me.

"Yup. He said they like to keep that shit quiet, but they're all about giving back. They just don't like it to be the head-line." Cinder chooses that moment to pounce on Watkins, and paw at his face with her little white declawed paw.

"And were you whining about being auctioned off when Bash told you this, Watty?" Maddie kicks at his leg from where she's sitting.

"Maybe." Watkins blushes, and it's adorable. "But I didn't really mean it." He raises his fist for a bump, and I smile and return it.

"Love you guys." Thank God for good friends.

Maddie and Watkins say goodnight, and my heart drops when Dixon doesn't say anything. Until he does . . .

"Night, D. Drive careful." It might not be much. But I'm grateful for it all the same.

MAX

"Any chance I can convince you to come back to bed, Daphne?" I know what she's going to say, but damn, she's so fucking sexy as she slides her legs into her shorts, my cock hardens again at the sight. Who the fuck am I kidding? That's my perpetual state around this siren.

"I can't." She looks over her shoulder at me and bats her lashes. "I've got to get over to the venue and make sure everything is set up right."

I cross the room and wrap my arms around her waist. "Need any help?" My lips skim over the bare skin where her neck slopes to her shoulder, and she melts against me.

"Max . . ." Daphne takes a tentative step away and grabs her shirt. "You're playing dirty. Keep your lips to yourself. I've got this handled." She leans up on her tiptoes and brushes her lips over my cheek, but I turn my head to capture them with mine.

Drinking from her mouth, I let her taste settle deep in my bones. "I'll see you tonight, siren. Call me if you need anything."

"Just you, Max. I just need you."

I follow her to the door and stay there, watching until she pulls out of the driveway, wondering if she has any idea how much I need her.

KINGSTON FAMILY GROUP TEXT:

Scarlet: I'm not feeling great, so I'm skipping the event tonight. But I've already given Daphne my donation. Have fun!

Hudson: You don't want to see me get sold to the highest bidder?

Sawyer: Ten bucks says no one bids on you at all, once they hear about the raging case of syphilis you got last year.

Amelia: Oh God. Gross.

Jace: You know they've got a shot for that.

Hudson: He's kidding Jack-off. But why the fuck do you know that?

Jace: Health class asshole.

Scarlet: Boys, boys, boys. Back to your corners. No one's spreading any rumors about STDs tonight. Tonight's Max's girl's night. Best behavior is expected. That means you, Becks.

Lenny: You're kidding right? You might as well have just thrown down the gauntlet.

Max: Nobody is going to fuck this night up. Right?

Sawyer: Nope. I'm looking forward to seeing how far the mighty have fallen, Maxipad.

Hudson: I'm volunteering my body for the good of the cause. I think that's all the support I can give.

Lenny: You're not a prostitute, Hud.

Amelia: Prostitute. Man whore. Potato. Po-tah-to.

Hudson: WTF?

Amelia: Stop screwing my employees, and I'll stop bothering you.

Jace: Ha. Would that require him to know their last name?

Sawyer: Or something other than their bra size?

Hudson: Where the fuck is Becket? He'd be defending me.

Becks: I'm right here and I can't help you with this.
Scarlet: Good luck Max. You're gonna need it.

When I get to the venue that night, the doors haven't opened yet, and the ballroom is quiet. The Ballroom At The Ben is a gorgeous old-fashioned space. I stop one of the workers. "Excuse me. I'm looking for Miss Brenner."

"Umm . . . Try upstairs. I think she was up there." The young woman points me to the back of the room, where the large wooden staircase sits between the wall and an ornately carved banister. I make my way around the tables and stop to admire the space. Daphne did an incredible job. High-top tables dot the edges of the main room with white flowers and red-and-blue ribbons adorning each one and a Revolution puck in the middle. They match the Revolution's logo that's lit up on the center of the ballroom floor in front of the stage set up for the auction.

Once I've climbed the stairs, I pass by table after table of silent auction items Daphne and her intern were able to secure. I donated a weekend at our house in Killington. There are tickets to Kings games and Revolution games. There are even Sentinels tickets, thanks to Brady and Natalie Ryan. Signed jerseys. Aiden Murphy and his wife donated an all-inclusive tour of Washington, DC, including a behind-the-scenes at the Smithsonian. Hudson is offering a private sparring session, and Sawyer donated a private party and bottle service at Kingdom. And all that is on top of the typical auction items you find at these events.

Daphne really outdid herself.

And just as that thought crosses my mind, the woman herself appears in front of me like something out of a dream. My siren, luring me in by simply existing, is breathtakingly stunning. Daphne's wrapped in a purple dress that hugs the curves of her body in a way I wish I were. Her hair is long and sleek, brushed back over her shoulders, and her expression is full of excitement and anticipation for her big night.

She's the most beautiful woman I've ever seen, and I hate that I have to share her with the world tonight instead of dragging her back to my bed. "Daphne."

Her head snaps up as she adjusts one of the auction sheets, and the smile gracing her beautiful face could bring a man to his knees. "This place looks incredible. I'm so proud of you."

"Thank goodness. I'm so nervous, Max. Look." She holds her hands up in front of me, her fingers trembling. "I'm shaking. I just want everything to be perfect."

I wrap my arms around her and hold her against me. "It *is* perfect, D."

She tilts her head back to look at me. "D, huh?"

"I figured it might help calm your nerves." My lips brush over hers. "Don't get used to it. It feels weird to say it."

Her fingers tug at the back of my hair. "No. I don't like it either. Not from you." Her mouth claims mine, and Daphne sinks into me until a whistle breaks us apart.

When I turn around, Becket stands behind us with Hudson and Jace. I place my hand on the small of her back possessively and glare at my brothers, wondering which asshole whistled like a dick. "Daphne, I'd like to formally introduce you to my brothers. This is Jace and Hudson."

"It's so nice to meet you both."

"You know," Jace is eyeing Daphne like a fancy new hockey stick he can't wait to hold. "If you ever want to trade up for the younger Kingston, I'm willing to entertain offers."

Hudson wraps his hand around Jace's face and over his mouth. "Ignore him. He's taken too many pucks to the head."

My siren bites down on her bottom lip and forces back her smile. "Thanks for the offer, but I've got no complaints."

Becket mumbles something that sounds like, "*I bet.*"

"And you've met Becket."

She reaches out her hand to shake his, but he leaves her hanging. She awkwardly lowers her hand and forces a smile I know is fake. "Nice to see you again, Becket."

I'm going to kill my brother if he ruins her night.

As the music begins to play downstairs, Daphne clears her throat. "Well, if you would all excuse me. I see Willow looking for me."

As she walks away, I turn to Becks. "What the hell is your problem?"

"*She's* my problem, brother. Has she told you her dad left town yet? That he sold everything they had to pay off a debt to Sam? That she's got nothing left? Not a penny to her name?"

"Becks," Hudson tries to interrupt.

"And it's not like her name means jack shit right now anyway. The old man owes everybody something. He even wiped out her trust."

"What the fuck?" What kind of piece of shit does that to their own kid?

But Becks is wrong. I know Daphne, and she's not her father.

Jace tries to stop his tirade too. "Becks—"

"You would have known that, too, if you hadn't left in such a hurry last week. If she isn't after your money, why the fuck would she be keeping it quiet? She's a gold digger, Max. And that tight, young pussy has you convinced you're in love." I hear the faint feminine gasp at my brother's harsh words and see red.

I rear my arm back with a closed fist and throw the first punch I've thrown in years.

His head snaps to the side.

A sickening crunch can be heard as blood pours from his nose, and he staggers back with a curse.

My brothers jump between us. Eyes wide, Hudson shoves me back a few steps while Jace grabs a napkin from a nearby table and hands it to Becket.

The roaring in my ears is all I know until Daphne's shaking hands grab my face. "Are you okay?" Her voice is strong and heavy with emotion.

"No." I push her aside. "I'm not okay." Becket stands across from me with a white linen napkin up to his nose, stained red with blood. "Apologize."

"Max." Daphne places her hand against my chest. "Your brother's right. My father made a mess of my finances, then left me here with nothing. But what Becket's overprivileged ass never considered is, even though he works, he's never had to work out of necessity. I've never had that luxury. I worked my ass off in college and got a job as soon as I could. I've put everything into making tonight a success because this is my *dream*. I've wanted this since I was a little girl, and no one, not even my father selling my damn life, was going to get in my way." She turns to Becket. "And if you think your brother handed me this job because we're together, then you're an even bigger ass for not having faith in him."

Daph turns around and slowly walks over to Becks, then slaps him across the face. "I've worked hard to get where I am. I've volunteered my entire life to help others. I've got a degree in Nonprofit Management because *that* is what I've always wanted to do. And I'm about to successfully throw my very first fundraiser, so I can help the less fortunate kids of Philadelphia have better lives. Tell me, Becket Kingston, have you ever done anything for those less fortunate than you, besides signing a check?"

She takes a step closer to Becks and doesn't bother to

lower her voice, letting anyone and everyone nearby hear what she has to say. "I'm also madly in love with your brother. So you better get used to having me around. Now, go wash your damn face. And bid on a fucking auction basket if you ever want me to forgive you." She grabs my hand and pulls me with her. "I want to see a lot of zeros, Becket. You can afford it."

Fury radiates off Becket in waves as Daphne and I leave him to stand there and digest his own actions.

Daphne practically drags me behind her, past one of the velvet ropes closing off an area. She doesn't stop until we're behind closed doors. But when we're in private and the adrenaline wears off, her legs give out beneath her. I catch her before she can fall and sit her down on a table in the corner of the otherwise empty room. "Jesus, Daphne. I'm so sorry."

"Stop, Max. Just stop. Those weren't your words. They were your brother's." She shakes her hand by her side. "And oh my God. I hit him. I've never hit anyone in my life. Holy shit."

I grab her hand and inspect it for damage as my mind replays her declaration. "You said you love me."

She stiffens and tries to pull her hand back, her eyes wide before they slide away from me like she's embarrassed. "Max, I—"

"Daphne." I slide my thumbs over her cheeks. "I love you more than I knew I could ever love anyone. You amaze me every single day. Your strength. Your grace. Your sheer will and determination. You're my world. And I swear to God, I will cut my brother out of my life before I ever let him say another word about you."

She leans her cheek into my hand and closes her eyes. "Max . . . I don't want you to cut your brother out of your life. I know how much your family means to you. Give him time to cool down. He'll come around when he sees that I don't want a penny of your money. If we ever were to get married, I'll sign whatever prenup the asshole wants. I always had money growing up, and it never made me happy like you do. I don't need money, Max. All I need is you and me for the rest of my life, and I'll be happy."

"You want to marry me, siren?" I don't know why, but hearing her say it surprises me. Not that the thought hadn't crossed my mind. But I hadn't considered it may have crossed hers.

"That better not have been a proposal, Max Kingston. Not after your brother just said what he said, and my hand is still stinging from the slap heard round the world." Her face pales. "Oh no. Did anyone hear us? Shit. Did anyone *see* us?"

"I don't think anyone was here yet." I lift her stinging hand to my lips and press them against her palm.

"I meant it, Max." Her silvery eyes pool with tears. "I love you. I'm sorry I told your asshole brother before I told you."

"Shh. Don't cry, baby." I cover her mouth with mine. "Do you think you can go back out there?"

"Of course I can. This is my event, and I'm not letting him ruin it." She stands from the table and wipes her face, then hooks her arm through mine. "Just stay close for a while, okay?"

"I wouldn't want to be anywhere else."

DAPHNE

IT'S WELL PAST MIDNIGHT BY THE TIME MAX AND I GET HOME that night. A night I'll never forget, for good or bad. We managed to double the goal for the night. And Start A Revolution is going to begin helping so many kids because of everyone's generosity. Including the generosity of the man arming the alarm next to me.

I slip my shoes off and moan as I stretch out my feet. "I swear, women should never be expected to wear heels for that many hours straight. I love shoes more than the average person, but that was just cruel and unusual punishment."

Max slips his strong arms around my back and under my legs as he scoops me up and carries me to his room. "You were great tonight, Daphne. I'm so proud of you." He stands me at the foot of the bed and unzips my zipper, then holds my dress for me to step out of it. "Do you want to shower?"

I shake my head. "I just want to sleep. Will you lie down with me?"

"I'll do anything with you. Just give me a few minutes."

I strip off my bra and panties and throw on one of Max's shirts. He's not going to have any left at the rate I keep stealing them. And as soon as I slip under the cool, soft sheets, I close my eyes and drift off.

I'm not sure how much later it is when I feel his lips against my skin.

"Hey . . ." I murmur, my voice raspy.

He wraps his arms around me. His chest is against my back, and he buries his face in my hair, a sigh leaving his lips.

"Max . . ." I know we need to talk about this. I've pushed it off as long as possible. "I'm sorry I never talked to you about my father. Maybe if I had, tonight could have been avoided." I roll over in his arms and rest my head on his chest.

His fingers drag up my neck. "Why didn't you tell me? I could have helped."

"I'm not sure. Shame maybe? Mixed with an insane amount of pain." I sit up and lean back against the headboard. "Seriously, Max. Your father is a legend, and mine got himself into so much trouble, he sold the team, sold our home, stole my trust fund, and ran out of town to hide." I pull my knees up protectively in front of myself.

Max pulls himself up next to me. "Jesus, Daphne. I can't believe he'd do that to you. I knew something was wrong. I should have pushed harder. I want you to be able to tell me anything. Everything."

"Pushing wouldn't have worked. I wasn't ready to talk then." I take in a shaky breath. I'm not even sure I'm ready to talk now. But I keep going. "He didn't even have the decency to tell me any of it to my face. He left me a note. Then, he called a few weeks later and demanded I sell my mother's wedding rings. Then he had the nerve to be furious when I told him no." Angry tears threaten to spill free, but I push them back down. I'm not giving my father any more of my tears.

"I wish you felt like you could talk to me about all this." His fingers lightly push the hair away from my face. "You can, you know? I won't judge. I might want to kill him for you, but I'll never judge." His lips gently skim over my head. "You know, Sam told me your dad left and that he owed a lot of money."

"What?" Embarrassment drags me down. "Why didn't you say anything?"

"It was the night of the bachelor party. It was why I came over. I was worried about you. But I got distracted as soon as I saw you. I find that happens a lot when you're around, siren. Sam's made sure your dad's enemies know you're off-limits. No one will come for you, even if he never pays his debts." He strokes my face with the gentlest touch. "You'll always be safe with me."

I crawl into his lap, straddling him, and cradle his face in my hands. "I know that now. I'm sorry I didn't trust you with it before." I grab his hand in mine and lift it to my lips. "I'm sorry I caused this issue between you and your brother."

Max's dick grows hard beneath me. "You didn't cause anything. Becket's a grown man, and so am I. I've been in a relationship before where all she was after was my name and what it could get her. Becks was there for that. He's been through it too. And it's hard to learn that someone you care about is using you. But that doesn't excuse his actions."

I wiggle in his lap. "I don't want to hear about your relationships, Max. I never want to think about you with anyone else." I plant my lips on his and sigh.

"Only you, Daphne." He tilts my head. "It will only ever be you." His tongue licks over the corner of my mouth before pushing inside as he drags his hands up my body and tosses his t-shirt that I stole down to the floor. Max angles his mouth over mine and cups my breasts in his hands before one slides down my body and into my panties.

He licks down the column of my neck, his teeth grazing as he goes, and it's the sweetest, slowest burn of torture. "Max," I keen. "I need you inside me."

"Not yet." He slips two fingers inside me and presses down on my clit with his thumb. "Come for me first, Daphne." The hunger in his eyes is intoxicating. "Drip your come all over my hand, then I'll give you my cock. Show me how much you want it."

I ache at his words and throw my head back, riding his hand as his mouth latches onto my hard nipple, and that slow burn turns into a five-alarm fire. My pussy pounds with need, and I'm so close. "I'm gonna come, Max."

"You fucking better. Come now, siren." He pushes his tongue into my mouth, and I tremble around him as I come so hard my toes curl until they cramp. But Max doesn't stop. No. He removes his fingers, then shoves them into my mouth. It's dirty and sexy. And oh my God, I suck them clean.

He doesn't even peel my panties from my body, just shoves them aside and pushes his boxers down, then he rubs the head of his cock along the seam of my hypersensitive sex, and I nearly shoot off the bed. "Oh my God, I can't take it, Max. It's too much."

"You'll take it, baby." He pulls back slowly, then pushes up with his arms wrapped around me.

Desire surges through me as I struggle to breathe. Panting and gasping. Matching each thrust of his hips with a grind of my own.

His mouth latches onto the soft spot between my shoulder and neck, and I cry out, desperate for more. I wrap my arms around his neck and fist his hair until his face tilts up toward mine.

"I love you." I swivel my hips again, taking him deeper.

His hot mouth closes over mine. And when he bites down on my bottom lip, my back arches and my world explodes, pleasure racing through my blood.

Max thrusts up again, and again, and again as I let him take all my weight, my body draped against him. "All fucking mine, siren." His hands on my hips hold me tightly as his powerful body meets mine, and he comes on a beautiful roar. My name is a beautiful plea on his lips.

"No one will ever hurt you again, Daphne. Not while I have a breath in my body."

I may not have wanted this man in my life when I met him, but I'm never letting him go.

When I wake up the next morning, my hand reaches for Max, but his side of the bed is cold. I roll over, and the sheets are rumpled. A quick check of the time, and I know I need to get up and get showered. It's time to function, and I promised the girls we'd meet for brunch so I could fill them in on why Becket Kingston had a black eye last night. But I'm really wishing I could cancel and spend the day in this bed.

I don't even want sex.

I'm too damn tired.

I just want Max.

But when I step into the shower and find my favorite pear soap and bodywash sitting on his shelf, I reconsider. Sleepy sex would be a great way to thank him for being so thoughtful. By the time I get dressed, throw a little makeup on, and braid my hair, I smell the coffee brewing downstairs and hear more than one voice.

These Kingston siblings take codependence to an entirely new level.

I wonder which one it's going to be this weekend.

When I walk into the kitchen, I realize that I managed to underestimate them. Because it's not just one Kingston. It's four. Well, four, including Max. Hudson, Sawyer, and asshole are all standing in Max's kitchen. Mugs of steaming hot coffee are in their hands with an assortment of breakfast sandwiches laid out on the kitchen counter. Acting like what Becket said last night didn't hurt should have won me an Oscar. There was no way I was going to let him know how much his words stung. But that doesn't mean I want to see him here this morning.

I ignore all of them, not quite ready to give a fuck until I've poured a cup of coffee, and say good morning to Max. "Why are you having a party this morning?" my tired voice cracks.

He drops a kiss to my head and looks across the island at asshole.

Asshole clears his throat. "My generous brother is giving me the chance to apologize to you, Daphne. And Tweedledee and Tweedledum over there are here to make sure we don't kill each other before that happens." He points to Hudson and Sawyer. "Max and me. Not you and me. But I do owe you an apology. I know Max has been hurt before. So have I, and I let that color my judgment of you before I ever got the chance to know you. It wasn't fair. And it wasn't right. Max told me that, and I wasn't listening. I guess I'm more of a talker."

"Bullshitter," Hudson coughs.

"Yeah. I guess. But I am sorry." He offers me a breakfast sandwich. "In our family, we say sorry with food. Not food we cooked because none of us are very good at that. Doesn't really work if the apology makes you sick. But it is a peace offering."

"I appreciate it. And I accept your apology, but I'm going to pass on the food. I'm meeting my friends for brunch and have to leave in a minute."

Max squeezes me to him. "Want me to drive you?"

"No. Maddie's going to pick me up. I'll grab some clothes and my car afterward and come back. Sound good?"

Max places a chaste kiss on my lips and squeezes my ass. "Yeah. Sounds good."

"It was good seeing you guys again," I tell Hudson and Sawyer, then turn to asshole and eye him.

"You really gonna let me off that easily?"

"I'm not one for holding a grudge. But just so you know, I'll be calling you 'asshole' instead of Becket for years to come. I might just have your brother's babies, so they can call you 'Uncle Asshole.'" I wave at the group of them as the brothers laugh at the asshole. "Bye, guys."

"Holy shit. Seriously?" I've just blown the girls' minds. But Carys seems to be the most surprised. "Am I the only one who thinks that's kinda hot?"

I laugh as I sip my sweet tea. "I don't think I was really in the right frame of mind to appreciate that aspect of the whole thing. But I always think Max is hot. So there's that."

"So, Chloe . . ." She waits dramatically for Chloe to look over at her. "Did D tell you Watkins asked for your number?"

"Um, no." Chloe eyes me with a smile. "But I'm pretty sure that's a big old no. Our inner circles are already a little too incestuous, if you ask me. I will not be dating your brother's work wife, Mads."

Carys slaps a hand over her face to hide her obnoxious laugh. "Oh my God. His work wife. That's great."

Chloe's phone vibrates against the table, and she silences it. "It's Nattie. I'll call her back. She probably just wants to make sure I'm going to watch the game. Like I haven't seen enough of our brothers playing football to last a lifetime."

The phone vibrates again, and Chloe blows out a breath, then slides her finger over it. "Nat, I'm out to breakfast with the girls. Can I call you after?" Whatever Nattie just said has Chloe's face going terrifyingly white as she looks over at

Carys. "Breathe, Nattie. I need you to breathe. Where's Brady?"

"What's happening?" Carys asks, but Chloe's eyes lock with mine, and my stomach drops.

Oh, God.

"Well, call his coach, Nat. Call Murph." Chloe sits quietly for a minute, refusing to meet Carys's eyes. "Hang up the phone, Nat. I'm calling Sabrina to come over until we can get Brady. Give me a few minutes, and I'll call you back." She sucks in a sharp breath. "I love you too, Nat. Call his coach. I'll get Brina there as soon as I can."

She ends the call, and it's as if all the noise is sucked out of the room, and the world tilts on its axis.

The only thing I hear is the beat of my own heart.

"Chloe . . ." Carys's whole body is shaking, her eyes full of unshed tears, waiting to break free. "What happened?"

Chloe takes a handful of money from her purse and throws it on the table. "We've got to go." She pushes Carys out of the booth, then grabs my arm. "Call Max. Tell him to meet us at Coach's house."

Maddie and I follow them outside The Busy Bee, the two of us holding hands like scared kids.

Carys grabs Chloe's arm with shaking hands and whispers, "What. Happened?" Her wild green eyes are wet and terrified, and her lower lip trembles as she waits for an answer.

"Let's go to your mom's, Care Bear." Chloe looks at me over the top of Carys's head, and Carys snaps as she vacillates between all of us. Her body is rigid as she grabs Chloe's arms.

"Chloe," she begs through the tears that are pouring down her face. "Please, just tell me. I need to know." When Chloe doesn't answer, Carys screams, "Tell me!"

Chloe grabs Carys's hands while Maddie and I stand on either side of her. "It's Cooper."

"Is he dead?" The words are barely above a whisper as Carys shakes where she stands.

Chloe tilts her head to the side, and a tear leaks down her cheek. "We don't know. His unit . . . They were captured."

The gut-wrenching cry Carys makes as she falls to the sidewalk is a sound I'll never forget as long as I live.

MAX

I'M SITTING AT THE KITCHEN COUNTER, ENJOYING LISTENING to Hudson give Becket shit for his black eye when my phone rings with Daphne's picture flashing across it. "Hey."

My brothers make cat calls and other annoying noises, but I cut them off with a hand in the air when Daphne lets out a horrific sob. "Breathe, Daphne. Breathe. Are you hurt? What's wrong?"

I push away from the counter and drag my hand through my hair.

Not knowing what happened or how I can fix it.

"Max . . . It's Cooper Sinclair. We don't have the details yet, but his squad's been captured. We're on our way to Coach's house now. I . . . I need you. Can you meet me there?"

"I'll be there in five minutes." She disconnects the call, and I grab my keys from the counter and look at my brothers. "Cooper Sinclair was just captured in combat. Daphne's at Coach's house. I'm headed there now. I'll call you when I know more."

I don't wait for any acknowledgement before I leave. And ten minutes later, I'm pulling up in front of Coach's house. I throw the car in park and see Maddie sitting on the front steps. "Maddie, why are you out here?"

She has tears streaming down her face. "Because it didn't feel right being in there. Daphne knows them. She's known them forever. I'm an outsider. I don't belong here." She grabs my hand. "I'm going home. I don't think they need a ton of extra people here. Will you bring Daphne home for me?"

"Yeah, Maddie. I've got her."

She drops my hand. "Thanks, Max."

I watch her walk back to her car, then knock on the door.

Chloe opens the door. "Daphne's in the other room with Carys."

"Thanks, Chloe." I step into the house, but she stops me.

"Max," she adds quietly. "Nobody knows."

"Knows what?"

"I figured D told you about Cooper and Carys." She's looking at me with expectant eyes, like I'm supposed to know what that means. "That they were together . . ."

"What?" I let that thought register for a minute before I start to frown. "They're stepsiblings."

As soon as the words are out of my mouth, I know they're the wrong damn thing to say. Especially now, when Chloe looks ready to deck me. "I'm sorry. You just . . . Daphne didn't tell me."

"The family doesn't know, so don't say anything." She brushes by me, annoyed, and I'm left standing there, stunned.

When I finally catch up and follow her into the family room, Katherine is sitting on the couch with tears streaming down her face, watching Coach, who's pacing around the room with his phone up to his ear. Declan and his wife are in the corner of the room with a phone between them.

Daphne looks up from the couch where Carys is curled in a ball with her head resting on Daphne's shoulder.

When Chloe sits down on her other side and wraps her arm around Carys, Daphne stands and walks into my arms. "Thanks for coming." She wraps her arms around me and kisses my chest.

"Max," Coach ends his call, and I offer him my hand.

"I'm so sorry, Coach. I don't know exactly what's going on. But if there's anything at all you need, it's yours." I run my hand over Daphne's back, anchoring her to me.

Coach's eyes are red and raw. I can't imagine the agony he must be feeling, knowing something has happened to one of his children. "Actually, I hate to ask . . ."

"Anything, Coach."

"Can I borrow the jet? I can pay you for it—"

"Take it. Where do you need to go?" My phone is already out, preparing to dial the airport to get the flight scheduled. I'd fly it there myself if it would help this man.

"Brady's game already started, and he and Murphy are playing. I told the girls to stay put until the game was over. There's no reason to pull them halfway through. But if we could send the jet down there to bring them home after the game, I'd appreciate it."

"I'll get everything set up now."

He pulls Daphne into his arms. "Thanks for bringing the girls home, D. I'm sure one of them will call you with an update."

"Thanks, Coach. Let me know if you need anything." She kisses his cheek, then takes my hand and pulls me through the kitchen and out a side door. Once we're outside, Daphne loses it. Completely breaks down. She throws her arms around me, and tears stream down her beautiful face. "Oh God, Max. They don't know where he is or if they're okay. Carys is a mess. I swear to God, she stopped breathing when Chloe told her. Actually stopped breathing. I didn't know what to do for her. I didn't know what to say. He's been the love of her life for years, and Chloe is the only one in that house who knows it."

"There's nothing you can do for her right now. That room

is full of her family. Check in with her tonight. See if they need anything. We can do whatever they need." I hold her to me, needing to feel her breathe. "Come on, let's go home. I'm sure Maddie wants to know what's happening."

When we get back to Dixon's house, Maddie and her brother are sitting at the kitchen table, waiting.

Daphne texted we were on our way when we got into the car. Then she dropped her phone and grabbed my hand so tightly, I wondered if I'd ever be able to feel my fingers again.

Maddie jumps up and hugs Daphne to her. "Is there any news?"

"No." Daphne shakes her head. "It doesn't sound good. It was an ambush. But that's all we know. Carys is a mess. She's practically catatonic. I think Declan knows something's up. But I don't think he knows what. Not yet."

"Jesus." Dixon blows out a long breath. "I can't even fucking imagine what they're going through."

For once, he and I are on the same page.

"I'm just going to step out front. I've got to make a few calls to get the jet ready for them." I take a step toward the door, but Dixon stops me.

He stands from the table. "You can use my office, Max. It's back this way."

I follow behind him into an office with big windows overlooking his back yard. A picture of him on draft day, standing with a Kings Jersey and hat in his hands, hangs on his wall. And another of him in his uniform with Maddie standing under his arm sits on his desk. Other than that, there's nothing personal in here. "Let me know if you need anything or if I can help in any way."

"Thank you."

He shuts the door behind him, and I make my calls.

By the time I rejoin the others, the jet is fueled and waiting. Coach Sinclair's assistant coach is ready to run practice without him tomorrow, and Scarlet has been filled in on everything that's happening.

Maddie, Dixon, and Daphne are all sitting on the couch, watching some old movie on the TV when I walk back into the family room. When I sit down next to Daphne, she lays her head on my chest and closes her eyes. She's asleep within minutes, and after an hour, I stand and lift her into my arms. "I'm going to go put her to bed."

"Hey, Max . . ." Dixon calls after me. "You gonna stay with her?"

I eye him, not sure how to answer. "That okay with you?"

"Yeah." He nods. "I think she'll want you here when she wakes up."

"Thanks, man." I take a step forward and realize I have no fucking clue where her room is. "Any chance you want to tell me which room is Daphne's?"

Maddie laughs at me. "Top of the stairs. Second door on the right. And make sure you shut the door behind you or Cinder will follow you in and sleep on your head."

Daphne moans and wraps her arms around my neck. "You don't want to share a pillow with our bitchy little cat. Now, can you please stop talking and put me to bed?"

Maddie yawns, then grabs the blanket from the back of the couch and lays down. "Good luck with that, Max. D's cranky when you wake her up."

Ha. She's not like that when I wake her up with my tongue between her thighs. But now's probably not the time for that.

After a minute, I've got Daphne in her bed, and I didn't

see Cinder follow us into the room, so I think we're safe from that fate. I pull off my shirt and pants and get in bed and pull her body against mine. "I love you, Daphne."

She kisses my chest. "Love you too, Max. Forever."

"Forever."

DAPHNE

By the time I'm locking my office door the following Friday, Coach and Carys are on a flight to Germany in the King Corp. jet, heading to the military hospital, and I'm about ready for bed. If I thought the week leading up to the fundraiser was brutal, it had nothing on the week leading up to Max's team party tomorrow, coupled with everything that had to be done after the fundraiser.

But life has a way of spinning you in circles, and with the bad comes the good. Willow and I have been fielding calls all week from sponsors, donors, and charities asking for our help. It's been incredible. And I've already started to plan for another event in the new year.

It's safe to say I'm exhausted. Mentally and physically.

I poke my head into Max's office to let him know I'm leaving for the night and am pleasantly surprised when he's closing his laptop already. "Hey, I was just heading out. You getting done early?"

He stands and grabs his suit coat from the back of his chair. "Yeah. I'm done. Let's go home. Want to pick up dinner on the way?" I've slept at Max's house every night this week. I haven't officially moved in, but that's because we haven't had a chance to pack up my things yet.

"Oh yeah. Let's get Fat Jack's. I'm in the mood for greasy food and the new season of that show on Netflix." He wraps his arm around my shoulders and walks me to the elevator.

"There's about a thousand shows on Netflix, Daphne.

Care to narrow it down?" The two of us step in, and he presses me against the wall. "Unless that was an excuse to Netflix and chill."

"Maximus Kingston. When was the last time you just chilled?" I swear his brain never stops. "Oh my God, did I tell you about this TikTok I saw earlier? Thee.Reading.Mom says it's 'chicken and dicken,' not 'Netflix and chill' when you're old."

Max growls. "I'm not that old yet." He smacks my ass. "First . . . you sound like my sisters when you call me Maximus." He takes my lips in a searing kiss. "And second, you're teaching me to chill. It's a lot easier to relax with you in my life, Daphne. I like going home at night when I know you'll be there with me."

The elevator doors slide open, and we step out. He walks me to my car and pins me to my door. "Marry me, Daphne."

"What?" I whisper. Scared of my answer. Scared of the question.

He drops down to one knee. "Marry me, Daphne Brenner. Let me love you forever." He pulls a burgundy velvet ring box from his pocket and cracks it open. A beautifully cut round diamond sits by itself on a platinum band. "I thought about asking Maddie if she could give me your mom's rings. But I wanted you to have something that was just yours. If you'd rather wear hers, we can have this made into something else . . ." He slides the ring onto my finger and brushes his lips over my hand.

"Promise you won't change your mind?" A sob is caught in my throat. "I can't lose you, Max."

"Is that a yes?"

"Yes." I nod my head uncontrollably and launch myself at him.

Max catches me and swings me around in a circle before he places me back down. "I always knew you'd either be my destruction or my salvation. Thanks for saving me."

My fingers tangle in the dirty-blonde hair curling at his collar. "I could never destroy you, Max. You pulled me into your orbit the very first time I met you, and I've wanted to feel your warmth every day since. Even when I thought I hated you, you pulled me toward you. I love you, Max. Every piece of you." He pins me against my car door and captures my lips in a kiss that sets my heart on fire.

My phone trills in my pocket with an incoming call I try to ignore. But as soon as it stops, it starts again. I pull it out and send the call to voicemail.

"Lets's go celebrate." Max smiles, and I swear that warmth shines so damn bright.

"Fat Jack's?" I ask as a joke, but I'm pretty sure that's what I actually want. When the phone rings again, we both glare. "It's Maddie. Let me just make sure everything's okay."

I slide my finger across the screen, not sure what to expect. "Hey, Mads. Now's not a good time—"

"Daphne, you've got to get to the house. Your dad is here. He was walking around the property, didn't knock on the door or anything. Brandon grabbed him and told me to call the cops. But when I saw who it was, I called you first. What do you want me to do?"

"We'll be right there, Mads." I end the call and look up at Max, who heard the whole thing.

"Come on." He wraps an arm around me. "Luka can drive us."

We get into the car, and I'm on autopilot, moving but not feeling anything.

Max fills Luka in as we head to Dixon's, but I tune them out.

My thoughts spiraling.

I've wanted to confront him since the day he left. But I don't know what to say to him.

Of course, my bastard of a father would come back today.

Why not taint one more memory?

Max holds my hand in his as we make the short drive to Kroydon Hills. I think he tells me to wait for him once we get there. I might even agree. But when Luka pulls the Range Rover to a stop in Dixon's driveway, I'm out of the car before the engine turns off.

Max catches up to me after a few steps. "Hey." He wraps his arms around my waist and picks me up from behind. "Slow down. Take a breath."

"Put me down. Now." I'm not ready to play around.

Max's arms grow tighter. "I need you to keep it together. Never show someone you're upset. It gives them power. I want you to breathe in and out a few times. We're going in there together. Got it?"

"Fuck." I wiggle in his arms to get down. "I really hate it when you're right. You know that?" After a few deep breaths, he finally sets me on my feet but links his fingers through mine.

"Ready?" Concern laces the corner of his eyes. "You don't have to see him if you don't want to. We can always leave it to the police."

"No. I want to see him." I steel my spine. "Let's get this over with."

Maddie meets us at the front door and pulls me in for a hug. "Oh my God, D. Brandon has your dad sitting on a chair in the dining room."

I push past her with Max hot on my heels but stop dead in my tracks when my dad comes into view. He's sitting at the table with Dixon standing next to him, massive arms crossed over his chest, and rage is rolling off him in waves.

Dix doesn't even turn to look at me. "He was trying to break into your window, D."

What the hell? I take a step back, right into Max. His hands cup my shoulders. "What are you doing here, Dad?" The look in his eyes is a mix of misery and hatred. Although, I can't tell if it's directed at me or himself. "What do you want?"

"I wanted to see you, Daphne." He looks tired. Heavy bags line his red eyes, colliding with his ruddy cheeks. "Can we go somewhere to talk?"

"Absolutely not." Max doesn't give me a chance to answer. Instead, he moves me behind him and stalks closer to my father. "You left her here, completely in the dark, with nothing. Not a clue of what kind of man her father is. No idea who you owed money to or that she could be in fucking danger." Max's entire body is vibrating with unleashed fury. "What if they went after her?'" He steps forward and grips my father's shirt, pulling him to his feet.

"Max. Stop." I pull at his arms. "He's not worth it."

"But you are." His deep blue eyes hold mine, promising me everything.

I step in front of him. "Did you pay Sam Beneventi back the money you owed him?"

"That's why I need those rings, Daphne. There's nothing left, and people are after me." His face perks up. "I need them so I can keep you safe—"

"The fuck you do," Max interrupts. "She doesn't need anything from you. She's safe. *I* made sure your shit will never touch her."

Dad deflates before my eyes. And I make up my mind without ever realizing I'd even considered the action. I walk out of the room, with everyone calling after me, and go upstairs into my bedroom.

Moments later, when I've returned, and everyone is

staring at me like I'm a bomb that's about to explode, I finally tell my father all the things that have kept me up at night since he left.

"I'm so mad at you, I want to cry. Not because I'm sad, but because I'm so angry, my emotions are simmering. For selling the team Grandpa loved. For selling the house I grew up in and not warning me or letting me take any of my memories before you did it. For making such horrifically awful decisions that you put us both at risk." I try to keep my composure and push through my emotions, but the red-hot tears are burning behind my eyelids. "I hate that you made me feel like I was unloved. That our relationship was a lie, and it was easy to toss me aside."

"Daphne—"

"No. You don't get to speak. Not this time." I reach out and place the rings on the table.

Maddie gasps, and Max and Dixon both call out to me, but I ignore them all. "Take them, Dad. Take them and leave. Pay off whatever debt you have and leave Philly. Don't come back. Don't call. Don't think there is any chance of you ever being involved in my life or my children's lives."

"Daph . . ." Dad picks up both rings and places them on his pinky finger. "Thank you."

"Don't thank me yet." I turn around and grab Max's hand. "Can you call Sam and find out exactly who he owes money to?"

"I don't have to." Max pulls me against him. "Sam bought his debt."

Now it's my turn to gasp. "Why would he do that?"

"Because he wouldn't let me when I wanted to."

This man is so much more than I ever hoped to have. "Could we ask Luka to take him to Sam's?"

"Daphne, you don't have to give him your rings."

I know if I asked Max for the money, he'd give it to me. I

knew it before he just admitted to already trying to pay off my father's debt. But I'd never take it from him. "I know. And I love you. But I want to do this." I turn back to my father. "This severs our ties. Don't come back."

Later that night, Max and I are cleaning up the dinner dishes after we finish our takeout. We didn't end up with Fat Jack's after everything simmered down. Luka took my dad to Sam and confirmed he was still alive and in one piece when they left after that. That's all I wanted to know. At least for now.

I guess this roller coaster of a day was an appropriate way to end this insane week.

At least, I thought it was over before the doorbell starts incessantly ringing.

Max closes his eyes before leaning his face up to the ceiling. "I'll get rid of them."

I tug on the pocket of the sweats he changed into when we got home. "Get rid of who?"

"Whichever sibling is at the door." He takes a step away, then stops. "Who am I kidding? There's probably more than one." I follow Max with my eyes as he leaves the kitchen, then decide "*Screw it,*" and follow him to the foyer, where he's now standing with a very pregnant Scarlet, flanked by Lenny and Becks.

The girls rush to my side, fawning over me. "Are you okay?" Lenny wraps her arms around me in a hug, and I may die a little on the inside. I'm not the biggest hugger if I don't know someone well.

"Back off, Len. We don't all like to be touched." Scarlet looks me over before settling on my hand and points. "What is that?"

My cheeks heat as I smile at Max, expecting him to tell

his siblings. But I'm learning anything goes when there's more than one Kingston in a room.

"How did you guys hear about this already?" He takes my hand in his and pulls me next to him.

Scarlet walks right into the living room, sits down on the couch, and puts her feet up on the ottoman as she rubs her side. "Sorry. This little girl has been killing me these past few days. Anyway . . . Amelia was with Sam when you called him. She may have overheard the conversation—"

"Even though we're not supposed to know that," Lenny adds.

"Yeah." Becks looks between Max and me. "She called Scar at work, and the three of us were together, so we figured we'd come check on you."

"Oh, God." I cover my face with my hands. "Does your whole family know?"

Becket laughs. The asshole. "Not yet."

"Yes, they do," Len corrects him.

"Ughhh," I whine.

Then I look at Max, who pulls me into his arms. "They're going to love you because I do."

"Ha," Scarlet scoffs. "They already love you because you smacked the shit out of Becket. Do you have any idea how many people would line up to do that?"

"Now," Lenny drops down onto the couch next to Scarlet, "What do you have to eat? And let's talk about that ring on your hand."

Two hours later, when the three of them leave the house, I feel like I've been in the center of a hurricane and survived. And as Max shuts the door behind him, throws the lock, and then arms the alarm, I think he might feel the same.

"You still wanna marry me? Knowing you're going to have to deal with them all for the rest of your life?" He picks me up, and I wrap my legs around his waist.

"I'd marry you tomorrow, Max Kingston."

He seals his lips over mine, and I melt. "We've got the team party tomorrow night. What about Sunday?"

"What?" I laugh as he takes the steps up to our room, two at a time.

He sits down on the bed with me still wrapped around him. "We've got a one o'clock home game. We could do something small here, after the game, and then, if you want something bigger, we could throw it together whenever you're ready."

"Really?" Hope blooms in my stomach. I love the idea of not waiting. "You'd be okay with something that small?"

"Baby, I want whatever will make you my wife. What do you want? Do you want a big wedding? We can do that too. It's completely up to you."

I push him back on the bed. "Nope. I just want you. Let's get married."

MAX

EPILOGUE

"WE DID IT." DAPHNE THROWS HER ARMS AROUND MY NECK and screams. "We won. We won the Cup!"

I squeeze her to me, appreciating her so much at this moment.

The cheers in the arena are deafening.

The energy electric.

It came down to game seven, but we won and got to do it on our home ice.

Red, white, and blue confetti litters the air as the team captain, Connor Callahan, raises the cup over his head, and our guys skate a victory lap. It might have taken us two seasons to get here, but everything about this was worth the wait. We came close last year but lost in the second round of the playoffs. It was a tense series that came down to a sudden death overtime in game seven.

They scored first.

It was a painful way to lose.

Our guys gave everything we asked of them.

The puck just didn't fall our way that night.

But we came back stronger this year. The team and the organization. There was a spark to this season from day one. Something special. O'Doul and I worked the entire off-season in what we turned into our war room, strategizing about who we needed and what moves had to be made to win. Making this victory all the sweeter.

"Why, Mr. Kingston. Are you crying?" Daphne's thumb brushes a phantom tear from my eye. She's been by my side every step of the way.

I bring her hand to my lips and press a kiss to her fingers. "No. Just happy." Sometimes it's still hard to believe that life can be this good. At work and at home.

Everyone knows we're together.

They see us at work, games, and foundation events, but we keep the rest just for us.

The two of us have crazy schedules, but we've learned to make every moment count.

Daphne has done so well with Start A Revolution that she's busier than all of us some weeks. She has a packed schedule, and that's with a full staff to help her these days. My hand slips down her back and squeezes her ass. "Ten more days, Daphne." We rented a boutique resort in Fiji for two weeks, and I can't wait to whisk my wife away. Sun. Sand. And Daphne in a tiny bikini.

Her mouth seals over mine. "Ten more days."

"How about we not be forced to explain to your nieces and nephews how babies are made?" Becks laughs at the two of us. It took a while for our relationship to get back on solid footing after Start A Revolution's first fundraiser, but we got there.

"Whatever, Uncle Asshole," Daphne murmurs just loud enough for Becket to hear as her eyes light up with amusement.

He's never getting rid of that nickname. But he's not wrong. We're surrounded by a ton of little ears in here. I decided Scarlet had the right idea, and we now have two boxes for the Revolution games, the same as the Kings games. One for the high-profile guests we have to entertain and another just for the family.

And the entire family is in here tonight.

Lenny's son, Maverick, tries running over on his chubby legs to high five me, and I scoop him up in my arms before he manages to fall flat on his face. At sixteen months old, I already have no doubt he'll be following in his father's football cleats one day. He's a bruiser. He's only a few months younger than Scarlet's son, Killian, and both boys try to do everything their older cousin, Maddox, does, even though Maddox is a year older.

Neither of them can keep up . . . yet.

One day soon though . . .

Lenny takes him from me and puts him back on the ground. "You've got to let him fall, Max. He's got to learn." Yeah. My sisters have given me this lecture more than once, but I'm not good at letting them fall. Some things will never change.

"Whatever you say, Len." She knows I'm mocking her.

Lenny links her arm through Daphne's. "I pity you when you get pregnant. He's going to put you in a bubble until the baby comes. Then he's going to have another one made just for them."

"Hey, Caitlin's here tonight, and she's not in a bubble." Amelia and Sam's daughter was born two months ago, and even she's here in a tiny Revolution onesie.

Amelia joins us by the window of the box overlooking the players on the ice. "Oh, please. You've noticed her daddy hasn't put her down once all night unless it was for one of us to hold her, right?"

"I feel like you're all ganging up on me. We're supposed to be celebrating." And right on time, the waiter starts passing around champagne flutes to everyone in the family. And the photographer has joined us, taking candid shots.

I raise my glass. "I'd like to make a toast and thank you all for being here tonight. The Kingston family legacy is across the street in that football stadium, but it's also down there on that ice as much as it's in each and every person in this room and all the generations yet to come. I love you guys. To family."

An echo of cheers rings throughout the box.

"Now, could everyone get together? I want a picture of all of us to commemorate the first time we won the Cup." It's going to sit on a shelf in my office until the day I retire. A permanent reminder of this night.

Everyone grumbles but puts down their glasses, and they do as I ask.

Gathering together in front of the windows with the celebration happening below.

Grabbing the kids and making sure we're all in the shot.

I wrap my arm around Daphne in the center of the group.

"Not all the kids are going to be seen in this picture, Max." She leans into me and brushes her lips over my ear. "But you and I will always know this picture was our baby's first family picture."

My mouth drops open, and my eyes grow wide as I jerk my head to look at her.

And that's exactly when the photographer snaps the picture.

"What?" I pick her up and spin her around, her laughter dancing over my skin. "You're having my baby?"

Beautiful tears shimmer in her eyes as she nods her head. "In about eight months."

"She's having my baby," I announce to anyone who will listen, and a round of cheers goes up throughout our family.

Daphne's hands frame my face. "Come on, Max. It's time to go down to the ice and celebrate with the team."

"I'd follow you anywhere, Daphne."

She wipes her eyes and takes my hand in hers. "I've never been more grateful for anything in my life than I am for you, Max Kingston."

The End

WHAT COMES NEXT?

Not ready to say goodbye to the Kroydon Hills just yet? Don't fret. Follow the remainder of the Kingston family as they each figure out what comes next while falling in love in the new series, Defiant Kings.

Hudson Kingston's book, Caged, will be releasing in 2023.
https://books2read.com/DefiantKings1

WANT A GLIMPSE INTO COOPER & CARYS'S DUET?

The Risks We Take duet will be releasing in summer of 2022.
Changing The Game - releasing August 24th
https://books2read.com/TRWT-1
Ending The Game - releasing September 21st
https://books2read.com/TRWT2

Prologue - Carys
Not all love stories have happy endings.
Romeo and Juliette died for love. I wanted to live for it.

I wanted a love that would set the world on fire.
But I never thought about the flames.
I never expected the burn.

A Bridal Party To Remember will be releasing June 14, 2022.

Love is in the air at this destination wedding, and Cupid's arrow is pointed at the bridal party!

Hit the beach with eight of your favorite romance authors as they introduce you to A Bridal Party to Remember. This collection includes all new stories that are so hot, you'll need a dip in the ocean to cool off.

Featuring
 Elle Christensen
 Hope Ford
 Hannah McBride
 Bella Matthews
 Kaci Rose
 Frankie Love
 CM Steele
 Fiona Davenport

Pre-order your copy today for just 99 pennies. Price will be going up after release!

Amazon Worldwide: https://geni.us/BridalPartyAmazon

Apple, Nook & Kobo: https://books2read.com/ABridalPartytoRememberAnthology

ACKNOWLEDGMENTS

M ~ I am forever grateful for you.

K. ~ No bigger cheerleader ever existed. You are the Nattie to my Belles.

D~ I don't know what I would do without your calls.

To my very own Coop ~ Cheers to forced friendships and everything that comes with them.

Vicki ~ I am so grateful to have you in my corner! Thank you for loving these books.

Sarah ~ Thank you so much for putting up with me.

To my Betas ~ Nichole, Hannah, Meagan, Shawna & Heather. Thank you for helping me make Max & Daphne everything they deserved to be. Our group chat is one of my favorite places to be!

My Street Team, Kelly, Shawna, Vicki, Ashley, Heather, Oriana, Shannon, Nichole, Nicole, Hannah, Meghan, Amy, Christy, Emma, Brianna, Adanna, Jennifer, Lissete, Poppy, Jacqueline, Laura, Kathleen, Diane, Jenna, Keeza, Carissa, Kat, Kira, Kristina, Terri, Javelyn & Morgan ~ Thank you, ladies, for loving these characters and this world. Our group is my safe place, and I'm so thankful for every one of you in it. Family Meetings Rock!

My editors, Jess & Dena. You both take such good care of my words. Thank you for pushing me harder, and making me better.

Gemma – Thanks for giving it that finishing touch.

Jena ~ you are so talented! Thank you for bringing these covers to life.

To all of the Indie authors out there who have helped me along the way – you are amazing! This community is so incredibly supportive, and I am so lucky to be a part of it!

Thank you to all of the bloggers who took the time to read, review, and promote Fallen King.

And finally, the biggest thank you to you, the reader. I hope you enjoyed reading Max & Daphne as much as I loved being lost in their world.

ABOUT THE AUTHOR

Bella Matthews is a Jersey girl at heart. She is married to her very own Alpha Male and raising three little ones. You can typically find her running from one sporting event to another. When she is home, she is usually hiding in her home office with the only other female in her house, her rescue dog Tinker Bell by her side. She likes to write swoon-worthy heroes and sassy, smart heroines with a healthy dose of laughter and all the feels.

Stay Connected

Amazon Author Page: https://amzn.to/2UWU7Xs
Facebook Page: https://www.facebook.com/bella.
matthews.3511
Reader Group: https://www.facebook.com/
groups/599671387345008/
Instagram: https://www.instagram.com/bella.matthews.
author/
Bookbub: https://www.bookbub.com/authors/bella-
matthews
Goodreads: https://www.goodreads.com/.../show/
20795160.Bella_Matthews
TikTok: https://vm.tiktok.com/ZMdfNfbQD/
Newsletter: https://bit.ly/BMNLsingups

ABOUT THE AUTHOR

Bella Matthews is a Jersey girl at heart. She is married to her very own Alpha Male and raising three little ones. You can typically find her running from one sporting event to another. When she is home, she is usually hiding in her home office with the only other female in her house, her rescue dog Tinker Bell by her side. She likes to write swoon-worthy heroes and sassy, smart heroines with a healthy dose of laughter and all the feels.

Stay Connected

Amazon Author Page
Facebook Page
Reader Group
Instagram
Bookbub
Goodreads
TikTok
Newsletter

ALSO BY BELLA MATTHEWS

57043210R00169